If

Sylvie

Had

Nine

Lives

IF SYLVIE HAD NINE LIVES

A NOVEL IN STORIES

Leona Theis

Freehand Books acknowledges the financial support for its publishing program provided by the Canada Council for the Arts and the Alberta Media Fund, and by the Government of Canada through the Canada Book Fund.

Canada Council   Conseil des Arts   Alberta◘   Canadä
for the Arts   du Canada   Government

Freehand Books
515 – 815 1st Street sw   Calgary, Alberta   T2P 1N3
www.freehand-books.com

Book orders: UTP Distribution
5201 Dufferin Street   Toronto, Ontario   M3H 5T8
Telephone: 1-800-565-9523   Fax: 1-800-221-9985
utpbooks@utpress.utoronto.ca   utpdistribution.com

Library and Archives Canada Cataloguing in Publication
Title: If Sylvie had nine lives : a novel in stories / Leona Theis.
Other titles: If Sylvie had 9 lives
Names: Theis, Leona, 1955– author.
Identifiers: Canadiana (print) 20200221426 | Canadiana (ebook) 20200221515 | ISBN 9781988298719 (softcover) | ISBN 9781988298726 (EPUB) | ISBN 9781988298733 (PDF)
Classification: LCC PS8589.H415 I32 2020 | DDC C813/.6—dc23

Edited by Deborah Willis
Book design by Natalie Olsen, Kisscut Design
Author photo by Shannon Brunner
Printed on FSC® certified paper and bound in Canada by Marquis

This is a work of fiction. Names, characters, places, incidents, or events either are the product of the author's imagination or are used fictitiously. Any resemblance to actual persons, living or dead, is entirely coincidental.

for Murray

As she danced, the image of a river came to her. A river branching into multiples of itself, no longer a single stream but a delta. And if her life were such a delta she might let the flow take her in a direction far from the current she was in now. If only there were more Sylvies, to ride the separate streams. The further she went, the further she'd be from herself. She could end up way down the shore, so far from this Sylvie, the Jack-marrying version, that all she could do would be to wave, and hope to be seen.

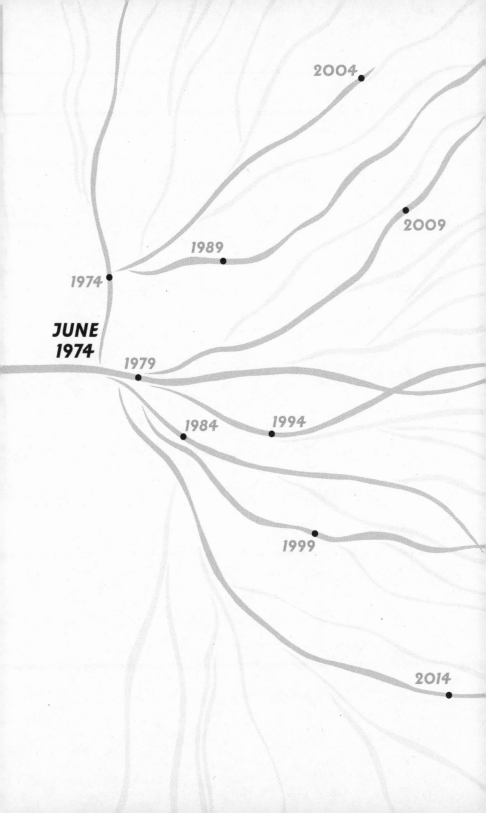

High Beams

TWO NIGHTS BEFORE the date printed in silver italic on her wedding invitations, Erik called, the guy she'd ridden with through all those dust-hung after-darks on country gravel roads in his mom's long Meteor, boat-like in the night. He was on his way through the city, he said. They should have a drink. In her right hand Sylvie held the clunky weight of the phone receiver, and in her left she held a half-made yellow wedding flower. Begin by stacking half a dozen squares of coloured, see-through plastic. Pleat the stack accordion-style, then bind it at the middle. Spread each side into a fan; fluff. Repeat four dozen times. Get married.

"Hang up the phone," said Margo. "Pay some attention already." She took the flower from Sylvie's hand and fluffed the unfinished side and handed it back. Among the rules for nuptials in 1974: decorate the wedding car with flowers the colour of the bridesmaids' dresses. Or, in Sylvie and Jack's case, decorate the wedding truck. They might have used Jack's Corolla, but rust had made macramé of its lower regions; Sylvie's dad's

Dodge pickup was the better choice, looking new except for a few pocks in the paint along the driver's side from stones and speed, her father's refusal to concede ample passage to oncoming traffic.

Sylvie angled the receiver away from her mouth. "I *am* paying attention."

"Course you are, it's just not all that obvious."

Sylvie held the flower to her nose as if she expected perfume. Somewhere in this city was Erik, also with a receiver in his hand and a cord leading away from it. Tug. She looked out the high, small window. Living in a basement suite, you see the lowest quarter of anyone walking around to the back door at the head of the stairs. She knew her friends by their legs, their shoes, the size of their feet. Here came Cynthia's sneakered feet now, cousin Cynthia arriving to help with the flowers.

Things get away on you, the better part of a year goes by, next thing you know your dad's booked the United Church back home and your aunts have made arrangements for the midnight lunch: assorted cold cuts and homemade buns and Uncle Davis's special pepper pickles.

"Yes, let's," Sylvie said into the phone.

"Good," said Erik. "I'll meet you at that club, what is it — The Yips?"

"Sure." Sylvie thought how he sounded like a hick, referring to Yip's as *The* Yips. She hung up and said, "Let's wrap this up, Margo. I'm going out."

"Without Jack?"

"Without Jack."

"Who then?"

"Not your beeswax." She went up to meet Cynthia. "Thanks for coming," she said, "but it turns out this isn't a good night for making flowers after all."

"But Sylvie, you only have tonight and tomorrow and then that's it."

Yes, Sylvie thought, that's true.

They used to drive at night, she and Erik, along the back roads near Ripley looking for parked couples. Once they found a vehicle, they'd train their high beams on the rear window for a bit, then back up, turn around and take off to find another car, laughing to think of Paulie or Stuart bare-assed in the back and Shelley or Beth struggling to do up her blouse, the buttons so big and the buttonholes so small and the fingers so suddenly fat. In the wee hours Erik would drive up Sylvie's street, head-lights off, and let her out three houses ahead of her own so as not to disturb Snoring Dad and Laid-up Mom.

("I get it, Syl. If you didn't love them you wouldn't give them nicknames."

"Think you know me?"

"Think I do.")

Sylvie and Erik called their game birth control. Let's go do some birth control tonight. Let's go do some *back seat interruptus* in Ripley, Saskatchewan, Playground of the Prairies. In those days Sylvie's Grandma Fletcher had in her living room a green satin cushion that dated from the forties. It was silkscreened with the *Playground of the Prairies* slogan and pictures of babes water-skiing and men golfing and fishing. In the real-life Ripley, there was no lake where a person could launch a boat or water-ski. There was no fishing hole, no river.

There *was* a nine-hole golf course that would flood in the spring, and for a week or so kids would put on rubber boots and go out and sink the rickety rafts they knocked together out of branches and tail-ends of lumber. These days, Grandma Fletcher's satin cushion sat on the couch in Sylvie and Jack's basement suite, a slippery joke.

The day after tomorrow Sylvie and Jack would get up and have breakfast, then take their finery, sheathed in plastic bags, four hours out to Ripley where they would tape the yellow flowers to the Dodge and have the ceremony. Tonight the boys had already come to pick up Jack. Took him out to party. The girls had given Sylvie a bridal shower last Thursday where they made her wear a tin pie plate with an orange pot scrubber stuck over to one side, supposed to look like a bow on a bonnet. They played parlour games. Margo won a Tupperware citrus peeler for having in her purse the item voted most unlikely to be found in a purse, specifically, a moo-cow creamer from the truck stop south of the city on Number 11. Tea and instant coffee and Tang had been the beverages on offer, so it was no wonder the thought that came to Sylvie's mind now was, You have to make your own fun.

"OKAY," SAID ERIK as they raised their bottles of Boh and brought them together in a clumsy kiss of glass. "Okay, you're already living with this guy anyway, and day after tomorrow you'll drive out to Ripley for the wedding, and then what?"

"What do you mean, then what?"

"Then you just come back to your same place?"

"No."

"No?"

"Too far to drive. We stay overnight at the Capri in Foster and drive back the next day."

"And you get up Monday morning and go to work at, what did you say, the basement of the library, same as always?"

"Yes."

"Is there a point?"

She stamped circles on the tabletop with her bottle. "Eight months in Edmonton pouring concrete for, what did you say, driveways? And now you're moving back to Ripley."

"The job was great, the boss wasn't. Bags of money, though."

"Anyway," Sylvie said, getting out of her chair, "this place has a dance floor."

THEY DROVE BAREFOOT in the long dark car, shoes and socks stripped off and thrown in the back. They took turns at the wheel. When Sylvie drove, the hard rubber ridges of the gas pedal and the brake pedal pressed into the sole of her naked foot, patterning her skin. When she was the passenger, she sat on her heel, switching legs when her knee cramped. They never once parked as a couple, though one night, after backing away from Paulie's old Buick and laughing at the idea of Paulie with his trademark white pants around his ankles — he wore them pretty tight and it wouldn't be an easy dance to pull them up in a hurry, wiggle waggle, and would he even care or would he simply carry on? — after turning around and a few miles later driving slowly past Panchuck's grain bins and seeing that no one had rolled the signal tire out to the middle of the lane to show that the spot was taken for the evening — Sylvie and Erik did each press a look on the other across the wide space between them in the front seat. Sylvie, sitting on her heel, allowed herself to grind against the bone. She wanted him to notice, and she wanted him to not. She told herself the rush and flush were no more than heightened feelings from the game. She and Erik were each waiting for the single, right match, the ones they'd be willing to be exposed with through it all — jobs and kids and grandkids and laid-up, hope-to-die. They had talked about this.

THE BAND AT YIP'S was midway through "Proud Mary." On the dance floor Erik leaned in close and said, "You didn't invite me, Syl."

"I don't hear from you for ten months, I don't know where you are, I'm supposed to invite you?"

He waved to show it didn't matter. "This guy then, you're fine about being naked in the headlights with him, yea unto glory-be?"

"Yea in the when and the what?" she said, stalling, standing on the dance floor, her hand palm-up, a blank where she dared him to put the specifics.

"You remember."

"Is this a test?"

"Come on. First the babies, then all the way through to the nursing home."

She was annoyed with him for mentioning babies. It was only a wedding; they were only going to see how it went. The band sang for Proud Mary's big wheel to keep on turning, and Sylvie began a slow 360 on the dance floor, arms in the air, moving only to every second beat in order to prolong the attention her movement called to itself. She was somewhat on the skinny side, but she was pretty sure Erik appreciated skinny, and what's a little appreciation between friends?

Proud Mary. A riverboat. By the time she'd finished her first revolution she was thinking less about the look of her hips under the strobe light and more about the image of a river that came to her as she danced. A river branching into multiples of itself, no longer a single stream but a delta. And if her life were such a delta she might let the flow take her in a direction far from the current she was in now. If only there were more Sylvies, to ride the separate streams. The further she went, the further she'd be from herself. She could end up way down the shore, so far from this Sylvie, the Jack-marrying version, that all she could do would be to wave, and hope to be seen.

Over the music, she said, "I guess we considered ourselves pretty important back then, to think anybody would be watching what we did. Nobody's exactly training their headlights on us, on me and Jack."

"Not even yourself?" Erik said. "Even you're not watching?"

"You think too much."

He shrugged, which was infuriating.

"Erik, just dance."

When Yip's let out they drove across town, she in the rusty Toyota, he following in the Meteor. His lights glared off her rear-view mirror and made her squint. They parked on Fourth Street in front of the bungalow where Sylvie and Jack lived downstairs.

17

She set a hand on the warm hood of the Meteor. "Great memories here. Just, I don't see how the old boat lines up with your motorbike and your Ski-Doo."

"Got it from Mom for cheap, which means I can afford my toys for boys." At the gate he reached in front of her and flipped the latch. "You lurch a lot."

She saw he was barefoot, carrying his shoes and socks. She said, "I'm not good with a clutch. Jack won't have an automatic." She slipped out of her sandals. The grass teased her naked arches. "Wet," she said. "There's dew." The pattern on the concrete tiles that led around back pressed into the soles of her feet. She unlocked the door. A quick inhale before taking the first step down; that old fear, hardly conscious by now, of falling. On down, then, past the furnace, the washer, the dryer, and into the suite.

"Bathroom?" he said, and she pointed the way. He touched her shoulder as he passed. It's the wedding coming up, Sylvie told herself as she waited for him to come out. Only tonight and tomorrow, and then that's it.

They didn't bother with drinks. They stood with their bare feet inches apart and ignored the half-finished heap of flowers on the table. Behind Sylvie was the stove. Beside the stove was a squat water heater and beside the water heater was the bedroom door, open. Erik looked up at the little kitchen window. "You live underground," he said as he moved his gaze from the window to the bedroom doorway. Those were the actual words, but he could have strung together any old combination of syllables and the meaning would still be, There's a bed in there.

"Hold on a sec." Sylvie went into the bathroom and closed the door. She sat to pee and whispered to herself, Think this through. But it wasn't the time of night for in-depth thought. She ran a powder blue movie that featured Erik. How his hardness would press into the hollow beside her hipbone, how his bare shoulders would feel new under her hands, like something she'd coveted on a walk through Eaton's and slipped into her pocket without paying. Different from Jack's, whose deepslanted shoulders might be her least favourite of his physical traits; the shoulders and the fact that one of his earlobes was weirdly long, which wasn't his fault, but still.

She flushed. Ran the tap.

"You get swamped by a motorboat in there?"

"Just a *sec*." Sylvie turned the slick bar of soap between her palms. There must be an equivalent, in Erik-terms, of the weird earlobe. Yes: the way his left knee angled outward when he walked — something you stop noticing in a friend once you've known him awhile, but that knee, in a boyfriend, would be more than itself. It would be the single thing you wanted to change and couldn't. Along with all the other single things. His inherited weakness of eyesight. Erik's eventual wife would be leading him and his white cane around before he turned sixty. Sylvie took a moment to dry her hands.

She came out of the bathroom and led Erik into the dark bedroom. Light from the street came in through the small window high above the bed. Erik pointed to the bell-shaped red decal stuck to the pane. "What's that?"

"The fire department gives them out to mark where they might have to come in and rescue someone."

"How would they get in through an eensie opening like that? And how am I supposed to get *out* through an eensie opening like that when your old man comes down the stairs?"

"He won't be home tonight." She knew about these stag parties. He'd sleep where he passed out, and she wouldn't see him before two in the afternoon.

Erik guided her onto the bed. He sat down and took her foot in his hand. "This part's already naked." He began to massage – his thumb inside her arch, his hand travelling from her ankle, up inside the leg of her jeans, his finger wiggling its way between the tight fabric and the back of her knee. Who knew the back of a knee could start a quiver that would travel out so far from the source.

She heard the scuff of shoes against concrete. Erik's hand pulled out, *interruptus*, and came to rest on her heel. Sylvie opened her eyes and saw in the pale glow from the streetlight three pairs of running shoes passing the bedroom window. Alex, shuffling along backwards; two other pairs of feet – Benj and Cyril? – shuffling forward. Clueless damn bozos. There was heat on the back of her knee in the shape of Erik's finger. Cooling. Gone. She put a hand to his wrist and the two of them held still.

She heard Alex say, "Lemme find his keys here." They were a noisy crew, shuffling and grunting and letting the screen door slap behind them. Then an uneven rhythm, step-thud-step, thud-step-step. Sylvie pictured them in the stairwell, Alex with Jack by the armpits, below him Benj and Cyril, each gripping an ankle. Don't slip, don't let go. Jack's inert body hitting the walls of the stairwell side to side. She looked at Erik, who was looking up at the emergency decal on the window. She had the fleeting thought that she could be the one to climb out. Stand on the metal bedstead, make herself small and shimmy through, run seven blocks barefoot and knock on Margo's back door. Leave both these guys in the basement. She could feel how the metal would press into the ball of her foot as she hoisted herself. Erik sneezed, sending a shiver through the bed, and the moment she'd imagined vanished.

"Shh. Stay put. He'll be out cold and the others don't need to see you."

She went to open the door at the bottom of the stairs. "Why didn't you let him sleep it off?"

Cyril said, "We thought he might be needed here tomorrow."

"Thanks a million." Sylvie pointed to the couch and they lifted him there and arranged him on his side. He groaned and rolled off, onto the braided rug Sylvie's aunt Viv had made "to soften those unforgiving tiles, dear." When his head landed, Sylvie felt a clutch in her gut and looked away. Just like Jack, to sideswipe her most vulnerable spot.

"Ouch, jeez," said Benj.

Whether to run up the stairs and away, or to see to his hurt.

"We could put him in the bedroom," said Alex.

"No, leave him." She knelt and lifted his head, curved her palm underneath it and felt its whiskied weight. There are falls and then there are falls. He would be fine. She reached for the satin Ripley cushion and slid it under in place of her hand.

"I don't suppose he's feeling any pain," said Benj.

"All the same." Alex looked toward the bedroom doorway.

Sylvie shook her head.

Once the three of them had tromped back up the stairs and the screen had slapped shut, Erik came out from behind the bedroom door. Sylvie let him take her hand and together they stood looking at Jack's oblivious face. Sweet, she thought. Sweet, but she'd seen him like this a dozen times and she knew he wouldn't be sweet tomorrow. Not horrible, not mean, but far from sweet. For a moment all her doubts attached themselves to his long, limp earlobe and the less than attractive line of his shoulders. But the earlobe and the slopey shoulders were nothing. Once you'd focused on them, you had to dismiss them, because it doesn't do to be shallow. You couldn't blame a guy for having a saggy bit of skin one side of his face.

Erik squeezed her hand.

"What was it we thought we were doing?" she said.

"Drastic times, drastic measures." He wrapped her in a hug. "He's not your man for the headlights."

"Don't go thinking *you* are." She wished he wouldn't talk as if her life from here to forever rested on what would happen the day after tomorrow. It was only a wedding. A party in the lit hall, little girls in ruffled dresses dancing past their bedtimes and half the town bellying up for their free drinks. It was what you did. It was what they all did, Shelley and Beth and Serena, and now herself.

"Oh, Syl. Maybe I'm not the one. Probably not." But when she started to ease out of the hug, he pulled her close and said, "Don't, not yet."

On the floor, Jack drooled onto a silkscreened babe on the Playground of the Prairies. "Everybody's got their faults,"

Sylvie said, her cheek against the green plaid softness of Erik's shirt.

"That's a fact."

"You have to back up now and drive away."

"That is how the game goes."

The strain in her head was like the strain she felt when Jack would interrupt a drinking party to get out The Riddle Game: people reading brain teasers off cards in their palms, and you couldn't muddle through to an answer and you'd think, At this time of night, who cares? There were the flowers strewn on the table, and the girls would be back to help fold and tie and fluff come morning. There was the dress, too, oh, the dress. She'd pinned and cut yards of ivory satin and spent a week of evenings stitching it up on the Singer she'd inherited from her mother. Things were in place. There was the hall booked, and the church, and Aunt Merry baking buns, and Grandma on Mom's side driving all the way from Calgary.

Erik pushed his toes underneath her naked arches and she stepped up and stood on his feet, skin over skin. They began a lumbering waltz, slow circles, each step coming down bare inches from where it originated. Sylvie felt the odd fit of her right leg with Erik's left where his knee angled outward. She felt the upward press of his foot against her arch, then the moment of release, then the settling of weight with each graceless landing.

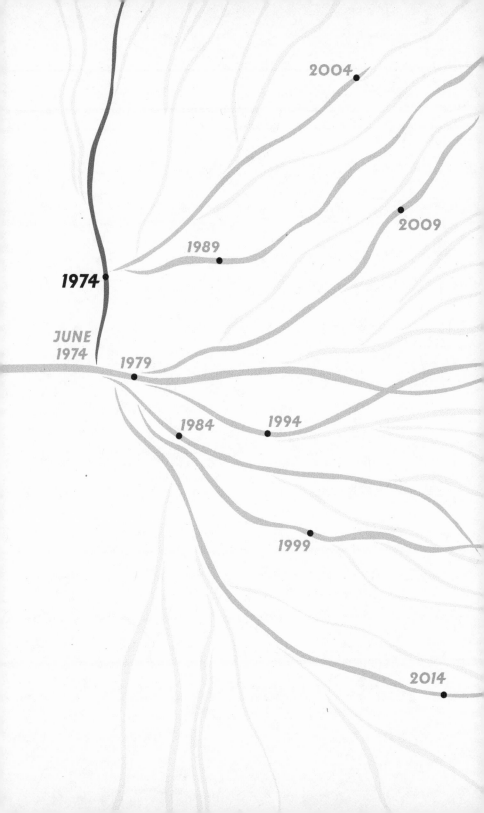

How Sylvie Failed to Become a Better Person through Yoga

WEEKEND AFTERNOONS during that hot, after-Jack summer, Sylvie and her roommate Lisa would wiggle into bikinis and slather themselves with baby oil and lie in the backyard under the sun. Periodically they wet themselves down using the hose in the shadowy space between the high walls of their house, where they lived on the second floor, and the neighbouring house.

Sylvie opened the tap one afternoon and held the hose above her head and closed her eyes while cold rivulets coursed her scalp. When she opened her eyes she saw the silver tabby that lived across the street. The cat arched its back and hissed at the stream of water issuing from the hose. Sylvie adjusted the tap so the stream became a trickle and propped the end of the hose on a cinder block. She called to the cat, coaxed, "Which of your nine lives are you in, kitty? Do you learn something every time, or do you get it wrong over and over?" Sylvie pinched a stalk of pigweed sprouting from a crack in the basement wall and shimmied it against the walk. The cat pounced. Sylvie moved the pigweed closer to the hose, and the cat followed. With patience she succeeded in getting the cat to drink. Lap-lap, lap. She shut off the water and kept her hand on the tap, at the ready. The cat stopped its lapping, sniffed, sat back and cocked its head, kitten-like. When want or curiosity made it lean in to sniff once more at the mouth of the hose, Sylvie cranked the tap and blasted the cat. It sprang from its crouch, letting out a yowl and landing two feet away. Sylvie's eyes followed the leap and saw the blunt toes of Lisa. Bits of grass from yesterday's mowing were scattered across Lisa's feet like candy sprinkles on cookies. How long had she been standing there? Sylvie's wet scalp puckered into goosebumps.

"That's a horrible thing to do."

As the cat slunk away with its wet whiskers and its grudge, Lisa picked up the hose, doused her strawberry blondness and her push-up bikini bra, and went back to lie on her towel. Neither she nor Sylvie mentioned the incident with the cat again, which didn't mean it was forgotten.

Sylvie and Lisa started out as roommates of convenience. They'd met at a bus stop and got to talking about the cost of living, and from there they put one and one together. Their suite was half a second storey in a house that might have been grand in the twenties. Access was by way of a jerry-built outside staircase. Sometimes, standing at the top and looking down, she would take a moment to check her balance. It was a bit of a project, living here, to conquer her fear of falling down stairs. She was making progress.

Sylvie and Lisa each ran with a different crowd, and they agreed this would make for a good relationship, each of them minding her own business.

In theory.

Sylvie envied her roommate on certain points: her hair, her twenty-six-inch waist, her collection of lacy, underwire bras. At first, the envy had especially to do with those brassieres, for Sylvie believed a girl had to be endowed in order to wear such a thing. Then one day when the door to Lisa's room was ajar, Sylvie caught a glimpse of her breasts and understood how a bra like that was the way to make a couple of unremarkable things remarkable. Later, when Lisa was out, Sylvie went into her room and tried the red one. Okay, she'd need to go one size down, but this would work. Next day at Eaton's, three bras, three colours, yes.

Lisa had moved into the suite a week earlier than Sylvie, claimed the larger bedroom and stacked three twelve-packs of Labatt's Blue empties on the floor at the end of the kitchen cupboard. Sylvie associated Blue with truck drivers and guys who went out to Alberta to work the rigs. As if to confirm, Lisa's fiancé Dave, a house framer, came by one night with three of his buddies who were home from Alberta for the weekend. All of them wore their hair short; one guy chewed the corners of his mustache; their fun appeared to come from drinking and its related games. Sylvie knelt and put Led Zeppelin on the turntable.

"Anybody mind?"

"Far out," said the burly guy in the quilted vest in the armchair, and Sylvie could sense the effort involved, like someone who'd never taken French at school trying to say *au revoir.*

She retreated to her bedroom and sat with her back to the door listening to the music. Static crackled through her hair where it rubbed against the wood. She heard one of the guys say to Lisa, "Wench, another beer!" These guys were not so different from Jack, and Sylvie had climbed onto a metal bedstead and shimmied out a window and left Jack behind, along with his Rod Stewart LPs, his running shoes he'd never run in, his coffee can full of bottle caps sitting in its rusty ring on the countertop. She missed him only on three-beer nights, and only then if she'd run out of friends for the moment. In her after-Jack life she'd latched onto a different sort of guy, the sort that wore dashiki shirts and seasoned leather hiking boots and knew the three best places to hide a dime bag in the alley.

Next morning from her bed, Sylvie heard the hungover rumble of Dave's voice, heard Lisa's hungover simper in reply, but couldn't make out words. Rumble, simper. She was hungry but wasn't about to walk through an argument between those two on her way to the cereal. Rumble, simper, silence. Silence stretching on. She heard Dave's heavy tread, heard the closing of the outside door and felt the slight shudder from his weight as he booted it down the stairs. Sylvie came out of her bedroom and tinkled Cheerios into a bowl, a sound to rinse the air. Lisa's face was red about the eyes and nostrils as she told Sylvie about the new rule: Lisa wasn't to speak to other guys unless absolutely necessary. Apparently, as the lamplight cast rainbows on the spinning vinyl and Robert Plant sang about what went on way down inside, Lisa had sat on one arm of the armchair and had a longish conversation with the burly guy in the quilted vest. Dave would have no more of this; likewise, he would not engage in conversation with other women.

"What did you talk about?"

"The price of jeans, his sister's horses. Shit, winter in Alberta."

Sylvie went to the bathroom, unspooled a length of toilet paper and brought it out to Lisa so she could blow her nose. A moment later she fetched another handful so Lisa could wipe her eyes.

From then on, nights when he stayed over, if Sylvie and Dave found themselves alone together at the breakfast table he made no sound but for the crunch and swallow of his Froot Loops.

THE GIRLS COAXED a signal along the rabbit ears and into Sylvie's little TV to watch *The Partridge Family*. The standing fan near the window pushed hot air at their sweaty faces. Lisa fetched her pins and elastics, did some fingerwork with her hair, and accomplished a twist arrangement on the crown of her head. Escaped locks floated in the breeze from the fan. "Here," she said. "I'll do yours. It's cooler." Sylvie slid down to sit on the floor in front of the couch, and Lisa positioned herself with her knees hugging Sylvie's shoulders. "You have the floppiest hair." She gathered and twisted, retwisted and pinned. "There. Finally."

Sylvie turned to say thanks, and a hank of hair came loose and drooped over one ear. They laughed together, and Sylvie made a little snort on the intake of breath. Lisa mimicked the snort, and the two of them giggled and gulped and giggled again. Another hank came away. "Oh," said Lisa, "I give up. But we'll have to somehow figure out your hair if you're going to be my maid of honour."

"Maid of honour?"

"Sure, why not?"

"Okay, yeah. Wow."

They heard footsteps on the outside staircase and looked over to see a hairy silhouette through the frosted-glass pane in the door.

"Looks like one of yours." Lisa turned back to *The Partridge Family.*

"It's only Will." With quick fingers Sylvie disassembled what was left of the updo, grabbed her Player's Lights, and went out to sit beside Will at the top of the rickety staircase. They'd first met at the laundromat on Avenue P and had gone down the block to Chin's to have coffee and wait out the drying time. They couldn't call it dating, she'd told him when they started hanging around together. She couldn't make out with someone who'd seen her undies sunny side up in a laundry basket before they'd even exchanged first names. She was joking, of course; she was eager, in fact, but Will seemed content simply to pass time together. Fine, she would have her adventures elsewhere.

Sylvie pulled out two cigarettes and Will flicked his lighter. Ah, that first drag. "I've been thinking," she said. Her leg bumped his.

He shifted casually away as he pocketed his Bic. "What's the topic?"

"Self-improvement. It's been brought to my attention I could use it."

"Uh-huh."

"You agree then?"

"It's an in-general thing, isn't it, not a Sylvie-specific thing."

Will worked at the used book store on Twentieth. He had a memory for titles and authors and the words of praise on the backs of the books, and so he could say things that made people think he'd read entire volumes. Sylvie would tease him: *You're so smart you could go to the you-knee-ver-settee.* She mocked the place because she couldn't see how a person would manage to rise beyond an everyday job — her own, for instance, binding journals in the basement of the campus library — to become an actual student. Someone should send out instructions. She'd been near the top of her class in early high school, but where did people find the money? What did they live on?

"Self-improvement." Will's voice was formal. For a few minutes they smoked in silence, looking into the leaves of the elm between the house and the street. Then he said, "You don't want to try this alone. Let's make a plan." He exhaled and looked to be sifting the smoke for an idea. He elbowed her in the ribs. "We could join yoga."

"Sure." She elbowed him back. "Let's go to confirmation class."

"Let's read *The Prophet*."

"I've heard of that."

The phone rang inside, and a minute later there was a rap on the other side of the frosted glass. Sylvie started to rise but stopped when Lisa said through the pane, "Dave called this afternoon?"

"Sorry. Forgot to tell you."

"You have to tell me. When he calls, I'm supposed to call him back."

And she was mean to cats. "Sorry, Lisa, I —" but Sylvie had no excuse to patch to the end of the sentence. Her thigh muscles, arrested between standing and sitting, burned. Lisa's ghost left the window, saying, "Now I'm in shit!"

"Now you're in shit," said Will.

A WEEK LATER, Will called to say he'd seen a poster at the laundromat advertising Kundalini yoga. They should go. Starts next week.

"I didn't think you were serious."

"I wasn't."

"Neat. Let's." She set the receiver back in the cradle and immediately the phone rang. Dave. Yes, he knew Lisa had gone to her cousin's place for supper, but wasn't she home yet? No, okay. Before hanging up he said, "Hell of a heat out there today. Burnt my neck so bad it blistered."

"Hot for sure. Did you just break the rule? The don't-converse-with-girls rule?"

"Now, Sylvie."

"Gotta go." She hung up, pulled at a thread in the couch upholstery, wound it around her finger until the blood built, remembered her Aunt Merry's warning about the little girl who'd lost a finger from tying a string too tight around it and leaving it there. She wondered what would happen if Lisa or Dave violated their new code and the other found out. Either one of them might just as easily throw their morning bowl of cereal at the person across the table, as scarf down what was in it.

SYLVIE WORKED WITH a drill press and a guillotine in the basement of the university library. She used the drill press, along with plastic pins, to bind a year's worth of journals at a time. Once the holes were drilled and the pins were in, she'd pull a lever to bring down a hot iron that melted the raw ends of the pins into rounded caps. *Voilà*: a book. The guillotine was the final step. She would push a button to bring down an automated blade that descended at a slow and certain pace and shaved away the uneven edges of the pages. Sometimes, as she pressed the button to bring down the blade, she'd think about sliding a finger on top of the stack of journals and into its path.

The sheared edges of the finished volumes were a fascination, smooth and sharp at the same time. They drew the hand. Her palms were nicked all over.

At noon she'd take her sandwich and find a patch of lawn out of range of the sprinklers and watch the university people as they carried their shoulder bags from one building to another. What would it be like to be one of them? To write the words in the journals that crossed her workstation. Even to read them. Maybe she would do that: begin to read them.

Her job, with its sunny lunch hours, was so much better than Lisa's. Lisa worked at the jeans factory in the north end. Her fingernails were stained indigo. She arrived home droopy-lidded after her hour-long bus ride, some days eating her supper at five-thirty and going to bed right after, only getting up again if Dave called.

He rang one Friday when Lisa had already caught the bus back home for the weekend.

"She went to her mom and dad's." Like he didn't know. Sylvie began to play with the upholstery thread she'd fiddled loose the other day. It was shiny and strong, with no stretch, no give. She rolled it between finger and thumb, a little rope anchoring her where she sat.

"Oh," said Dave. "Forgot." Liquor-laced enunciation. "How about I talk to you instead. Better yet, I'll bring over some beer."

She twirled the thread in a tight motion so it wound around the tip of her finger.

"I've never seen inside your room," he said.

Sylvie moved her hips in her chair, rising to his words. She twirled the thread once more and then again. "You won't be seeing my bedroom anytime soon." By now she had a tight band around her finger, and the tip swelled red.

"Be a sport, Sylvie."

"I'm just on my way out."

"Sure you are."

"It's true. Yoga." She worked at the thread with her thumb, trying to roll it off the end of her finger. The more she pushed, the more it twisted around itself and held.

"*Yo*-ga. Well."

"Bye, then." She hung up. With her other hand free now she loosened the thread and slipped her finger out. The relief was out of all proportion, travelling across her palm and shivering along the inside of her forearm all the way to the crook of her elbow. She got up and locked the door, came back and lay on the couch. The pleasure she took as she moved against her own hand over the next minutes would remain her own; she'd no more get into bed with Dave than she'd give up a digit for a more intimate knowledge of her guillotine. Still — would he be rough, and would she like that? She wondered if she'd stumbled right past one of those moments that could send a life sideways. She wondered, if not for the foolishness with her swelling finger, whether she might have said, pretending innocence, Sure, let's have a beer.

ON A SWEET-SMELLING EVENING, Will came by to pick up Sylvie, and they walked half a mile to City Park and found eight or nine people their own age or a little older sitting on the lawn of a bungalow painted powder blue. Peasant blouses and water buffalo sandals — the kind that are meant to be soaked in the sink overnight and worn wet into the day so as to take the impression of your sole.

"Hi," Sylvie and Will both said, and the others smiled or nodded. Sylvie lit a smoke. A woman on the steps in a voluminous purple shirt said, "Such a yang thing, smoking." What did it mean, for a thing to be yang? Two more puffs and Sylvie bent to grind what was left of her cigarette on the scrubby lawn, "the big ashtray," as Will called it. After a moment the woman in purple extracted a pack of smokes from the drapery of her shirt and lit up. Soon the door opened and a young, blond-bearded man in loose white pyjamas looked past the others

37

toward Will and Sylvie and introduced himself as Animesh and the woman at his side as Satya. The two of them shone in the dark doorway. "Come in!"

They met twice a week in Animesh and Satya's rented house, sweating on the maplewood floor of the unfurnished living room, evening sunlight filtering through the philodendrons and spider plants on the windowsill. They engaged in a range of poses and stretches, but Sylvie could see that the chanting and the silences were just as important as the movements. One evening as she entered the room, Satya smiled and locked onto her eyes. Sylvie did her best to return the gaze. An itch built in her left eye. Satya's gaze wouldn't let go. Sylvie's eyes began to water, momentary relief from the itch. She had the idea she was to look harder, past the brown-sugar irises and into Satya's essential being. She managed not to giggle. A dozen pinpricks across her eye now, and she scrunched the outer corner to bring another tear. These people didn't explain anything. The itch was too much, and she closed her eyes.

Later that evening as the group sat in silent meditation, Sylvie snuck a glance at Will, whose eyes remained closed, his expression steady, no twitch of his lips under his shaggy mustache. This gave Sylvie confidence that with time she might feel the way the other people in the room felt. Appeared to feel. Between one yoga session and the next she would sometimes think of Satya and Animesh as they'd looked that first evening, shining in the dark doorway. Followed, without apparent logic, by the thought that she hadn't taken a five-finger discount on anything in months, not a magazine from the corner store, not a sweater from Eaton's, not a pair of panties, not the change off Lisa's dresser. Maybe she'd left that impulse back in her Jack life, and maybe it would stay there.

Yoga practice was routinely followed by Sharing of Food, which Satya called by a Sanskrit word Sylvie couldn't pronounce. Leftovers stayed with Animesh and Satya, who looked as if they could use them. Raisins, dates, dried apricots, sliced apples. Will and Sylvie learned to add the suffix *ji* when they addressed the people in the group. Brian-*ji*, Marianne-*ji*. In Hindi, Animesh told them, this meant *respected*. It was clear most of these people had known each other for some time, and it was kind of them, the way they made Will-*ji* and Sylvie-*ji* welcome.

One night Earl-*ji* brought a fresh pineapple for Sharing of Food. Animesh went to the kitchen. He called out, "Brenda, where's that knife with the red handle?"

Satya called back, "Look in the drawer by the stove."

Sylvie whispered, "He calls you Brenda?"

"It's an old name. Once in a while he forgets."

"Does he have another name too?" Will said.

Satya's neck reddened. "He's Animesh now."

"Where are you from?"

"Swift Current."

"And Animesh?"

"Gimli. Manitoba."

That night as Will walked Sylvie back to Bedford Road, she said, "Animesh could tell us the way to show respect in Hindi is to say *ting* and we'd say it. Marianne-*ting*, Earl-*ting*." Will laughed and Sylvie let the back of her hand brush against his.

Will moved to make a little more space between them on the sidewalk. "Will?"

"Yeah?"

"Do you get it? I mean, 'the deep mysteries of yoga'?" Her voice mocked both her words and herself, but only lightly.

"Which?"

"Any of it."

"I don't know. We have the books at the store. The idea is, you get your mind and your body communicating with each other. You open up these," he searched for a word, "these centres. Inside. So the life energy will flow through."

"But do you *get* it?"

"Takes practice, I suppose."

ANOTHER HOT BACKYARD DAY, and Sylvie lay on the beach towel with the big blue anchor; Lisa lay on the bath mat, a dishtowel overlapping it to make it longer.

Lisa said, "I need pop. D'you want anything?"

"Nah. Thanks." Sylvie opened her eyes to see Lisa pull on her cut-offs and leave for the corner store. A few seconds later she heard a rattle. She propped herself on her elbow and looked next door and saw the screen on the basement window move. Fingers curled out and gripped one side of the frame, angled the screen and pulled it inside. From the cavity emerged a young man's head — long dark hair, small moustache, happy eyes. People came and went from these houses.

"Hello," they both said, their voices bumping each other.

"Want to come over?" he said.

"You could come here." She lay back down.

40

He climbed out and sat cross-legged in his jeans on the bathmat. "I have come, My Lady, as you commanded."

One of those. Almost forgivable, though, now that she saw his happy green eyes up close. His was not the sort of gaze that would try to see all the way inside her.

"But here under the sun," he said, "it is hot and bright and —"

"That's what makes a good day for sunbathing."

"It is hot and bright, I was saying, and lacks . . . privacy." His bare chest was smooth and skinny. His fingers played with the stray hairs that curled close to a nipple.

"So come with me, if it please you." He stood and held out his hand.

She followed him to his basement window and through it, feet first and backward the way he showed her, and when her toes landed on the chair he'd placed below the window as a step, she felt his hands on her backside. Leaving at that point was a choice she was aware of, but the feel of those hands through her bikini roused her in the way she'd been missing.

In the heat, lying on a grandma quilt on a mattress on the floor, they had sweet, slippery sex. Their after-dozes overlapped, and then they both were awake once more. Sylvie placed a hand on the painted concrete floor to gather its coolness. She set it on the guy's chest, fingers spread, a gift. She asked him what he did for work, and he said he was presently without gainful employment, My Lady. She told him about her own job and how, when she pushed the button on her machine, the blade would descend and slice through the booklets without slowing down, and it would follow through right

41

into the slot in the work table. "It's a force. I get to start it up, and I get to turn it off."

The guy raised himself on one elbow and took two of her fingers into his mouth. He said around her fingers, "Speaking of forces."

Later, as she climbed back out, his hands boosted her backside and followed her legs all the way to her ankles. They gripped there, tight around bone and tendon, and Sylvie sensed she was about to be pulled back down, on his terms. She tensed. His grip slackened then, and she dared to look around. He smiled a My-Lady smile. She gave his chest the smallest kick as she shimmied out. It wasn't the first time she'd crawled through a window to leave a man — or two — behind, but it was the first time she hadn't even learned a name. He caught her toe and pinched, hard, and then he let go.

Lisa was lying, eyes closed, on the towel with the anchor, which she'd relocated to profit from the late-afternoon sun. An empty pop bottle lay under her limp hand. As Sylvie moved the dishtowel and the bath mat into the sun, Lisa lifted her head and squinted, then let her head fall again. Another month and Lisa would be married and gone, no longer there to see Sylvie climb in a window or out. Sylvie closed her eyes, the better to bask.

A YOUNG MAN, Bimal, arrived from Edmonton, and there was much excitement when he agreed to lead a chanting session at the powder-blue bungalow where Animesh and Satya lived in their pyjamas. They would create energy, the group of them, energy that hadn't existed before, energy they would — and

he emphasized the words — *bring into being.* As they sat on
the hardwood in half lotus, he directed them to turn their
heads to the left, shouting "Wah!" then to the right, "Guru!"
They began slowly and sped up. "Wah guru! Wah guru!" Their
shouts crescendoed, fell, crescendoed, fell. Sylvie grew dizzy
from swinging her head. The vibration in her chest felt deep
and rich, but the speed was frantic. She stopped and looked at
Will, whose hair lashed his face with every turn. She resumed
her head-swinging. Afterward, she had a job of it to stop her
limbs from shaking.

During Sharing of Food, Bimal told them stories about his
recent travels with beloved spiritual leader Mata-*ji*. "We were
driving through the mountains, and suddenly Mata-*ji* held up
her hands. 'When The Deluge happens,' she said, 'the water
will come this far, and no further.' Then we got out of the van
to see the very place where the water will stop. The very place."

"You're so lucky," said one of the *jis*.

"Far out," said another. Sylvie bit the insides of her cheeks.

Later, as she and Will walked back to Bedford Road she
said, "We're just fucking tourists, aren't we, with this yoga
thing."

"So far."

LISA'S BROTHER PERRY hit town on a Thursday. He was moving
back from Calgary, looking for his own place, but in the meantime he would crash on the couch. By the time Sylvie got home
from work on the Friday, Lisa had already gone to meet Dave
down at the bar. There was Perry alone on the couch, a bottle
of Blue sweating on the coffee table. "I took the empties in for

cash." Grin. Sylvie looked toward the end of the counter and saw that the stack of cartons had been replaced by a new box with a couple of empties already inside.

"In the fridge," he said.

Sylvie opened a bottle and turned so she was three-quarters facing him. She took a swig and felt his eyes.

"Too bad," Perry said.

"Too bad what?"

"Nancy's coming in from Calgary tonight. I'm not a free man."

"You should be so lucky." Sylvie walked toward the couch, moving her hips in a way she had, not too much, you don't need much.

The phone rang. Will. "Are you coming to yoga?"

"You go ahead."

"You missed Wednesday."

"I know, but I've had a beer and I wouldn't keep a straight face, and that would be rude."

"Don't want to be rude," Perry said after she hung up.

When Lisa got back from drinks with Dave, who dropped her off and drove away to see a man about a dog, Sylvie and Perry were eating deep-fried shrimp from the takeout window down the block, and Sylvie was telling stories. She imitated the expression on Satya's face as Satya had tried to tunnel through her pupils to find the essential Sylvie. She told Perry about Mata-*ji* and The Deluge and said she bet Mata-*ji* was from Moose Jaw. Lisa stood at the kitchen counter opening and closing doors, making noise with a cup and a spoon. She boiled the kettle and let it rise to a full shriek before taking it off the burner. She poured hot water and made a show of not looking their way. Squeezed her tea bag and plopped it in the sink. She looked at her brother. "Nancy'll be here by nine, I suppose. You and her can have my bed, I'll take the couch." She went into her room and closed the door.

Nancy arrived within the hour. "Nance, sweetie," Perry said. "This is Roommate Sylvie." He stopped speaking and looked to be biting the insides of his cheeks. Sylvie offered Nancy the last of the battered shrimp, but Nancy said no, she and Perry would go out, thank you. The next day by four in the afternoon they'd found him an apartment to rent.

ON A SATURDAY MORNING, Sylvie walked up the outside staircase with her groceries and opened the door, and there was brother Perry on the couch with his arms around a sobbing Lisa. She was supposed to be out at the lake with Dave in his slant-floored trailer. Perry tilted her head forward so Sylvie could see the back of it, parted her hair here and here with his fingers to show the swollen places and the gashes and the confetti of dried blood. He gave her the story: early this morning while Dave was snoring off the booze, Lisa had snuck away. It took her hours to hitch the sixty miles to the city. "She called me half an hour ago. That asshole bashed her head against the cupboards. Bastard." He said the word *bastard* tenderly, while stroking Lisa's hair. "Four times," he said. "Once for each cupboard door in that shit trailer of his."

"Capital asshole," Sylvie said. Lisa looked up, and Sylvie saw the dark bruise on her cheekbone, the red marks on her jaw. She pictured Dave's fingers cupping that small face. The

45

skin at the back of her neck pulled itself tight. She shuddered. Revulsion, chased by a fleeting twinge of arousal. She went to the fridge and opened the tiny, clogged freezer at the top and chipped at the frost with a knife until she'd freed a bag of frozen string beans. She slapped it twice on the counter to make it pliable, and handed it to Perry. "She needs to go to the hospital."

Perry looked at Lisa, who shook her head. He left the beans on the couch and went to the bathroom and started to run a tub. Sylvie sat down beside Lisa and moved her hands awkwardly, trying to think how to touch her. She picked up the beans, steadied Lisa's forehead with one hand, and used the other to hold the bag against the swelling at the back. The cold sucked at her fingers.

After a moment Lisa reached up and lifted away Sylvie's hands. "It's all right." Perry came out of the bathroom and Lisa went in, her steps small. Sylvie brought from her own room the bulky cardigan that served as bathrobe for both of them and handed it around the door. The next morning she made a point of bundling the fabric she'd cut for her bridesmaid dress and stowing her sewing machine under the table.

Two weeks later Lisa was back out at the trailer with Dave for the weekend, and the wedding was on for the following Saturday. She hadn't cancelled a thing, not the church, not the food, not the alterations to take in her whipped-meringue dress one more time at the hips. Sylvie wanted to tell her, I know it seems like you can't stop a wedding in its tracks, but you can. Once you do, relief rushes in. She found Perry's number on the list pinned to the wall and called him and asked, "What should we do?"

"Mind our own business."

Own business, hell. Sunday night when Lisa returned from the lake, apparently unharmed, Sylvie sat her down on the end of the couch where the springs still held up. She told her about Dave on the phone that other day, how he'd suggested he come by with beers, what he'd said about wanting to see her room. "He's a gold-medal jerk."

"Don't —" Lisa said, and she made a show of breathing in and out and in again — "Don't make the mistake of thinking that just because he said those things it means he likes you. He doesn't *like* you. You should *hear* what he says about you."

"Lisa! That's not —"

"You haven't got a frickin' clue. And prancing around for Perry. He told me about that."

Sylvie was the first to look away.

"I've had in mind," Lisa said, "that actually Nancy should be maid of honour."

"Oh."

"She's practically family."

"True."

"And maybe two bridesmaids instead of three. Simpler all around."

IN THE DAYS LEADING up to the wedding, Lisa bunked over at Dave's apartment, dropping by to pick things up or leave things off at times when Sylvie wasn't in. Sylvie still felt sucker punched, nursed the sensation for days. At least she knew better than to marry one of these guys. The scatter of dried blood on Lisa's scalp, the wince the next morning as she brushed her hair. The long baths in the evenings, Sylvie having to come in for a pee the one night and seeing how Lisa sat up quickly, steam rising, hair dripping, as if she'd been trying to scald shut the gashes.

On Friday morning she wrapped a wedding present, thinking, This will happen again to her. The gift was three brass candlesticks in graduated heights that she'd found at the Whole Earth Store. Almost a set. She'd enjoyed their lovely weight, a secret in the bottom of her purse, as she walked on past the smiling woman at the cash register who wore dangling silver earrings and a lustrous brown braid draped over her shoulder. *Those earrings are the mint,* she'd said to the woman. *Thanks, yeah, I'm loving them.* Candlesticks, because she remembered Lisa saying Dave's basement suite was cold, and though a small flame doesn't give off much heat, it might lend warmth of a different sort. Or. Push came to shove, she could use one to strike back. Sylvie tied a silver bow and left the gift on the table.

When she got home from after-work drinks the package was gone, and under the pepper shaker were three twenties and a note: *Last of the rent money.* In search of a breeze, Sylvie went to sit on the landing at the top of the outside staircase. She looked down at the street through a lace of elm leaves. A red pickup was parked at the curb, running. The dark-haired basement neighbour with the happy eyes appeared, slid a duffel into the open bed of the truck alongside two cardboard boxes and a mattress already there, and climbed into the passenger seat. Sylvie smoked a cigarette and then a joint and went inside to call Will. It was too long since she'd seen him. He, however, was on his way to yoga. Did she want to come?

"Maybe next time. Could you come by later?"

"It might be late. Things, you know, not sure when."

The living room was stifling, the bedroom worse. The fan that used to stand by the window had belonged to Lisa. To create a cross draft Sylvie opened the outside door at the top of the staircase and the window above the couch. She stayed up till eleven watching TV, but Will didn't show. Wearing only her panties and hugging a rolled-up blanket, she fell asleep on the couch. The next morning, the phone woke her. She pulled the blanket around herself and got up to answer it, still groggy.

"Sylvie?"

"Hello, Lisa."

"Thank you for the present."

Sylvie let the blanket drop and stood, panty-clad, in the already warm morning. Across her shoulders, an itchy film of sweat. "You're welcome." Crooking her neck to hold the phone, she opened the freezer and looked for the bag of beans to cool her forehead. It wasn't there. She remembered tossing it after using it as a cold pack.

"Sylvie, I didn't want things to finish up this way."

"Me neither, Lisa." She put her hand against the inside wall of the freezer, where it melted a print in the frost.

"Me neither, Sylvie."

"No." It was the only word to find its way out from among all the things she might have said, all the possibilities for counterfeit cheer or honest questions or best wishes that, though they might not be affectionate, would at least have been sincere. Sylvie heard the line click and she, too, hung up. She thought, She has a brother. Sylvie touched her cool hand to her throat, her forehead, the back of her neck, turning her head as she did so, and from this new angle she could see into her bedroom. The pink sheet on her bed made a long hill, and the shape of that hill was a lying-down body, and her first instinct was to run screaming in her underwear down the shaky stairs to the street. Then she saw it was Will, his tangled hair standing out around his sleeping head like a curly cloud of joy. She took a couple of deep breaths while the jolt of adrenaline subsided, then bent to grasp the blanket from the floor and pull it around herself. She went to the bedroom and put her hand on the sheet where it lay across Will's shoulder. He opened his eyes, already in possession of himself, and she guessed he'd been awake for some time.

"Tell me something wise," she said. "Anything."

"You shouldn't sleep with the door open," he said. "You never know what could happen."

"That's fairly basic."

"And yet you didn't know it."

She nudged him to move over, which he did, dragging the sheet, still around him, and leaving a shelf for her on the narrow bed. I am abandoning her, Sylvie thought. I have abandoned her. Still wrapped in her blanket, she settled herself in the narrow space. A girl could walk out of a safe, upstairs apartment and into harm's way and pretend that wasn't what she was doing. A girl had to watch herself. She touched her cool hand to her forehead, wishing for ice.

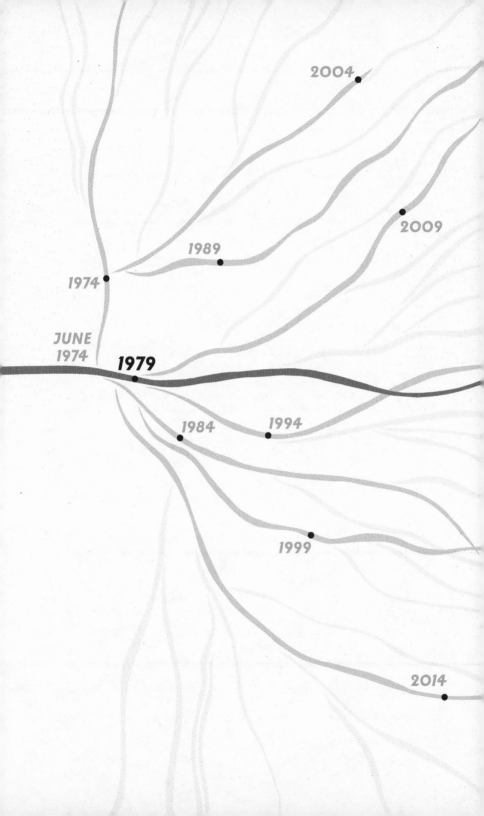

The Last Days
of Disco

MARGO AND BENJ necked lazily on a sand-strewn blanket. Alex and Penny lounged on web-woven lawn chairs, Penny with her eyes closed, white-blond hair twisted tight in a towel, tanning as if she was going for an A. Sylvie sat low in the canvas sling of her beach chair, the crossbar at the top pressing into the back of her skull, chair-bone to head-bone. And Jack, well, Jack was pacing. In their five years of marriage he might have walked all the way to Antarctica if he'd straightened out his hairpin turns and followed his toes where they led. But he wasn't one to light out for parts unknown; nor had Sylvie been when despite her doubts she'd joined him at the altar, age nineteen. Sunburn bloomed above his tight blue trunks.

This was new for the six of them, to be outdoors together in daylight. They knew each other in dim bars and night-time kitchens, in scraggly, moonlit yards around smoky fires where they threw their bottles in among the flames to watch the labels scorch.

A hardcover novel she'd brought from work rested in Sylvie's lap: *The Last Enchantment,* thick as a brick. She ran her fingers across the impressed lettering on the cover. This was one of the things she loved best about the world, the physical feel of objects, the changes in texture under her fingers. It was what redeemed her job, mending books in an unwindowed room on the second floor of the university library. No more stacking journals in the basement. Now she worked with the loose weave of binding tape; the sharp splinters of crystallized glue that hid along the edges of a separated cover waiting to nip a finger; the dependable firmness of a replacement spine. Her job was to keep a thing going past its time.

Jack halted. "It is time, people, to raise your beach bums, your sandy asses, off the sand." Sylvie watched to see if his peculiar magic would work, as it so often did. She opened her book and ran her palm across a page, feeling the faint indentations the trails of print left in the rag paper.

"It is time," Jack said, "for your lesson in line dance Hustle! Form yourselves into a single line, my friends, on the dock if you would." He was not — as Sylvie had reminded him last night when she and he were in the screaming thick of the worst of it — a man of vision. "You can see about as far as the bug screen strapped to the front of your Corolla." Sometimes, though, he did show evidence of a vision for the next fifteen minutes or so.

The dock where Jack wanted them to line up was a good size, a pier leading out to a square patio that stood above the water on stilts, but it wasn't nearly big enough for five people to dance the Hustle in formation — or not for long. Sylvie dug her toes in, and the fine spill of sand across her feet was reason enough not to leave her chair — the grains against her skin, their slide, their heat.

Jack stooped to tug at the corner of Benj and Margo's blanket. "Repossess your tongues!" Benj kicked at Jack's hand, but he got up and hoisted Margo after him, her limbs sun-honey languid. Jack grabbed Penny's chair by the legs and dumped her sideways. She gave the others a flash of breast as she slipped it out of its cup to shake away sand.

Jack's reply to Sylvie's accusation last night (in the screaming thick of the worst of it) had been to say he did *too* have imagination, he had a semi-trailerful. People were always telling him he had a real sense of fun. Sylvie had made for the bedroom, turning her back on the living room and the insults they'd flung at each other.

"Are you gonna just walk away?" he'd said as she walked away.

The sand so warm, and she was so sleepy these days. She closed her eyes. "Hi-yo, Sylverie." Alex's sweat-wet hand was on her knee. She flicked the sand off her toes and followed him. Below his cut-offs, the backs of his pink legs were embossed, criss-cross, from the webbing of his chair. She bit back on the urge to put a finger to his skin and trace the pattern.

"YOUR TROUBLE," Jack had said last night — he'd whipped past to face her in the hallway — "your trouble is, nothing's ever enough. You're just plain greedy." He put one hand on his hip and leaned his opposite shoulder against the wall. "That was it when I met you, and that's it now."

"So arrest me." She put a hand on her hip in mockery and leaned against the wall as he did.

"I wouldn't bother."

"Exactly!" She slapped the wall hard. "You wouldn't bother."

"Exactly." He slapped the wall a bare inch from her face. She felt the wind from it like old breath.

THE FIVE OF THEM lined up on the dock under Jack's direction, blinking in the sun, their ripening beers abandoned, bottles aslant in the sand, bubbles expanding inside them. Benj performed a showy stretch, arms out to either side, pecs proud. "We can't dance without music."

"*I'm* your music," said Jack. "Just follow the count of eight, over and over." He clapped it out: *one*-two, *three*-four . . . Not exactly Soul City Symphony, but one thing you could say about Jack, he had rhythm.

The rhythm method, that was another story.

Still, as of last month they were five years married. Anyone would say it was time.

"Idiot-proof," said Jack. "Now, as you Philistines may not know, Van McCoy died last week." He mimed grief with a downturned mouth and took on an emcee voice. "Remember that date: July 6, 1979. This ceremonial tattoo we are about to perform on Uncle Walter's dock is the least we can do in honour of the man McCoy. Without him we would not even *have* the Hustle." He did the party trick where he bulged his skinny belly so it ballooned above his trunks, skin stretched taut, and used his fingers to tap out a drum roll. "Sylvie, dear Sylvie, kindly educate these novices in the steps."

The conjurer's lovely assistant. "Which combination?" she said. *"Master,"* she added, in the manner of *I Dream of Jeannie*, the clear-eyed woman in harem pants on the small screen who would swing her blond ponytail and pretend she wasn't the one making the decisions. As a kid Sylvie used to feel as if she was in a conspiracy with Jeannie against all the boys in the world.

"The one with the heel-slap, dear Silly."

It was the most teachable of the combinations the two of them had learned in ballroom dancing classes at the gym in the school down the block from their apartment. A short pattern, repeated, repeated, and four reps would make a square. Except: the rolling grapevine sequence tended to loosen when you stepped it out but tighten when you reeled it in, which meant the square would shift along the dance floor by a foot or so each time through. Then you turned ninety degrees and the pattern wanted four steps back. In the school gym one evening, Sylvie had danced backward into the grid of a metal light cage mounted on the wall, head-bone to light-bone.

This afternoon she would play Jack's game, sure, show off her own sense of fun. Earlier in the day, as Sylvie floundered in water up to her armpits, Margo had said, "You're not exactly fluent as a swimmer, are you?" It was a fair comment, but she could keep her head up. Jack couldn't swim to save his life. You could bet that once the dance was done he'd be standing dry and alone on the dock.

One-two, *three*-four. A dazzling disco sun above, Jack clapping the beat, Sylvie leading the other four in the simple sequence, forward two, back two, kick, turn, and on. They caught the pattern with hardly a misstep. One pair of cut-offs and one pair of bulging Speedos, three pairs of breasts slung into bikini bras, Penny's with the most generous swing on the turns, the most emphatic bounce when it was time to rise on tiptoe and slap her heels together. Sylvie had less bounce, less swing, but a pretty sweet bikini. And her breasts would swell by a cup size at least, she expected, over the coming months. Sweat trickled down her back, wicking to either side where it met her bikini bottoms. She'd been sick to her stomach at five a.m., then brushed her teeth clean of evidence and stolen back into bed beside a sleeping Jack. She'd woken again at seven, her insides settled for the day if the pattern of the past couple of weeks was anything to go by.

The beat of the dance, kick, turn. *"Dis*-go here," she said, to make Alex laugh beside her as she stomped a foot, "and *dis*-go dere." Alex did laugh, and Jack said, "Hey, it's my show." She glanced along the weathered boards: still a few feet of dock between dancers and water.

Last night, raw from shouting and sex, she'd said, "You know *your* biggest problem? You never think *What if?* about anything. Not your job, not your tooth decay, not your brand of beer. It's like you can't imagine how any of that could change." For a year and a half, roughly the gestation period of an elephant, she'd been preparing to say that or something like it, then letting her lips go dry with her own silence. "Don't you think that by twenty-four you should be deciding what you want to be when you grow up?"

"I did that," he said, "long ago. Don't you think that if *you* didn't you're kinda late?"

FIVE YEARS AGO, as she'd stood holding Erik's hand while Jack, passed out and moaning, rolled from his back onto his side on the braided scatter rug in the basement suite, she'd said, "Jack makes me laugh."

"Ha. So do I."

She'd let go of Erik's hand. "All I want," she said, "is an ordinary life, nothing fancy. An ordinary job, a little house, kids one day. Save up for the big holiday in Hawaii five years from now."

"I don't believe you."

ON THE DOCK Jack clapped a final *five*-six, *seven*-eight and handed off the beat to the slap of ten bare soles on wood. Sylvie tapped forward twice, back twice, swung her leg through and looked over her shoulder to see Alex's back foot lose its toehold on the boards. He fell butt-first into the water with a great flailing splash. He started to shout, *Ffff—!* but his head went under and the word got dunked. The others laughed but didn't break their rhythm. On the next sequence Penny made a show of balancing on the edge and then let herself fall. They'd seen this from the start, of course they had, and still they were game.

BACK THEN, Erik had used a gentle palm to turn her gaze away from Jack and toward himself. "We're nineteen years old, Syl. Why do you want to know your whole future?"

"Doesn't everyone? How else would that woman on Twentieth with the big glass ball and the little stars from the teacher store sprinkled in her hair — how else would she make a living?"

"How do you know she's got stars in her hair? Have you been to see her?"

"She has a window right on the street. Anyone can see her sitting there."

"What did she tell you?"

"You're infuriating."

BENJ, dancing behind her now that the line had turned, said, "Don't you have the most lickable dimples just above —" *Splash.* Sylvie was next in, laughing, pinching her nose. She panicked, almost, then collected herself. Treading water should be just another dance step. Benj swam up as if to rescue her and nuzzled her neck. Jack, on the dock, flipped the finger at Benj and all three of them laughed, Benj's breath hot on her skin. Cross-couple flirting was one of her favourite things about the six of them, harmless and open, always in plain sight. She managed with her faltering tread to keep her head above water.

Margo finally danced herself in, surfaced, and swam two strokes back to the dock, where she rested her manicured fingertips and looked up at Jack. Last man standing, he mimed Travolta, bouncing in his snug blue trunks. Sylvie felt Benj's hand touch her knee under the water, felt it slide up her thigh. On the dock, Jack was more energy than style, ending with a one-eighty spin, an arm raised, pointing toward the disco ball of a sun. He held the pose, puffing.

Margo was still looking up at him. "You gotta dance yourself in."

"No way. I'm the music."

In bed last night, when neither the fighting nor the sex had ended in a release that satisfied either of them, Jack had said, "Does this mean you're not coming to the lake tomorrow?"

"Oh, I'll come. They're expecting us. Fun in the sun. And such."

"Christ, Sylvie. I mean, Christ."

Now she stayed close to Benj, feeling the absence where his hand had left her leg. Jack said, "The Sunshine Band, *uh-huh, uh-huh.*" Sylvie reached an underwater hand toward Benj, closer, closer. He stared deliberately ahead and she saw how he was waiting, expectant. She stopped short of touching, maneuvered herself away from him, felt a pleasant lurch inside.

Alex swam past, hiked himself onto the dock, took a run at Jack, shouted, *"Boo-yah!"* and they were in.

"Jesus!" Sylvie shouted. "He can't swim!" Alex surfaced, showering her with a flip of his wet hair. No Jack. The others were oblivious, at play. Benj ran a fast hand over the water, driving a jewelled arc toward Penny.

"You guys!" Sylvie said, but then hesitated while it flashed that Jack could be gone, so simply.

Benj, behind her now, gave her ass a hard, angry pinch. The jolt brought her back to herself. "He can't *swim!*" She put her legs and arms into clumsy motion, trying to propel herself toward the place where he'd gone under.

Jack flailed his way to the surface and gasped for air. Alex said, "Whadya mean, can't swim?" and he laughed and put a hand to the top of Jack's head and pushed. "How's that saying go? Drowning, not waving?"

"Jesus!" Sylvie did a frantic, ineffectual dog-paddle. Jack came up again, still out of her reach. Slipped under. "You *guys!*" "Holy, you're serious!" Alex dove, his feet strewing water-gems. As the ripple from his dive spread, Jack burst the surface, sputtering. He coughed, took in a rough breath, went down again. Sylvie got hold of his arm. He flailed in a fury. Alex broke the surface. "Stop with the windmill, man. I'll get you to the dock."

But Sylvie had to be the one to get him there. Alex was laughing and nothing was funny. "Bugger off!" she yelled. Legs churning, she tried to get an arm around Jack's chest from behind as he went down again.

"Sylvie, jeez," said Alex, reaching.

Jack pulled her under and she lost him, came up coughing, her throat burning. Alex had him now, an arm circling his chest. So close to the dock, just a few more feet. Jack was flailing less now, sputtering more.

Sylvie's ass was a weight, her legs were weights. She gulped in air just before slipping under again. The burn deep in her nostrils. *Tell me, water* — tell me what happens next for me and this child. If she were to open her mouth and let the lake fill it, and fill her throat, and her lungs, her head, too, then the water would tell her. She closed her eyes. She readied herself. She opened her mouth. A violent spasm seized her throat, and she thrashed. She felt arms lift her and she stiffened and then surrendered. When she broke the surface she thought she would cough her whole insides out. Penny said, "Okay? Okay? Let's get you out, Syl." Sylvie was aware of the others, the commotion as Alex and Margo and Benj hefted

Jack to safety. Penny's arm pressed up underneath her tender breasts.

"I'm okay, okay?" She slipped free of Penny's hold. On her back in the water now, she gathered herself and pushed out a single, sudden frog-kick to propel herself to the dock, but she misjudged her own power and bumped her head on a post.

"Ouch, Sylvie. Let me help you up."

"I'm *fine*." She wanted to say, *Leave me the hell alone.* "But thank you." She hoisted herself onto the boards, clumsy with the effort, suffering the scrape of the wood against her bare midriff. She made her way on hands and knees to where Jack lay shuddering on his stomach, spitting onto the silvered timbers.

Alex stood and used the side of his hand to squeegee water from his belly and his legs. "Are you gonna live, Callaghan?" He shook his head to scatter drops across Jack's back, where they caught the light like a party going on. Sylvie felt a clench in her gut, a swelling in her eyes.

"I gotta go take a crap," Alex said. As he made to leave, Jack grabbed at his ankle with little ambition and missed. Weak and hollowed out, Sylvie lay down on the warm dock and curled an arm and a leg around Jack. "Stupid trick for a guy who can't swim."

"Yeah," he said. "People who can't swim shouldn't throw glass at houses."

She put her lips to his spine and kissed a bump of bone. Her main trouble wasn't that she'd seen, for an instant, a clear space. Her main trouble was how familiar the moment was, the wanting: afternoons when he was hours late getting home from work and she waited at the kitchen table for The Knock. Nights he crashed on a buddy's sofa without calling. Hunting season. She pressed her mouth harder against his spine.

Behind her Benj laughed. "Get a room!" Sylvie felt the shake through her hip and her shoulder and her quivering thighs as he stomped past on the dock, and she felt it diminish as he walked away.

IN A PARKING SPOT Sylvie paid nominal rent on, in back of a bungalow near their apartment building, sat the rumbly Meteor Erik had sold her years ago for a dollar after watching her struggle with the manual transmission of Jack's Corolla. Maybe he'd expected, even as he tossed her the keys, that she'd one day use it as a getaway car. Last week she'd purged her closets and heaved into the back seat a giant garbage bag bound for the thrift store at the YW — flared jeans and wrap-around skirts, blouses with Peter Pan collars, a pair of pink panties with red lettering — *enter to win* — that she'd stuffed in the pocket of her coat on an amble through the Army & Navy Store. That bag was still in the car. She could be gone tonight, wouldn't even have to enter the apartment.

Last Sunday when Jack went out the door on the way to Uncle Walter's acreage to cut grass, she'd locked the deadbolt behind him and even slid the chain into its slot. He might be gone three hours. She'd felt a letting-go in the muscles of her upper back. She was on her way to the bedroom to get back into her pjs and slump into bed to experience the spread of the entire mattress to herself, and the expanse of air above, where her breath and thoughts could rise and meander without hindrance – when she heard him in the hallway again. He tried the door, resorted to his key, and was stopped by the jerk of the chain. "The hell?"

She opened for him. He'd brought his mug in from the truck, and he filled it with coffee for the road and poured in a drizzle of rye, one corner of his mustache sucked into his mouth in a way that made her want to reach and pull it out for God's sake. He was teasing when he said, "You locking me out, Syl?"

No. Trying to lock possibility in. She took the bottle from his hand and splashed rye and then coffee into her own mug and thought, there's something we have in common, whisky. Leaving could take years. It already had.

ON THE DOCK she tucked Jack's wet hair back around his misshapen earlobe and whispered, for her own sake, "I saved your life." She felt the hot spot of soreness where Benj's angry pinch had twisted her flesh. If he hadn't startled her just then, would she have woken to the moment? She tried going back for a second to check how that moment had felt, but the door was closed. She couldn't imagine being a person who would let another person drown. Some things you just had to act on: saving a life, leaving a life. There were other things that would happen if you did nothing. All it would take was for Sylvie to do nothing and this cell division, this multiplication going on in her womb would change itself from accident into person. Let life happen. The money they'd saved for Hawaii would have a new use. She moved her hand along Jack's arm, her palm fitting itself to the small bulge of his biceps. This is my husband. These are the people who know me, or think they do.

Jack had his job at the bus yards; he had his personal cause in helping out old Walter, which seemed to come naturally: Uncle Walter who'd handed over the keys for this Sunday afternoon to the cabin Jack hoped to one day own, along with sixty feet of shoreline and the mossy, rotting roof and the septic tank that was possibly, probably, cracked. Being written into Walter's will was more in the nature of bonus than calculation. But he did have his plan, Jack.

Spooned together, they fell asleep on the unforgiving boards and woke to the sound of jangling keys, and Alex's cool shadow falling over them. "I do believe," he said, "I've stumbled upon the keys to Walter's formidable ninety-horse cruiser. Just hanging inside the shed, they were, as if on offer."

Jack raised himself on one elbow, leaned over the edge of the dock, hocked and spit. "Get me something to drink. "

Alex offered the beer he was holding, a third full.

"Water was what I had in mind." Jack reached for it, chugged what was left, and let the bottle roll. "Put the keys away. You're in no shape."

He lay back down and Sylvie circled her arm around him, her fingers memorizing the feel of him for the times she would need it. From over on the sand she heard the indistinct voices of the others trailing through the threadbare afternoon. None of this would go into the Meteor: not Alex and his loud *Boo-yahs,* nor Benj's breath on her neck, nor Margo's hot and cold friendship, nor the smell of the lake nor the rise and fall of Jack's belly against her palm. She would have to replace these with other things. Her hip relaxed against the dock as she allowed her weight to shift and settle.

She was almost asleep again when she heard the motor rumble. Jack jolted upright and shouted over the noise — did Alex know the definition of asshole? Penny was on the run from the beach. She vaulted into the boat before it veered away. "I got him!" she said, fighting for balance, breasts swinging.

Jack held his hands to his temples. "Christ."

Alex ceded the wheel to Penny, who steered the boat back around in a wide arc. "Everything's all right," Sylvie said to Jack, and she was struck by the familiar shape of the lie. "Everything's okay." She felt the hard slap of water against the dock from the turn of the boat. She ran her hand along the weathered planks, rough under her palm. She was hoping for a fat splinter, the kind that's easy to pull out once it's quickened your blood.

Three Mothers

"**I NEED A LITTLE HELP.**" The long-distance call came at a quarter past noon, when her niece knew Merry would be home for her half-hour lunch break. Sylvie delivered two pieces of news, fastened like a hook and eye. After Merry hung up, half a dozen old troubles, old joys, stuttered to mind, a jumpy reel of sad and glad, and one image in particular she could barely look at sidelong. For the moment she flicked them all away but this: Sylvie ten and more years ago, midway through junior high, limping into Merry's yard wrangling a fender-bent bicycle that belonged to the banker's daughter. Howard had told her time and again she wasn't allowed to borrow that bike. Her forearm and her shin were pocked with tiny ground-in pebbles, but she was trying her darndest, and crookedly, to smile.

"Jeez and crackers!" Merry said as Sylvie laid the bike on what passed for a lawn. "Let's see that skinned leg. Like poppy seeds in rising dough."

Sylvie's mouth lost its grin and found it again. She'd made it all the way, she told her aunt — head high so that her hair fell back and Merry could see a bright, berry-sized gash on her forehead — she'd made it the eight miles to Flat Hill and the same eight back without a sniff of trouble until she was half-way down the slope the other side of Ripley's railroad tracks.

"Why *that* road? You could've avoided the hill altogether."

"*Help* is what I'm looking for, Auntie."

"You don't make it easy. Inside, now, and scrub yourself up. I'll find the salve." Merry had helped Sylvie knock the fenders straight again and repaint them, in league with her in the lies they told both Howard and the banker's daughter, whose trip to summer camp had been the only reason she'd agreed to loan the bike.

Today on the phone when Sylvie broke the news she was leaving Jack, had already left him in fact, and Merry said right off the top, "This will not go down well with your father," Sylvie came right back with, "*Help* is what I'm looking for."

At the garage after lunch Merry lay on her back on the Jeepers Creeper underneath the jacked-up Dart that belonged to the school principal. The radio at the other end of the shop sent out a slender skein of country music. Glen Campbell yet again. She reached toward the oil plug, and the odd little bump at her tailbone dug into the hard platform of the Creeper, a little stab of pain to keep her awake. What Merry loved about her work was not this tedium, but all the business that couldn't be seen through the undercarriage — the intricate anatomy: *engine-bone connected to the crankshaft, crankshaft connected to the tranny, tranny connected to the drive shaft.* The life of the thing. But here she lay, only inches above the floor, while Howard monopolized the hoist replacing a differential.

The Dart's underbelly was caked with mud, baked on solid. Drives it like he stole it. Merry pictured the principal, his Peter Fonda hair, his aviator sunglasses, the way he'd spin out and make for the highway as if with the next clutch and shift he'd manage liftoff and leave the plain old plains receding. Any other man in Ripley who owned a set of wheels like this would take it to the alley, slide underneath on a piece of cardboard and change his own oil, but not Bert Siding.

With any luck Merry would be looking at more than dirty oil. When Bert handed over the keys he'd mentioned that his noisy car was even more noisy lately, and not in a good way, and could she let her brother know about that? Well no wonder — the way he bossed the transmission it was sure to be shredded. Once she'd finished the oil change she'd take it for a spin, town and highway, take a listen, play through the gears, talk to Bert about an overhaul. Hustle the job for herself.

She used a gloved forefinger to flick away a pebble embedded in the grey crust of dried mud that surrounded the oil plug. Another image of Sylvie: age six, standing on the back step and offering a mud pie, silver grey and sunbaked, stretching her twiggy arms to hold it high. "For you, Auntie." On the top, embedded with care, were swirling ferny fronds from the yarrow that grew in the ditch.

"It's beautiful, honeypickle." The sudden catch in Merry's own voice had surprised her. She motioned for Sylvie to back onto a lower step, then swung the screen door open. Gingerly she lifted the pie from her niece's grubby hands and set it on the table. "It's as fine as feathers on an elephant."

Just the night before, when he heard Merry tell the girls their backyard cleanup effort was as pleasing as trout in a jellyroll, Howard had said, "They don't think it's funny, you know. When you call on your Muffins from Heaven or your Princess Meg in a Wheelchair or your Fish in a Christly Jellyroll."

"They know love when they hear it."

Her mud pie delivered, Sylvie scampered off, letting the door bang shut. Merry nabbed an ant speeding away from the pie and washed the critter down the sink. Out the window she saw the small curved backs of Sylvie and her sister Mavis hunched side by side in the bare triangle at one end of the garden where she'd meant to seed late lettuce. Borrowed miracles, the two of them. She watched as Sylvie, without breaking her crouch, measured out tiny steps sideways, crowding her sister. When Mavis pushed back Sylvie braced herself on hands and knees, determined to claim all the earth her four limbs could reach. Mavis, older by a year, conceded finally and wheeled away on her oversized tricycle. It was the younger girl with her fierce attachment to that patch of dirt who made Merry ache to go outside and win a reluctant hug. "Look," she wanted to say, "what is it you want? Just ask." Sylvie lowered her face closer to the dirt and stayed that way for a long moment. Maybe she was watching an earthworm, but she might just be breathing in the mix of odours the hot sun pulled from the soil. A tonic. Merry understood. For her, the heady traces of gas and oil and grease that met her at the door of the shop said *Welcome home*.

Merry left those few square feet of garden unplanted for several years. After a time Sylvie lost interest in mud pies, but she was still a dirt girl. Summer evenings she'd squat there shaping a hill with her hands, driving toy cars around the base, then straight up the slope, watching how the wheels left a flowing wake. The mechanics of soil. Merry, nearby, thinning carrots and slapping mosquitoes, said, "Little scientist." The girl didn't hear or didn't care, lost in her head until Howard three houses down whistled her in for bedtime snack.

"When might you help with the weeding, Your Exalted High Princess of Dirt?"

"Um. Tomorrow?"

UNDER THE DART, Merry worked the tip of a screwdriver around the lug to loosen the dried mud, turning her face to the side to avoid the fine sift. It had taken her years to convince Howard the garage was more than a hobby for her. Hadn't they *both* inherited the place from their father?

"A girl mechanic?" he'd said. "We'll lose business." They had, and then they hadn't.

"You'll never find a husband."

"Second husband," she'd reminded him, and that was true so far, but marriages fail anyway. A man can vanish in a minute to the sounds of the back door falling shut and the engine of his Studebaker catching and tires on gravel as he makes for the city, where he might already have a job and almost certainly has a woman. And the babies you'd always expected to birth from him and hold and love can vanish in that same simple minute. *Vroom.* Merry took up the ratchet that lay across her stomach, loosened the plug, and listened to the glug of oil as it began its long drain into the catch-pan. She could inch her way out from under, or she could relax a minute and listen to yet one more Glen Campbell song. She bent her knees further to take the pressure off her back. Rhinestone Cowboy.

"*HELP IS WHAT* I'm looking for."

"Yes, honey, sorry. Whatever I can do."

"Being as how I'm pregnant."

"A baby, oh. Honey. Listen, how about I come to the city for a day or two. Later in the week, say. We'll get a few things figured out? Your dad can bring in one of the young fry to cover for me. Honey, I've got to get back, but I'll call again just as soon as I'm home for supper. A baby, that's — it's wonderful."

"Are you going to tell my Dad?'

"No, dear. Aren't you?"

She didn't mean to make a tally of her envy, but there it was. Children: Howard two, Merry zero. Grandchildren: Mavis with six-year-old Chad whooping and running about and two-year-old Kayla studying her picture books; now Sylvie with a wee bean floating warm inside. Howard three, Merry zero. Once tallied it was fact, and manageable. She would do what she'd always done, hammer it into help. Swords to plough-shares, that was the teaching. Still: Sylvie one, Merry none.

AS THE WEDDING DANCE was winding down those years ago, Merry and Sylvie had slipped out the side door of the town hall into the fresh June night, Sylvie still catching her breath after a frantic round of butterfly where she'd twirled counter-clock-wise with Jack, then clockwise with Erik Salverson, her friend since mud pie days. She bent and lifted the skirt of her long dress and used it to wipe her forehead. "I finally feel like I've left home for good."

"That you have."

"Mom always told me the best thing to do was get out of this town. It's the most important thing, she said."

"It isn't all misery, you know — Ripley." But the mom is the mom and the aunt is only the aunt. Even on the wedding day, and with the mom gone — and tragically — almost two years, the aunt was only the aunt.

"'Leave it behind,' she told me."

"Is that why young Erik never figured into your plans?" In his high school years, Erik had hung around the shop in the late afternoons just the way Merry had years before, hoping for jobs, hoping for *something*, picking up an old piston or a piece of broken tie rod just to thunk it back on the bench. Fetching a tool the moment before it was asked for. His wishbone leg — the left one, was it? — seemed to crank his steps with restlessness. He might have this town inside him, but he had other things inside him too. He was here for the moment, but soon enough he'd be knocking Ripley's dust off his workboots, you watch. Merry wondered, not for the first time, what life she might have found if she herself had left. But for her brother's girls needing her, she would have. Wouldn't she? The pulse of unfamiliar streets, department stores with shelves and racks and dressed-up windows, high-ceilinged rooms downtown where a man might ask a woman to dance.

Sylvie reached up and began pulling hairpins out of her updo. "Erik was never that big a deal." Her side ringlets were limp, brought low by the hours and the dancing.

"Is that right?"

"And I did it, you know. I moved to the city and I found a job, and I met a pretty good guy, and now look." She swirled her ivory satin.

Merry slid a hand along her own skirt where the fabric was damp with rum and coke. Would anyone even care that a middle-aged woman's skirt was no longer fit to swirl? At the finish of the butterfly the groom had stumbled into the table where she and two aunts from his side were sitting, their drinks half-full. Crash, splash. Living with Jack, Merry thought, might turn out to be a lot like living in Ripley, except in the city.

SHE BRACED HER FEET to wheel the Creeper out from under the Dart, get off her back and stretch her shoulders. She began inching her heels along the floor but stopped when she heard footsteps, a relaxed tread. Looking to the side she saw a large pair of moccasin loafers pause near the front of the car, and she heard Greg Thompson say to Howard, "Got your girl mechanic changing oil on Bert's hot rod."

Howard said, "*Woman* mechanic, is what I understand I'm supposed to say."

Merry held her heels steady. She would spare herself the cat's eye view up past those loafers, along the soft crease of Greg's Fortrel pants to the white plastic belt he was known for, the swell of his waist, and past that the pale underside of his chin, and above that the dark hollows of his nostrils.

"Just *mechanic* is fine." She watched the last of the flow into the catch-pan. Lit by the trouble light, even dirty oil had a shine to it. Small rewards.

DARN THAT GIRL. Darn her now and darn her years ago. Take the night Merry went over to help Sylvie boil fudge for the Sunday bake sale.

"You drop just this little bit into a cup of cold water. See how it makes a tiny ball?" Merry's voice competed with Foster Hewitt's eager play-by-play. Howard was watching the Leafs in the other room.

"Ha!" said Sylvie. "A little turd!"

"That's how you know it's ready. You have to pour it right away, or —"

"Bitch!" There was Mavis, standing in the doorway from the hall and glaring at Sylvie. "Damn bitch!" In her hand was a tin globe the size of a grown-up fist. Her piggy bank. "You raided my paper route money again!" Her thin hair clung to her cheeks in static wisps. She heaved the bank at her sister. It bounced off Sylvie's thigh and fell and rolled, and the pedestal, meant to keep the coins inside, twisted loose and spun across the floor. A nickel and a penny twirled on the linoleum.

Sylvie grabbed up the globe and tossed it back fast and hard, and Mavis raised a forearm just in time to shield her face.

"Snakes in a cake, Sylvia Fletcher!"

"I didn't mean to. It slipped."

"Howard," Merry called, "this one's yours."

He stomped around the corner, all six feet of him. The fudge boiled on and the soft ball twirled down through the water. Howard yanked a chair away from the table, sat and waved for the girls to sit opposite.

77

He pointed at Mavis. "You. You watch your mouth!" He pointed at Sylvie. "You. You are a hankering child." He jabbed at the table with his index finger. "Ever since the crib."

June's voice floated out from the bedroom at the far end of the hall: "Mavis? Sylvie?"

Howard leaned across the table. "Now you've bothered your mother." He looked at Merry. "They've bothered their mother."

"It'll be all right." She moved the pot off the burner.

Howard softened, leaned back in his chair. "Put your little bank on the table."

Mavis did so. The globe wobbled, then settled on its side, steadied by a dent where the equator passed through Africa. From where Merry stood, Howard appeared to be looking directly at the two girls. She knew, though, that he'd have crossed his eyes, and to the girls it would be as if he saw each of them, but with the opposite eye. It was a way he'd had since they were small. He used to say, "I got my eyes on you, one each," and they'd collapse in giggles.

"She took your worldly goods," he said now, tapping the globe. Neither girl laughed. Howard looked down, picked at the threads that feathered from a hole in his trousers. A square inch of his long johns, their waffled knit, showed in the opening. The angle of his jaw gave him an extra fold of chin, grizzled with seven-o'clock shadow. A wisp of hair far back from his forehead, what remained of his young-man's pompadour, had fallen forward. His height was in his legs, and sitting on a kitchen chair he never did look like a six-foot man. In the next room Foster Hewitt's voice sped to a shout.

The crowd hollered. Howard shifted. "You got to figure this out. Together." He was standing now. "Your aunt will referee." He glanced in at the game before going along the hall to look in on June and ration out yet more Aspirin against her arthritis pain.

Referee, I don't think so. Merry waved the girls out of the kitchen. "I'll need a pick-axe to chip this out. Come back when you've settled up and we'll start this candy over."

The girls took turns shoving each other along the hallway.

"Are you gonna give me back my money?"

"I spent it."

"Jesus God!"

"It isn't like I was going to keep it forever."

Merry shook the wooden spoon at their backs. "Jug feathers. Shush!"

Ultimately Mavis split her paper route in two, giving Sylvie the right to deliver half until she earned out her debt. The idea was that each would do her own loop and they'd finish in half the time, but in fact Mavis walked Sylvie's loop with her, the two of them bundled in parkas, before going off to do her own alone. After the first few days they were walking the entire route together, helping each other with scarves and mitts. What was it about those two? Was Sylvie a forgivable sort of girl or was Mavis the sort who easily forgave? Or was it that a sister — that other, ever-empty space in Merry's own life — was a vein each girl's blood ran through on the way to its own heart?

MERRY ROLLED SLOWLY out of the shop in the principal's Dart. A gold Swinger 340 and he'd ponied up extra for a bumblebee stripe and four-on-the-floor. She went for a spin, a little bit town, a little bit highway, grass skirt swaying on the hula girl suctioned to the dash. Shifting took more muscle than it ought to, and she could feel the grind from third to fourth and hear it, a transmission just crying to be taken apart. She'd make sure her brother was well out of earshot when she spoke to Bert, or he'd swipe the job out from under her. Later though, about 4:30, Howard told her the principal was coaching baseball at the schoolyard and wouldn't be by till late. At 5:00 he told Merry to head home, he'd tuck the keys on the visor for Bert. She took a last glance at the Dart, for now, and headed across the street and along toward the grey bungalow she'd owned since her nieces were in diapers, title transferred to her at the time of the divorce. In the kitchen she held the phone receiver to her chest a moment, letting the dial tone hum through her bones. Out the window she saw two jays poking their beaks into the pea patch. She took a deep breath and whistled it out slowly and tried not to think of the transmission job she might be giving up completely, and good luck to Siding next time he tried to take flight. She'd have to tell Howard to look into it. There was the business to think of, to say nothing of a girl mechanic's reputation. Darn it, Sylvia Callaghan. She dialled Saskatoon. Her niece wouldn't need her right away this minute, not necessarily.

"I can get there later this week. We'll go shopping for maternity blouses. That discount centre at The Bay. Or Simpsons, you can always get a good deal at Simpsons."

Silence.

"Or if you're thinking about, um. We can talk about what —"

"I'm keeping it. Maternity smocks are not my biggest problem."

"Sorry, honey. Yes." The darn jays were still in the pea patch. Merry itched to run out the door and across the yard to shoo them. "Are you planning to come home? Have the baby here?"

"You're kidding, right?"

"But where are you staying?"

"Will you sing to me, Aunt Merry?" Sylvie's voice was high and not at all steady. Her plea called back to a bedtime tradition from her childhood.

"Can you hold on for just a moment, Sylvie? I won't be long, I just have to . . . I'll be back in a jiffy." Merry set the receiver on the counter, hurried out the door and down the steps and clapped her hands at the jays. One took off and the other stayed, cheeky, its head cocked just for her, she'd swear. "Yeah, it's always you, isn't it? You, you, you." She had to stomp right to the edge of the garden before the bird finally took flight.

Stop. Look now. Look that image in the eye: teenage Sylvie trembling in her cut-offs and T-shirt, framed in the bright rectangle of the office doorway at the garage, her back to the sunlight, her features a scribble on a shadow. The room smelled of carbon paper and empty wrappers from Howard's daily chocolate bars, with only hints of the heady mix of gas and grease from the shop. Howard was off in Foster on a parts run.

Sylvie, her voice wavering, said, "We need some help."

The voice on the transistor radio said, "Here's a timeless favourite," while Merry groped for the knob and twisted it to Off.

"We need help."

Mavis ran in, pushed past her sister and pressed her hands on the desk, breathless. "Mom — she fell." She wiped her nose with the hem of her T-shirt.

Sylvie stepped in close beside Mavis. "The basement stairs."

"Why would she even — ?" Mavis took a deep breath. "I think she might, she might —"

Sylvie reached for her sister's hand. "She isn't breathing. Mom isn't breathing anymore." They didn't look toward each other, they looked toward Merry.

Oh, my girls, my girls. You've had a measure of longing stirred through every one of your liquid days from childhood on.

BACK INSIDE, Merry lifted the receiver again. "I'm sorry, Sylvie, I needed to — never mind. Where were we?"

"I was asking you to sing."

"You'll find I'm no better a singer than I was back then."

"Please, Auntie."

When was the last time Sylvie had called her 'Auntie'? Merry cleared her throat and obliged with a tuneless, meandering *la-la-la*, on and on, the way she used to do, a non-song, though sweet, until she heard a small laugh over the line.

"As a singer, Auntie, you make a pretty good mechanic."

"Just so." Sure. At times she'd even tried to see it that way — her job was her child and no need for lullabies. A thin argument. "Your turn, my girl. Let's hear it."

"Tonight, maybe. Try singing myself to sleep."

"Oh, sweetheart, I can get away tomorrow. I'll leave first thing in the morning. Here, hold the receiver to your chest now. I want you to feel this in your bones."

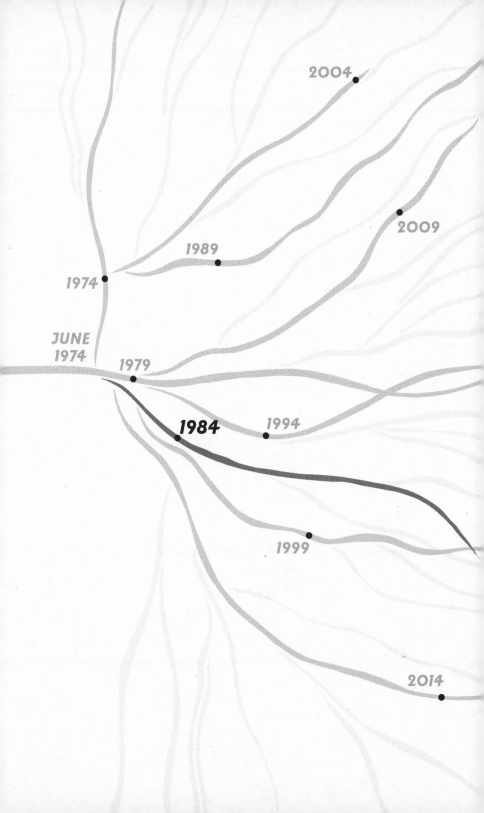

Naked Bodega

THE SHEET THAT LAY draped over her head and torso was thinning, polyester and pilled. Underneath it Syl's breath swirled in a sour microclimate.

"What in blazes?" Aunt Merry had said last week when Syl invited her to the city for the fundraiser. What in fury and blazes did she think she would prove, competing in a beauty contest at twenty-nine?

"I wouldn't call it a contest so much as a pageant." Syl's voice reached for irony. "To showcase our stunning legs."

"Well, honey, you do have those."

"And I wouldn't call it competing. I'm participating."

"And a way with words."

Now Syl's lower limbs, along with those of six other good sports, were on display and chilly. Fourteen naked legs, seven pairs of high-heeled shoes. A giant truck tire, fresh from the factory and smelling of it, lay on its side in the function room at the community centre, and the women's bare legs rested at a slant against the hard-edged knobs of its tread. Their upper bodies radiated out, flat on the floor, covered with mismatched sheets from their hips to the tops of their heads, a shrouding meant to ensure the judges would concentrate on the limbs in question, the whole of the limbs in question, and nothing but.

They waited.

Gams, Erik liked to say: "Your prize-worthy gams. Just one more reason I had to step in. Woo you."

Ten years earlier, after deserting her fiancé a day and a half short of the walk to the altar, Syl had decided within weeks that yes, she would marry Erik. "And I already have the outfit." She reached into her closet, brought out the ivory wedding gown she'd spent so many hours stitching, and swirled its generous skirt.

Erik pretended shock. "You can't wear the dress you would've worn for Jack."

"Suppose I alter it."

"Cut it shorter, maybe. Show off those beauties."

She'd been the only bride whose knees Ripley United Church had ever seen.

IN HER AWKWARD POSITION Syl felt an annoying stretch along her right hamstring. From her hips to her ankles she was goosebumps, from her waist up warm and itchy. When they'd tried out this arrangement last night at rehearsal, Marilyn had caught the heel of her shoe in a crevice between treads and sworn quietly, then laughed and said, "We're doing this for the children. Sure. Okay."

Once you angled yourself into the right mood it was a

rationalization that almost worked. *Ask me what I wouldn't do for my kids.* When Adam was born, after Syl had cuddled and fed him, and the nurses had rolled his bassinet away so she could rest, she'd said to Erik, "All along there's been this club called Parents, and we had no idea what a huge, important, staggering deal it is." Three years later, there was Brycie. "Imagine," she said to Erik. "There are people who don't even know."

"Imagine."

SEVEN WOMEN BREATHED into their sheets, waiting for the eighth pair of legs to arrive. Janet had been slow to change into short-shorts, slow to slip into open-toed stilettos, slow in the bathroom. "It's like I have to pee," she'd said from inside the stall, "but nothing comes out." She'd emerged with her purse tucked awkwardly under one arm. When she leaned at the sink to wash her hands, the purse fell, and makeup, hairbrush, tampons and pens clattered across the lino.

"Damn zipper doesn't work."

"I know." Syl knelt to help her gather her things. "Purses these days. Let's get a move on."

"I can't." Janet tugged her short-shorts down and sat on the toilet again, stall door hanging open. "I just can't."

"You can, Janet. By now, we have to."

IN THE WHIRL of a freak snowstorm in mid-October Syl had slipped on an icy stretch of sidewalk down the block from GetAway Tours. A common FOOSH, the doctor called it: Fall On Out-Stretched Hand. There are falls and there are falls.

Once that knife of pain dulls, a broken wrist is nothing more than inconvenience. Before returning to work left-handed she'd treated herself to a few days' recuperation downstairs on the comfy red couch, her arm in its cast resting on a throw pillow. The best was History TV — easygoing, put-your-feet-up fare, and Syl did in fact prop her feet on the kidney-shaped footstool she'd found at Rose's Auction and fitted with a slip-cover. A program about the fifties showed footage of a legs-only beauty pageant. (*Footage*, said Erik when she told him about it.) Eight women lay on the floor (eight *lay*-dees, he said) like the spokes of a wheel, covered but for their naked legs, which rested on a circular ramp that made Syl think of the poster at work of Mount Fuji, its simple geometry. Eight dainty pairs of high-heeled shoes met at the summit.

"What do you think?" she'd asked Erik that night after they'd tucked in the kids. "Would I make a fool of myself even suggesting it?"

He was the one with his feet up now, as he studied the new remote control. He ran his free hand along her thigh. "You'd be going out on a limb. Or two."

"I'm asking a serious question."

"You can answer it better than me." He pointed the remote and, with some concentration, progressed through three channels. "Look at that, we don't even have to walk across the room." He congratulated himself by raising his glass and knocking back what remained of his rum and coke.

AFTER A DISPIRITING START, Syl had managed to work her way through every binder of the Accredited Travel Consultant Course from Wellspring Correspondence. Now, with the kids into their school years, Brycie swaggering every morning in her forgivable way into the grade one room and Adam slipping quietly in among his grade three classmates, Syl was once again in that happy club of the fully employed. Back when she'd made her eleventh-hour decision not to marry Jack she told herself her decision had nothing to do with his slopey shoulders and his funny earlobe, and everything to do with a settling fear that his lack of drive gave her a ready excuse not to find her own. Drive. Well, she *had* made something of herself. But among the other moms from the Beamers Swim Club she was surrounded by gynecologists and wives of gynecologists and lawyers and wives of lawyers and the wife of a newly minted judge and — who knew? — possibly his mistress. To make herself valuable she'd joined the fundraising committee. She wore button earrings to meetings and made the effort to match them not to her blouse but to one of her dozens of scarves. Took care when speaking not to slip into vestigial small-town turns of phrase. Cleaned her nails meticulously, though she stopped short of polish, and she sometimes thought, resting her hands on her notebook, that the group could use a little, I don't know, *life*. At the November meeting, and with no clear notion of how they might use the idea to raise cash, Syl described the pageant she'd seen on History TV. Chairwoman Leslie's lips spread into a wide grin. "This is what comes of watching television during the day." Her nails with their neutral polish tapped the table. "You're not proposing a fundraising event in this vein?"

Janet, more pale than usual, said, "I'm a swim mother, not Miss Swimsuit."

"Exactly," said Carol. "We're not body parts."

"No, no," said Leslie, "It'll be fabulous."

"Right on," said Marilyn. "It's the eighties. Why shouldn't we have a little fun?"

Typically the swim parents raised money by working bingos, moms and dads patrolling the aisles in a smoky hall, taking orders from impatient players: "Over here! Today, all right?" Work a bingo, go to bed with your nose plugged from cigarette smoke. Wake up the next morning and spit yellow in the sink. And the house takes fifty percent. Home from the hall one night, Syl leaned in to kiss her sleeping daughter and heard, "You smell."

Sometimes, too, they sent the kids door to door selling spiced cashews, little Brycie rushing up front walks in her tiny yellow running shoes and using her wide smile and bouncing pigtails to sell bagloads. She wasn't a swimmer, but she'd begged to help. Adam trotted along the other side of the street and never matched his baby sister in sales. Syl drove them block by block and waited with the motor running. She had to watch to make sure Adam didn't skip every second house. "Maybe square your shoulders up." She loosened the zipper of his jacket by an inch. "Here. Switch out your mitts for gloves."

You had to peddle a lot of nuts to pay the expenses involved with hosting a swim-meet. The vote for the pageant had been six in favour, two against.

WITH A FORCEFUL EXHALE Syl wafted the sheet away from her face for a moment's relief from the stifling polyester. She felt the insistent press of a tire tread against the soft flesh of her calf. This sort of discomfort hadn't come to mind when she'd envisioned the event. What had come to mind was the fact she had killer legs and this was the youngest they'd be from here on in. Sell the people a six-ounce glass of Naked Bodega, red or white, offer them a slip of gouda on a Wheat Thin and let them bet on which pair of limbs would win, place or show. *Do it for the children,* their winking invocation at every planning meeting.

"Help me understand," Janet had said one evening, "how this will make money?"

"Tickets," said Syl. "Wine sales."

"Yeah, but the main thing," said Leslie, "is the betting. Look at these parents: we've got a radiologist, two gynecologists, at least three dentists. There's Hinton, just been made a judge. There's your high-end kitchen builder," she said, meaning Syl's Erik. "People will bet big. They'd be embarrassed not to."

A high-end kitchen builder, Syl refrained from saying, does not necessarily make high-end profits, what with the home-owner (who's just been made a judge) demanding the granite be recut and the range reinstalled one-point-five centimetres to the left; what with light fixtures shipped from Italy and broken before you open the box and two insurance companies facing off over which, if either, will pony up close to a thousand to cover the claim.

"We'll need three men for the jury." By way of adjournment Leslie lifted the shoulder strap of her purse from where she'd slung it on the back of her chair. "None of our husbands, that goes without saying. How about Greg S., Chris M., who else?"

"Tony?" said Syl. "Tony S.?"

JANET AND HER LEGS were still in the bathroom. Stalled in the stall. Syl felt a shiver along her thighs. Was there an outside chance goosebumps would make her legs attractive in a vulnerable sort of way? Doubtful. Did the small blue vein that flowered inside her left calf offer a hint of the exotic? She'd meant to mask it with a dab of concealer.

Hesitant stiletto steps telegraphed Janet's approach across the battleship linoleum. A *floof* of fabric as a sheet a couple of spokes around from Syl rose and settled, then Janet's whisper: "Brrr."

"You'll be fine." Syl's sheet puffed as she spoke.

DRIVING TO THE community centre she'd said to Erik, "Suppose next year we have the dads compete: best rear end." He smiled, his face half-lit by the glow from the dash — his receding blond brush cut, the shine of his close-shaven cheek. "You guys," said Syl, "can begin the same way we will — parade across the stage in running sweats so as not to reveal too much in advance, and the bettors can place their bets. Then you can retire to another room where you strip and stand in a circle shielded in sheets except for a cutaway to show the pertinent view."

"Better my ass than my legs, babe."

True. His turned-out knee, the way it shortened his left leg.

"You know me: I'm just an ordinary gimp from Ripley, Saskatchewan."

"Stop it, Erik. And please don't say that in public anymore."

"People like a little humour, babe. It's good for business."

"No, honey, it isn't."

"Disputable. My ass, though," he said, turning in at the parking lot, "is some kind of all right."

"As firm as the very first time I saw it." Stag night ten years ago, when Syl's fiancé was out partying till tomorrow with assorted rascals and she'd led Erik to the bedroom, the press of his finger at the back of her knee had set off a current that melted her sense of who she was. She'd known him since she was four, and their fifteen years of friendship had flipped other-side-to in half an electric minute.

UNDER THE MISMATCHED SHEETS, giddiness among the contestants surged, then ebbed. Erik went to call the judges. Tony and the other two would have a private viewing, the better to concentrate before the hoi polloi were let in. Syl suppressed the urge to scratch her nose. Do not disturb the tableau. So many had contributed so much, Leslie had reminded them as they strapped on their heels. The truck tire that supported their legs was courtesy of Wheels on 51st. Later it would remain on exhibit, in all its naked strength and beauty, to remind the people who owned the BMWs and station wagons and the dated Ram truck (Erik's) in the parking lot to think of Wheels when their tires wore thin. Eight shoe stores, all with thumbnail ads in the program, took credit for the open-toed stilettos. Pedicures were courtesy of Marla School of Beauty, as announced on a placard near the platters of gouda.

AT THE FINAL planning meeting Syl had said, "I like this whole idea, but —"

"You better," Janet said, "it's yours."

" — but I don't understand the betting."

"Have you ever been to the races?" Leslie said.

Syl had not.

"It's the way the purse divides. You have to understand parimutuel."

"Ah," said Syl, not understanding parimutuel. "It's the wine sales I'm counting on. I'll need half a bottle once it's over with."

"Oh but Syl," said Marilyn, "you have gorgeous legs. You'll probably win."

Actually, no: Marilyn would probably win.

SYL LIFTED ONE ANKLE a whisper away from the tread and flexed her foot to reawaken the nerves. The trouble with a truck tire is there's no *give*. She wiggled her toes. Normally she avoided polish, not wanting to draw attention to the unbecoming trait her podiatrist called Morton's toe: the second digit of her right foot was longer than the big toe. Would the oddity bump her to third place, even fourth?

She'd been the parent on mornings this week, getting Adam to the pool for practice by 6:15 — "Go, Adam! Push!" — and both kids to school after that. Erik took care of evenings, supervising homework, supper, soccer tryouts. After Syl came in from her day at GetAway, heated her 6:30 leftovers, listened to one trouble from each child and played good cop or bad cop, whichever Erik said they needed, she was free to take long baths. Pamper the gams. Every second day she'd shaved her legs, lifted them out of the water by turns and admired the glisten as bubbles slid along a calf. One night she discovered she was singing in the tub — not a proper song but a tuneless meander, the sort of non-song Aunt Merry used to sing if she were the one to tuck her in.

"That's not a song, Auntie," little Sylvie said one night.

"I don't know much about music, but I know a thing or two about mechanics: Sing any old way — it doesn't matter — and the hum will spread through flesh and bone to soothe you. When soothing's what you need."

Sitting in the tub, Syl watched a shiver spread across the surface of the water as she sent her voice low to deepen the vibration. For five minutes at the end she turned on the jets. By any reasonable reckoning it was a good life. Two weeks in Florida every winter — who knew citrus could taste so good? — the ranch-style house in River Heights, season tickets for three plays every winter and four symphony performances expensed to the company. She'd learned to dress in neutrals for the symphony, a simple frame for the music. She'd found Erik a charcoal suit from Elwood Flynn and a silk pocket square in a quiet shade of green. ("You'd never guess I'm just an ordinary gimp from Ripley," he said one evening to a client before the performance. Well you would now, Sylvie didn't say.) Sidelong glances from people in neighbouring seats had taught them not to applaud at the end of a movement. The networking during intermission had landed Erik a contract or three, otherwise he wouldn't have suited up to be there. Then again, he might have, for the concertmaster was a dark-haired beauty in a flowing black dress with a scoop neck that revealed a slim, rich shadow of cleavage. Syl didn't so much mind where Erik's glance went so long as other parts stayed home.

One night as she sat in the tub, just as she'd paused in her quiet chant to lean forward and whisper to her knee, "Don't ever get old," Erik opened the bathroom door without knocking, his evening measure of rum in hand, and sang out in his rusty voice, "You're so vain!" Her sudden sideways slide resulted in a bruised hip. "Am *not*," she said to the door as it closed, and immediately wished she hadn't taken the bait. Tonight she'd managed to cover the bruise with the short-shorts supplied courtesy of Sally Girl Sport, tugging the Spandex just so. She did this once more now, by feel. She was relieved, after all, that Aunt Merry hadn't been able to come.

She felt in her bones the tread of the judges as they approached. A male voice — it sounded like Tony's — said, "Sh-boom, sh-boom!" and heat rushed her neck. She'd had more than one dream featuring Tony last winter when Erik was away in the mountains snowmobiling with the guys, taking chances for real, gunning it straight up snow-covered slopes. The risks Syl dared to take happened under the covers while she slept. Now she felt as if those dreams might be there to read on her naked flesh.

When they'd paraded earlier, she and the others had been fully covered from espadrilles to shoulders in unrevealing togs courtesy of Running Threads. Tony's eyes had passed over her as he tapped his pen on his adjudicator's clipboard. Late-day stubble, shining black curls.

The footfalls circled closer. She tried to picture how the sheets draped, whether they drew attention to her breasts:

size, asymmetry, slump. One of the judges said, "Cross left," and she crossed her left ankle over her right, imagining the look of her calves as they moved and then settled, the disarming curve of ankle, the liability of the small blue flower of vein. She pictured her teal patent shoes, her coppery toenails, her unfortunate Morton's toe. A new pressure spot troubled her hip. She shifted her pelvis with the slightest movement she could manage, to relieve the pain and because the idea of Tony so close made her want the pleasure of movement. Between her legs she felt a sudden soft ring of ache.

EVENTUALLY CAROL HAD REFUSED point-blank to be in the pageant. "This is not what I want to teach my boys."

"But the kids won't even be there," Leslie said. "We're not billing this as family night."

"Exactly."

Syl had recruited her cousin Cynthia to fill the gap between three o'clock and six. "More than happy. An electrician doesn't have so many opportunities to shed her Carhartts and show off her legs."

Small noises came intermittently from the spokes on the floor — laughter held back or sneezes stifled or the beginnings of asthma attacks. Listening to the judges' campy *Oh-la-las*, crossing her ankles the other way now on command, Syl felt giggles fizz inside her, then fizzle. Leslie, who lay at three o'clock to Syl's noon, said, "Hands off, buddy." Her tone was four strands teacher and one strand tease. "You can look, but you can't touch."

"This pair's a winner." Tony, his footfall close. A finger landed on Syl's ankle and began to trace a tickle up her leg. She kicked it away — "You heard the lady" — but she wasn't so good at getting the teacher into her voice to overrule the tease. Her cheeks burned; no doubt they shone right through the damn sheet.

AFTER CAROL HAD walked out of the meeting in protest, Syl had retreated downstairs to her comfy red couch. The whiff of last night's popcorn was a comfort. A person has to follow through, she'd learned that much. Back when she was stalled with the travel correspondence course, staring in despair at the costly binders every morning and searching herself on a failed quest for the will to open them and do the work, she'd been saved by a ringing phone and the price of a cappuccino. Margo, a woman she hadn't spoken with in years, not since the days of her almost-marriage to Jack, and whose friendship had never seemed a solid thing, was on the line and desperate. She needed to connect, she said, with someone, anyone, from the days before her life went sliding sideways. Why the slide, Syl asked her. Because she'd failed at life — her words. Hadn't finished secretarial school, couldn't even apply herself for ten short months to make herself employable. Again, her words. Her husband's question as he walked out: Where was her self-respect?

"If I had any before he asked me that, I sure didn't after."

"How long ago did all this happen, Margo?"

"Eight years."

"What have you been doing since?"

"So now guess who he's with. He's with a waitress he met at Smitty's. I mean."

"Margo. What have you been doing since?"

"I'm at my mom's."

"Coffee's on me," Syl said. It took a week at least, but it happened. She looked at the Wellspring binders and told herself, You have to follow through.

Which was what she would do now. She pulled the kidney-shaped footstool close to the couch. It was a 1950s original, from the same era as the pageant that had so charmed her that day in October. She'd bought it for its lines, but the shade of orange was, as Erik said, vomitous. By sewing a tan slipcover with red piping, she'd brought it forward into the eighties. An elastic run through the casing was meant to hold it in place like a fitted sheet, but the fit was slightly off, and when she rested her feet the fabric often shifted, as it did now, exposing the ugly original vinyl along the inner curve. Before settling to watch *Family Ties*, Syl tugged it into place, an effort that made her think of how she was forever adjusting the drape of her scarf when she dressed for a meeting with the swim parents. She hummed through the first commercial break, no particular tune, just a deep vibration in her chest.

THE FLOOR TREMBLED as foot traffic multiplied. A chatter of voices. The riffraff were in the room, upper-middle, middle and some percentage plain middling. The bets had been laid earlier, and these few minutes of exhibition stood in for the drama of the horserace. Footsteps circled. Her earlier, unruly pump of arousal had vanished. A bright light flashed past her eyes. She heard Erik say, "Who called the TV people?"

By now the judges were supposed to be saying, "Show's

over, folks." They were supposed to herd the onlookers to the other room so the beauties could crawl out from under in privacy and chase their shivers with four complimentary ounces of Naked Bodega, choice of white or red. Instead, here were rolling cameras and her pale and naked legs as if they were all she amounted to, and a bruise at her hip like the end of a sentence.

Air, she needed air. She took a deep inhale and the fabric plastered itself against her cheeks, her nostrils, her open mouth. She overcame a gag reflex and rolled her head to the side. The women to her left and right were restless, fidgeting. Maybe they should all stand up and wrap themselves in their sheets. How would they look, wrangling double-wide fabric, legs streaked with black from the tire, dizzy from lying down, trying not to fall off their stilettos?

A small noise separated itself from among the stifled giggles and coughs, an edgy little laugh a couple of spokes counterclockwise from Syl. Janet? The laugh rose in volume, loosening as it grew, unlacing until it became a high-pitched sob. Janet for sure. She couldn't just take herself in hand. The sobs subsided, but not so much they were easily ignored. To drown them out, Syl began to sing, *la la la la,* her voice meandering to no particular tune. One of the other women began to sing too, to her own tempo. More and more spokes of the wheel joined in, an aural maze of notes and rhythms, accompanied by gasps as the women sucked air through the sheets. The sobbing couldn't be heard for the hilarity, or the sobbing became part of the hilarity. Giggles fizzed inside Syl again and took over briefly before she stifled them. A tear or two followed the giggles. Her thighs so chilly and her face so hot, how could they belong to the one body? *La la la la,* gasp, *la.*

She heard the familiar voice of a local TV personality. "Is somebody crying?"

She heard Leslie's husband. "I'm sure you have all you need now."

She heard Erik. "Step this way and I'll show you the space-age calculator we used for tallying bets. Some nifty features."

AN HOUR LATER they were at home on the couch. She'd pinned her second-place ribbon to the leg of her sweats, and Erik stroked it with half a mind while they waited for the news. The club had raised over fifteen hundred dollars. That should keep the kids out of the sales racket for a few months. After the spectators left the room, Janet had taken a long moment before bunching her sheet to the side and kicking off her shoes. She stood then, barefoot, hair shielding her face while she pulled on the sweatpants Syl handed her. Her husband put his arm around her and the two left quickly and quietly. She didn't win, didn't place, didn't show. If there was a conversation anywhere in the room about the singing and the sobbing, Syl didn't hear it. Marilyn, who had just the best legs and so it was no shame to come in second to her, gave Syl a hug. "Wasn't that fun?"

The pageant appeared in the soft slot at the end of the news. "We leave you with this." The voice-over commended their novel approach. "Good sports, these women." The screen showed the tire and the legs and the pretty shoes, a faint singsong in the background as the closing credits rolled.

The camera zoomed in on coppery toenails before tracking along a pair of shins.

"Your blue-ribbon legs!" Erik made a drama of kissing Syl's hand. "Love them. Love you."

"Love you too."

A wide shot again. Long legs and short, skinny legs and shapely. She recognized her own, but with no feeling of ownership, the way sometimes you see an old snapshot of yourself and for an instant you see just a person, an anyone. There they were, an anyone's legs.

She rolled the hem of her sweatpants to her knee and flashed a calf for Erik, who wasn't looking. The station had cut to commercial and he inspected the remote as if he might discover a new function. "Are you getting a drink, babe? Can you get me one, too?" He'd parked his glasses on his forehead, nose pads digging in just above his eyebrows.

"I wasn't, in fact." She reached for the footstool, pulled it close and tugged the slipcover into place. Before she could put her feet up, Erik's clunky size elevens landed. There was that damn orange vinyl peeking out. "Cripes," Syl said as she leaned forward, lifted his heels — not a simple business from this angle — and pulled hard at the fabric. She let his feet fall and slapped his sock foot. "This is what I keep telling you. It has to line up just so, or it may as well not even be there."

"Aw, babe. Come here." Erik swivelled his head and his glasses dropped and settled at the tip of his nose. "You worry too much, Sylly."

Soon she'd feel a stitch in her neck, but for now she nestled under his arm. "Someone has to."

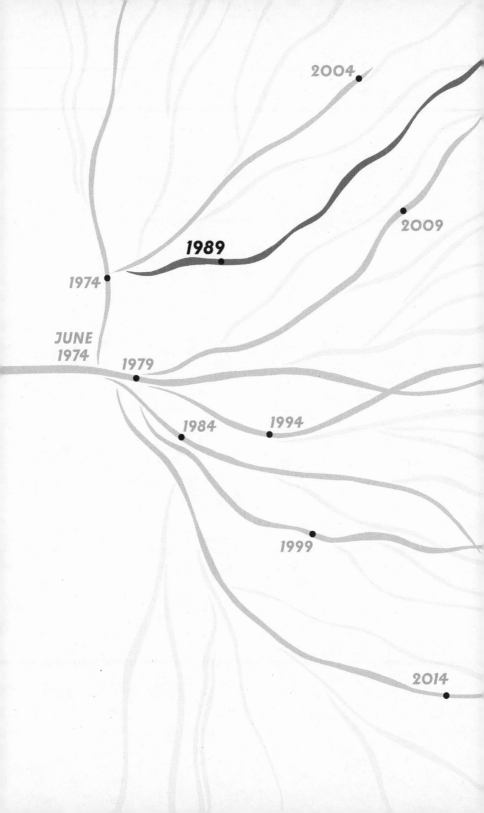

Our Lady of
Starting Over

SYLVIE WATCHED through her sister's kitchen window as her teenage nephew lifted his bike onto a sheet of plywood propped on four stacks of tires. He climbed up after it, and the platform jiggled on its rubber pillars as he readied himself to ride down a do-it-yourself ramp and into the deep end of the swimming pool.

"Your Chad's about to break his neck," Sylvie said to Mavis, just now home from her shift at the Co-op. She reached for her coffee mug and held it tight. "I know I'm just the never-married aunt, the family spinster, but."

"I haven't heard that word in a while."

"Spinster? I'm trying it on. I like that it sounds chaste."

"So it's chastity now?"

"I could use some."

Mavis poured herself a coffee, uncapped the bottle of Bailey's on the counter and poured a dose into her own mug, then Sylvie's. "A belt for chastity." She reached out to clink cups. "Chad's fine. A typical afternoon's entertainment."

"How can you bear to look?"

"I don't."

Sylvie did. She watched as he pushed off and sped down the ramp. Waterslap along his shins and full on his knees, his face. A huge and glorious splash, the far drops falling on the tin chairs and the pot plants beside the pool. The ripples settled and the view into the water cleared. Chad came up for air, dove deep again and began to maneuver the bike up the slope toward the shallow end. Sylvie's breath came quick with the effort of watching him push through water. Such a leap. She wondered if Mavis had ever told him what happened to his Grandma Fletcher. He leaned the bike against the wall and hiked himself onto the pool surround. She went out to help him heave it onto the concrete.

"Glad to see you're alive." Still, the way he'd let go and flown down that ramp, the thrill and pain of hitting the water hard and sure yet knowing it wouldn't break him. She lifted a towel draped over a chair and handed it to him. He took it but didn't use it, stood dripping in the sun, grinning; shook water beads from his hair onto his mother's pot plants, shivering their leaves. Potted pot plants, the sort you could

- harvest and
- hang ten days or more in a box and then
- cure in a mason jar

Tall, lush and lovely, layer over layer of hand-like fronds. Fat drops of water sat on their green fingers, trapping sunlight, turning it silver.

"Say, Chad, I'm looking for a favour."

"Yeah?"

"Your mom says you need opportunities to use your week-old licence with an adult in the vehicle."

"Yeah?"

"Can you ferry me over to your Uncle Geoff's so I can look at this building of his?"

"Lemme get some pants." He went dripping into the house.

Sure, she thought, barrel along back-country gravel with a stunt boy. How did he come to be old enough to drive? More sobering still was a reminder that often surfaced when she saw Mavis's eldest: if she hadn't had the abortion, her own child would be only a couple of years younger.

Beside her lay the shining wet bicycle, the tilt of it leaving the rear wheel free of the ground. She spun the tire and watched the blur of the spokes and wondered just how much it would hurt to poke a finger down through them and stop the spin, and would the hot jolt be worth the pain?

THE QUONSET BUILDING stood at the verge of Geoff's abandoned farmyard. Sylvie took the heavy padlock in hand, slotted the key past built-up rust, coaxed until it sprang open, and slipped the lock free of the heavy chain that passed through the handles of the double sliding doors. The long end of the chain made a single loud clank as it hit the door. A sound that said *take note*, like the drumbeat at the beginning of her favourite Dylan tune.

The best thing about Sylvie's apartment in Saskatoon was that the concertmaster for the symphony lived next door.

All sorts of music would float through their shared wall, but most often it would be one of three types: classical recordings; or the concertmaster herself, practising; or Dylan tunes. Sylvie recognized most of the Dylan. Of the classical she was familiar with little but happy to listen, even to the practising – the repeats, the pauses, the occasional soft curse. She admired the concertmaster for the effort she invested, her perseverance through the difficult parts. Sylvie's old stereo from RadioShack was toast, and until she could replace it with something up-market she was doing without. She'd moved her bed so the headboard was against the common wall. Some days, even if *Mary Tyler Moore* was about to come on, or if she'd just opened *Maclean's*, when she heard music she'd go to her bed and let the sound float her weightless. Occasionally she'd unzip her jeans and slide in a hand and move to the melody while she imagined a man: sometimes a former boyfriend; sometimes even her old friend Erik, who lived on an acreage near Ripley not twenty minutes from Mavis; sometimes – though less and less often – Barry. Less and less often Barry because until recently she'd been sleeping with him for real.

At times, listening as the hesitations of practice built into smooth passages, she imagined the touch of the concertmaster. She pictured her fingers on the frets. If Sylvie could reach through the wall she would massage the tips of those fingers. Yet another new beginning, exploring a woman. After all, she knew the map.

She and the concertmaster had a shared love for *Highway 61 Revisited*. What made it through to Sylvie was faint, and she never could make out the single drumbeat at the beginning of

"Like a Rolling Stone," but memory delivered it, sharp like a shot. Get ready, it said. Swing out of the holding pattern. Find a different job in a different place, and no Barry to stand in her office doorway radiating expectation. Better yet, invent a job. Hence this trip home to Ripley, this scouting of a padlocked building that belonged to her brother-in-law's brother. Maybe she would convince herself.

She pulled the chain free of the handles and let it slither into a coil on the ground in front of the Quonset. Chad helped her slide one of the doors open, lean and push, lean and push. The place smelled of old dust and still air. Inside she made out irregular shapes, the jumble of decades. Chad's hand searched the wall for a switch. A row of incandescent bulbs, unshaded and spaced at long intervals, lit up. The accumulation of junk cast new shadows now.

"Wow. I don't suppose, Chad, that you and your buddies are looking for summer work? Help clean this out."

"What's the pay?"

"I'll have to see. It depends whether your uncle Geoff will back me."

"Maybe, sure. D'you need anything else?"

"Don't go far." She handed back his headphones, which she'd confiscated in the car once she saw he planned to wear them while he drove. He pressed *play* on his Walkman and waded through wild oats in the direction of the dugout. He had his dad's wide shoulders. His finely shaped nose was patterned after Mavis's, as were his deep-set eyes, both traits that Sylvie shared with her sister. Never a child in her own life, not yet; the most she might see of herself in the next generation would be that shape of nose, the set of those eyes in Chad, and the long, slim line of leg she'd noticed in Mavis's daughter Kayla.

The light from the doorway had a short reach, and the naked bulbs strung from the ceiling were weak. Of the three side-by-side panes that should have constituted a window over the workbench a few yards in, one had been replaced with plywood and one with a piece of tin. The third was encrusted, the colour of parchment, yielding only a soft glow that burnished the scatter of wrenches, nails, bird droppings and drill bits on the bench. She tried to imagine the window replaced, and the flat expanse of a well-lit cutting table below it. Come on, what are you afraid of? Fabric? Measuring tape? Scissors?

MAVIS HAD HELPED Sylvie unpack the car after the four-hour drive from Saskatoon. "Let's see these, then. The — what did you call them?"

"Prototypes."

Sylvie dragged her giant vinyl suitcase to the living room and opened it on the floor. "You *have* to like these." Not only did her sister have to like them, she had to think they would fly off the shelves, because it was Mavis's job to convince her husband's brother Geoff to put his unused building and some several thousand dollars at Sylvie's disposal.

"What I'm asking for — the figure isn't so high," Sylvie said. "Not compared to the numbers when he was farming."

"Still. A lot of dough."

"Not even the price of a grain truck." Well, more, but this was the placeholder Sylvie had conjured to make the number less frightening.

"I'm working on him."

Sylvie would need more than money, more than practical, stylish designs and more than her sister's faith. At business-readiness seminars she'd seen the bright world of commerce projected through a sequence of overhead transparencies, the screen lit time after time with the message that crucial to her future success would be

- market reach

One of the perks at the community college where she ran the office was the invitation to drop in for free to any evening class that piqued her interest. She'd soldiered through four business seminars, bulleting notes in her scribbler, her grip on the pen sometimes firm, sometimes quivering with anxiety.

A couple of nights, stepping quietly as if she had to sneak past herself, she'd turned left instead of right and found a chair in the front row of Classics for Canucks. This was a more soothing place to be, with a less intimidating instructor. Sheilah had a tiny stud in her nose, waist-length grey hair and an eye for a designer find at the thrift store. She rested her bum on the table at the front of the room and talked about Sophocles. In her old job at the university library, Sylvie had occasionally picked up a classics journal and taken it to lunch, dropping sandwich crumbs on the ancient Greeks with their heroes and myths and their dramas that turned on the idea of an otherwise smart person getting the crucial thing wrong — what Sheilah called Error, straightening the hem of her Chanel-cut jacket. A capital *E*. Something the character has to get through so as to move on. The business prep seminars told Sylvie there was no room for Error in the first place.

UNZIPPING ONE OF THE prototype handbags she'd pulled from Sylvie's giant suitcase, Mavis, who hadn't even been to a single seminar, had said, "We need to get you on Oprah."

"Why didn't I think of that?"

"I'm serious. That woman from South Dakota selling the high-waisted pantyhose that snap onto your bra — she made it to Oprah."

"I tried those pantyhose. They don't breathe."

"So why not you, Sylvie, with something beautiful *and* practical?" She picked up the current *TV Guide* with its cover shot of an impossibly sexy Winfrey draped in gauze and perched on a hill of greenbacks. She tossed the magazine so it fell on the open suitcase lid and slid to the lip, Oprah-side up.

"Right. Call Chicago for me."

WATER HAD LEAKED in here and there, and Sylvie caught a whiff of damp earth that lifted her out of the Quonset, landing her elsewhere and else-when. She'd once snuck into the skating rink with Erik, two kids in a prairie spring taking turns holding the loose door out at the bottom just far enough to make a triangle of space to crawl through. Once inside, kneeling in the mud the melted ice had left behind, they'd performed the first-ever kiss for both of them. Twelve years old, a practice kiss between friends so they wouldn't be smooch virgins when it came to the real thing. The musty summertime rink was a cave of escape from the house, her mother having one of her low months, Sylvie and Mavis apologetic about every creak of the floor, every little bicker between them, each clatter of knife against sink. "Tongues too," Sylvie said to Erik, and so they

114

explored. Thrills coursed through from her lips to her kneeling knees. And then they made a promise: that was that. They never needed to kiss each other again. Why? she thought now, breathing the smell of earth and dampness. Such a cautious beginning, and she'd turned into quite the adventurer in the years since, and what was wrong with that? She could tell you what was wrong with that: touring from one mattress to the next certainly could distract a person from noticing that the only thing changing in her life was her lover.

A few more steps into the shed, and she smelled oil from a row of old cans. Another whiff of memory — her dad's hands, her aunt Merry's hands, the honest waft from their overalls when either of them gave Sylvie a bear hug at the end of their day at the garage. And another scent memory, of the man she'd almost married. He'd spent the afternoon at his uncle's acreage puttering with the lawn tractor, and he was about to shower. "No," she'd said. "It's working-man's cologne." But if she wanted to put six or eight people in here and have them operate sewing machines hours at a time, she'd have to rid the place of its odours.

A few steps more and she caught the reek of old rubber from a leaning stack of tires. She'd crafted her samples entirely of cloth but hoped that with a generous backer she'd manage leather trim. Until then, braided rubber shoulder straps?

It was hard to see the consumer going for that, unless — well, she'd learned such things depended on

- sexy marketing

She sits on Oprah's talk-show couch, angled toward Our Lady of Starting Over. "I was standing in a shed on the prairie feeling daunted. Having so little money, I asked myself — let me rephrase: I asked the Universe, How will I manage? And I saw that stack of tires, and the Universe answered: *Recycle, Sylvie.* So I consider this business to be, in some small way, helping to save the Earth."

Applause. The Universe strikes a chord.

Sylvie heard the wing-beat of a frantic sparrow high under the galvanized arc of ceiling. It fluttered into light and then shadow. I can't help you, little bird. She felt a shrinking inside herself. Parts of her story fell short of Oprah friendly. All those years ago, tangled half-naked on the couch with her room-mate's fiancé, two bottles of Blue on the coffee table open and untouched. Dave had known full well when he called that she was alone, and Sylvie knew he knew, and still she hadn't declined when he said he could be there with beers within minutes. The decrepit *couch* mind you — bad springs, loose threads and scratchy upholstery; between the two of them they hadn't mustered the etiquette to make for the bedroom. And in walked Sylvie's best friend.

"What the hell?" Will kept his voice low and quiet. He raised a hand and pulled at a tangle of his curly hair as if pulling would undo things.

"Relax, hippie boy," Dave said. He zipped up and walked out the door and shambled down the stairs with his shirt still open. She didn't even like him, never had.

"But don't you think —" Sylvie said once she'd zipped her own zipper and buttoned her blouse with shaky fingers and both she and Will had calmed a little. "Don't you think Lisa should know what this guy's capable of?"

"Do I hear you right?"

She burned with shame. But she wanted. More touch more thrill more people paying attention more of what she couldn't even name.

Will walked out of her suite and down the outside staircase leaving the door open. Out of her life. She never climbed past her defences to ask him back into it.

How did people fill the void?

Sheilah, at the front of the Classics class, long grey hair tucked behind her shoulders, said, "Look." She reached into an insulated black bag on the table, then held out her cupped hand, palm up. "Sophocles talked about desire as pleasure and pain intermingled. A ferocious bite, and at the same time a hot melting." Sheilah lowered her hand and the class saw that she cradled an ice cube.

THE FIRST KEY to a successful venture is to

- find a void in the marketplace

Easy. No one made a decent bag. Purses, shoulder bags, book bags, clutches. The deep end of Sylvie's closet was stacked with her rejects, some paid for, some not, some she hadn't even granted a day's use to.

Still. The first key implied a second key. Every one of those workshop leaders with their laser pointers had put up a transparency that said

- What's your hook?

See above. The rejects piled in her closet had too few pockets or too many, pockets which at any rate were the wrong sizes and in the wrong places. Zippers that failed. Zippers that opened too far or not far enough. Zippers you had to clamp in your teeth at one end if you needed to close the thing single handed because of the sloppy Fudgsicle in your other hand. Had any one of those folks responsible for the design of the purses for sale from Eaton's to Saan Stores to wobbling tables at summer craft markets ever tried to *use* one? Had they ever looked for a Kleenex to stop a nosebleed with one hand still on the steering wheel, or suffered a sudden tickle in the gullet when their niece's Christmas concert was about to start, or searched through four likely pockets in search of a pen when one pen-likely pocket would do?

What, then, was her hook? Only to make a purse that would be what a woman needs it to be.

After another day of pretending busyness on the phone each time she heard the approaching tread of Barry's soft-soled shoes along the corridor at work, she'd hefted her mother's old machine onto the small table in her apartment. She cut apart a winter coat she was bored with and plotted a design. The coarse run of the fabric under her fingers on its way to the needle delighted her. The flick of the presser-foot sounded like possibility.

She had taught herself to sew when she was seventeen and hankering after a new outfit. Her mom had one of her good weekends and was, she said, more than happy to demonstrate backwards and forwards on the Singer and the best way to pin a pattern. "We'll make whatever you want. Pants, dresses, skirts." More than happy, but then her arthritis took her low again and she went to her room to rest her joints and Sylvie knew she might not walk again for weeks. On Monday after school she loaded the machine into the wheelbarrow and trundled it over to her Aunt Merry's. When her aunt came home from work Sylvie was at the table ripping out a mistake. "Dad says to work here so I don't bother Mom. Can you show me how to attach the sleeve into the hole?"

"I'm not much for sewing. I know you need to gather it."

"Gather?"

"Pull it into a ripple."

"I'll figure it out." Sylvie dug through the linen closet, found an old sheet, cut it up and experimented until she'd solved it. Late the next afternoon by the time her aunt was home and shrugging out of her overalls, Sylvie was ready. She stepped into the kitchen modeling a blue minidress that pleated open at the front to show a pair of shorts sewn in underneath.

"You're not going to wear that creation to school."

"It's hotpants. Everyone has them."

"Is it supposed to have that extra tuck, there on the left?"

"I had some trouble on that side."

"Principal Siding lets you girls walk around like that, all legs?"

"If you ask me, he *wants* us to walk around like this."

FURTHER INTO THE Quonset Sylvie smelled mouse bait, a faintly sweet whiff she recognized from the elevator of her apartment building. Encounters in the elevator were the only times she saw the concertmaster at close quarters: olive skinned, a serious and shapely mouth, flowing dark hair, a fashionably cut black trench coat, her long fingers gripping the handle of her violin case as she said a neutral hello. The local daily had recently made reference to her talent and the offers she received from elsewhere. What did the concertmaster see in that moment she said hello to Sylvie? Someone more kempt than she'd seen a year before. There had been

- the shapeless hair
- the oversized glasses
- the ten redundant pounds

Until along came

- a stylist who knew her scissors
- new technology in contact lenses
- cross-country skis left behind in the laundry room

(Sylvie was pretty certain they'd been abandoned; surely they didn't belong to anyone who still lived in the building).

Barry for one had noticed the changes. He'd been soft-soling past her office door for ten years and one morning quite suddenly he stopped to chat and didn't even pretend it was to do with work. He made brief jokes about construction noise and weather, followed by, "Drinks?"

"All right," she answered, not even pretending to think it was a bad idea.

ALONG THE SOUTH WALL the Quonset smelled of wet cardboard. Sylvie pulled aside a flattened carton and watched a garter snake slither through its own little exit to the grassy world beyond. She used to bite the insides of her cheeks in order not to laugh as Will tried to explain to her, as they walked together to yoga class, what he knew about the Kundalini, the force coiled inside a person like a snake, the force that could bring self-healing, higher awareness, creative genius. She could use a little Kundalini now. Was there any hope that a tour through the past could deliver a person to the future?

Drawn by the mellow light sifting through the single intact windowpane, she made her way toward the workbench. She lifted a rag, shook out the stiffness, and used it to clear a space at the centre of the pane. Through the swirl of grime that remained she saw Chad, Walkman in hand, dancing on the gravel laneway.

In the beginning, with Barry, that was how it felt. Dancing inside, where no one could see. Passing him in the coffee room without so much as a brush of the hand. The thrill of the clandestine and the sweet pain of impossibility.

They'd sat one evening at her small table, a candle burning low. For atmosphere she'd turned off the ceiling light and left the bathroom door half-open offering a second-hand glow. Making do. (She was good at making do. It was how she'd managed, without benefit of formal training, to work her way from receptionist to crack office manager.) A simple meal, pasta, salad and wine. Playing house. She'd planned a chocolate fondue to follow: chunks of banana, a cake from Safeway cut in cubes. They had the time, his wife out of town and not due to land till 1:00 a.m., but after a few bites of pasta he set down his fork. "Forget dessert." He took her hand and coaxed her out of her chair, kissed the inside of her wrist once, then reached between her legs. He worked her with his fingers, through her jeans.

She heard a catch of classical music. "Do you hear the violin?"

"Hmmm?" Pulling her to the bedroom doorway. "There's a rumour she's leaving."

"There's always that rumour."

In the morning the second pillow was empty but for the scents of sweat and shampoo. In the kitchen, dry white cubes of cake and chunks of slick banana sat browning on a plate. Sylvie picked up the jar of chocolate sauce, twisted the lid and heard the pop of the vacuum seal. She slid a spoon into the goo and pulled it out, covered in chocolate, and sucked.

ON THE WORKBENCH lay the skeleton of a small bird, collapsed onto a spread-eagled pair of pliers. The fine bones of the bird and the jaws of the spread pliers seemed as if they might once have supported the heavy and light parts of the same creature, a dead grotesque with an open beak. She set the soiled rag on top of it and looked instead at the boy out the window, dancing alone. He flipped open his Walkman to switch tapes. Sixteen. Her own would have been fourteen. Girl or boy, it did no good to speculate which. She wasn't sorry, just sometimes she wondered, that was all. She slipped a thumb and finger into the pocket of her jeans — the fit was getting snug again — and pulled out the skinny joint she'd helped herself to from the baggie inside a coffee tin in Mavis's cupboard. She flicked her lighter. Sharp crackle, fast burn, and the smell, that welcome green funk.

"THIS IS WRONG, wrong, wrong," Barry had said a week ago in the ten minutes they'd stolen in the alley behind the A&W close to the college.

"It's true. We should never have begun."

"It's time to do something right."

Uh-oh.

"My son is settled in his own apartment." Barry had a practice of not using the names of the members of his family, not wishing to pull them into the affair. "My daughter will be off across the country to U of T in a couple of months."

Uh-oh.

"I've told my wife she and I need to talk. She said, Yes, we do. So come the weekend, we'll talk."

Sylvie hadn't thought it necessary to say she wouldn't want to play house if there actually were a house and the two of them free to play in it.

"Sweetheart?" he said. "Things are changing."

"Changing."

"Sweetheart, I'm leaving her."

"I wasn't really — We should get back to work, do you think?"

He passed his hand through his hair in a nervous gesture, and she watched the way his bronze curls fell against his forehead. Handsome. Sylvie kept her eyes on those curls because she couldn't meet his eyes. He was a good man. She wished she could have loved him. He didn't even know he'd overlapped with others. She wished she could have loved any one of the good men she'd known. Some people seemed to manage it, or at least to fool themselves into it. Love, children, satisfaction. A full glass.

She made her way back to the Quonset's entrance, flicked off the lights and strained to close the heavy sliding door.

SYLVIE STOOD BAREFOOT in shorts and a T-shirt near the edge of Mavis's pool, holding a gin and tonic. "Coward," she said under her breath. She fished out the wedge of lemon, put it in her mouth and felt its sour sting. She tipped her glass and slid the three ice cubes up the side and into her hand, held them there and braced against the cold bite. She felt the surprise on her toes as the melt dripped onto them, then slid dark onto the concrete.

Mavis had been the first one down the stairs that long-ago day, the one to find their mother; Sylvie the first to run for help. They were both just home from softball practice, Mavis right field, Sylvie left, lowering their voices from field volume to the necessary hush of home as they came up the back steps. But Mavis, in the door first, spoke out loud. "Why's the basement door open? Why's the stair light on?"

Ruth Fletcher, a woman who, on a good day and relying on two canes, struggled to manage a single-floor path from bedroom to bathroom, kitchen to living room, had for reasons unknown attempted to navigate a narrow descent. Whatever she'd been after, from shelf or trunk or rickety wardrobe down there, she could have asked either girl and they'd gladly have fetched it. Gladly. The errand that took her to the stairs that day died with her, a stubborn knot inside her husband's and her daughters' separate hearts.

"Chad?"

He lay by the pool, half-shaded by the pot plants, a corner of his damp towel lying over his eyes in a skinny twist. "Mm?"

"Can I borrow a bike?"

He lifted the towel away from one eye, and that one eye looked to be considering how to say no to an aunt.

"Not one of your good bikes. The one you rode into the pool yesterday."

"Cool. Are you going for a ride along the grid?"

"No, um, can you help me lift it onto your platform?"

"Aunt Sylvie, I don't know if—"

"I'll be fine. If not, you're not responsible."

He did help. He even held the bike steady while she got on. She swung her leg over the rear wheel, lowered herself onto the seat and struggled to sit steady. "People do some reckless things, don't they?"

He shrugged. "Auntie, straighten your handlebars."

"How's this?"

"You sure you want to?"

Sylvie pictured him speeding into the pool the day before, knowing water couldn't break him, finishing with a glorious splash. "I've taken stupider risks." She settled one foot on the lower pedal, where its serrated metal edges pressed into her bare sole. She raised her second foot to the other pedal. The bike listed and Chad wrenched it back into balance. "Oh Jesus," Sylvie said. "Oh Jesus, Jesus." She tightened her grip.

"I'm letting go now, Auntie S. Okay! Go-go-go!"

Love it! Love it! the whooshing no stopping, *love it!* The wheel slipping sideways, sideways. Pull back, pull back! Just before the pool's edge the front wheel skidded off the ramp. She careened in sidelong to the wall. Watersmack, neck jerk, head against concrete, hard, hard. The bicycle dropped away below her. She was under water with a fury of pain in one shoulder. Nose burning. Don't move that shoulder, don't! Up. Up now. She kicked to spin herself around, grabbed the edge with her good arm and hung there coughing out water.

Chad helped her into her car and floored it to what passed for a hospital in Ripley. He left her with a nurse, who called the doctor, while Chad sped off to the Co-op to track down his mom. Sylvie had torn her rotator cuff. She might need surgery. In the meantime the doctor fitted her with a complicated sling that included a tie to wrap around her waist. She was not to move that arm, strictly not. The doctor feared a concussion and ordered her to wait under observation while he went off to do whatever small-town doctors do between emergencies. Observing her in his absence was nurse Beth, who'd been Sylvie's classmate from grade one through to graduation. They'd never been close, but they'd been to the same parties. They'd hardly seen each other since the final day of high school. Still, their shared history might support a small request.

"I don't suppose you could rustle up a joint?"

"You've got opioids in your system. And don't go asking Mavis, either."

"Please. I bet you've got one in your pretty pink pocket."

"I bet I haven't had one in my pocket since 1974."

A shame. A little green would have eased their awkward catching up, especially when Beth said, "Office work, huh? That's nice. We always thought that out of the bunch of us you'd be the one that got to university."

Sylvie tried to guess who Beth might mean when she said *we*. The whole bloody town? Seven hundred-odd people she'd let down by bootstrapping up the lower rungs of administration.

"And here *I* did," said Beth.

"Life is funny."

"Yeah, you have to laugh."

"Sometimes" — Sylvie shifted in her bed and winced — "it's the best strategy."

Mavis appeared, in her collared Co-op shirt with her name above her left breast. "Look at you. Mascara smeared halfway to your chin."

"Yours too, sis."

Mavis took a tissue from the squat cabinet by the bed and looked at Beth, who left the room on her quiet white shoes. "I told my kid to take the ramp down. Jesus, Sylvie. What got into you? I mean, *what?*"

"I don't know. I needed to get past a few things."

"Things. Now would be a good time to be specific."

"It isn't what you're thinking. Just that I need to put my more — my recent past behind me."

"There are other ways to move from A to B."

Sylvie closed her eyes, felt a nudge to the bed as Mavis shuffled her chair closer, felt her sister's hand close over her own. She found it best to concentrate her attention on the feel of that hand and little else. They sat this way for a good long moment. When the time felt right, Sylvie opened her eyes. "I'm sorry to take you back there. It wasn't even in my mind."

"It was a long time ago, Sylvie. I'm okay. Are you?"

Sylvie shrugged with her good shoulder and smiled as best she could. "I'll have to put my business idea on pause. Possible surgery. Can't operate a machine."

"I thought the idea was you'd be the brains, hire the brawn."

"Brawn costs money."

"Yes. And I have news. Geoff was at the Co-op when Chad came barreling in. We were having yet another conversation about your idea. He still wasn't sure, then Chad bursts out with your escapade. Well. Anyone with the spunk — Geoff's word — to ride down a ramp into a swimming pool at the age of thirty-five —"

"Thirty-four."

" — he said that would be a person he's happy to support."

"I tore a body part I'd never even heard of."

"By now I'm running to my car, of course I am, thank you very much Sylvie, and he follows me out and what he says as I'm closing my door is that he likes a risk taker."

"A risk taker who can't steer."

"I know. Take it or leave it."

And take or leave the city. This month's rumour said the concertmaster had landed a position in Hamilton. The city was an empty room with no more music threading through the wall. The city was her hollow kitchen with its drying cubes of cake and browned banana.

She was afraid. Afraid to borrow money, afraid to be the boss. These, she had learned at a business seminar, were

• typical fears

and could be dealt with.

But to circle back to Ripley? A town the same but different, where people thought they knew her but they didn't; where Erik, who'd helped her practise how to kiss, now managed the gas station and lived on three acres with a wife and four kids; where one of his brothers worked in the grocery store and the other at the rink, which was a year-round facility now, with artificial ice and hockey school in July, no longer a place for dusky trysts; and where the house that held her childhood had long ago been torn down and replaced.

Her elbow was restless, held close at her side by the strap that circled her waist. "Watch yourself," Erik told her more than once, years past. Well, she never really had. Maybe if she were on her own awhile she would. Maybe for the time being the person to get close to was herself. Suppose, though, her new friend disappointed her? This was the real fear. Suppose her new friend wasn't enough to fill the void. She strained against the binding at her elbow, and hot pain shot from her shoulder on down.

"Mavis?"

"Yeah?"

"Get in touch with Oprah for me, okay?"

"I'll find the number. You can make the call."

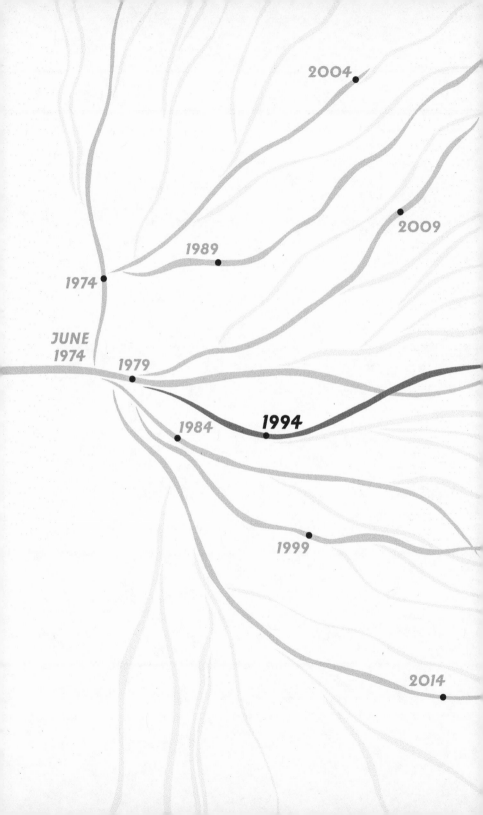

Honestly,

...**I DO WONDER** why the fiftyish man with the clipped beard in colours of rust and salt has left me alone in his office as if I can be trusted with all the private whatnot: company books, confidential records, almost certainly pills and elixirs in the squat cabinet where I've set my folded jacket. Over there's a monitor, the word *dozing* in pale blue letters sliding across the screen on the diagonal; up on the wall a clock with a brown surround that reminds me of the one in the principal's office from my sixties childhood. Maybe, unprepared to deal with a case such as me on a Saturday morning, the man stepped out to collect himself. He did look nervous, kept squeezing one pale hand with the other. I just now saw him go into the bathroom – Employees Only – past Shampoo and to the left. *Are you still squeezing your hand in there, Mister, or are you squeezing something else?*

Think I'm funny.

He's left me here to consider my sins. All right. I watch the second hand as it jerks, jerks its way around. I am not, at the core, a dishonest person, though others have their doubts and at times appearances support their view. Sometimes I think I do it just for the feel of a thing under my fingers. A new and secret friend among the monotonies.

When something urgent needs figuring out, I find it's helpful to walk through it as if I were trying to explain my actions to a person who loves me without question, say my kind and wonderful Aunt Merry. Tell my own side of the story on the way to seeing its possible other sides. What would I say to my aunt if she were to walk in here and vouch for me — if, that is, she weren't at the moment sunning herself on a beach in Martinique — if I could see the shine of her silver pixie cut under the fluorescent lights as she strides up the alley between Baby Care and Foot Care to arrive at the four steps that lead to the glassed-in office where I sit overlooking this two-bit pharmacy? I didn't mean to say two-bit; I meant to say modest.

If Merry were to negotiate my release on an aunt's recognizance, I'd feel compelled to present her with the entire sequence of events. I would begin with the simple facts, not just this drugstore-cowgirl incident today, but last night's dilemma as well: left to my own devices, what would I have done with the money I found at Top of the Evening?

It would be best, in fact, to begin as far back as Wednesday: Jack and I got married in 1974, which on Wednesday made twenty years, a remarkable accomplishment. We don't often go out on work nights ("school nights," Jack calls them; he likes the joke because, aside from occasional training junkets the city sends him on, neither of us has been to school in decades), so we decided to delay our celebration, with a reservation for

Friday evening at The Tavern on Twenty-First. It didn't seem right, though, to let the actual date pass without recognition, so on Wednesday Jack suggested I stop after work at the video store. I rented *Drugstore Cowboy*, which had Matt Dillon and company laying waste to small-town pharmacies, scooping up brightly coloured pills to brightly colour their brains. I loved this movie, the attitude it took for granted, the on-the-road feel, even the flying pigs; Jack, on the other hand, did considerable head shaking. After a while, things didn't go so well for Matt and his friends. This was the part where I didn't like the story so much any more and Jack began to enjoy it, nodding along to the dark horrors of poetic justice.

The machine was still on rewind when we left for the bedroom, where we stripped each other in a hurry. A special occasion will do that for us, even now and even on a work night. Once naked, though, I had trouble surrendering to the moment. The movie, with its other world, had given me a thought that seemed bound right in with the passage of our twenty years, and just as my attentive husband was heading southward under the sheets, I said, "You know —"

"Huh?"

"Sometimes I think about how there are so many different doors a person has the choice to walk through, and if you happened to —"

"Shush, honey."

I don't suppose that, if I included this scene in my explanation to Aunt Merry, she'd be comfortable looking in on my bedroom goings-on, but it's so much a part of the story, this wondering and wanting. And she is, after all, a grown-up.

"But Jack, don't you ever think about a set of doors like that? Don't you ever look at all those choices and think, This one looks interesting, but this one grabs me in a different way, and, wow, what about that yellow door?"

"Gee, Sylvie" — he lifted the sheet so he could see past the spare geography of my body to my face — "why don't you just get a bag of frozen peas and wrap it around my parts?"

"Sorry, sorry."

Later, coming back from the bathroom, I saw how he'd pulled the sheet to his neck and was holding it taut with his stubbled chin as if he was afraid a draft would find its way in. One of his eyes was lit yellow by a slice of light that angled in from the hallway. He said, "I always knew which door I'd go through." This wasn't news to me, but still I felt disappointment roll and resettle low in my gut like a handful of marbles.

"Twenty years of marriage, and my wife thinks she'd be better off with a dark-eyed dope fiend."

"Aren't we dramatic."

"Aren't we."

I wanted him to know it was nothing to do with him. I love him, I almost always have, though sometimes more and sometimes less. Truly I didn't wish I'd turned the handle on some alternate door. Couldn't he see that the mulling was about how a person only gets the one, single door, and she has to fit *every-thing* into the room she finds beyond it? And the fact you can't try them all — those other lives you'll never, ever know — didn't that make him sad? A little? Jack is not the sort of person a woman would say that to, so I said, "Don't worry, babe."

And now we come to last night, Friday, and the dilemma of the money. There was a moment in the early evening when I feared our anniversary dinner at The Tavern would be pre-empted. Jack got in at 7:00 and immediately switched on CNN to follow the same slow drama I'd been watching before I left work. A group of us from the basement offices at the university library, with the full consent of department head Patrick, had gathered around a TV on a cart in the hallway to track the progress of a white Ford Bronco as it rolled along the freeway between Disneyland and LA at thirty-five miles an hour, OJ Simpson in the back seat, cops behind, helicopters above.

Jack settled into his habitual hollow on the couch and I sat down in my lesser hollow beside him. Black and white police cars were strung out behind the Bronco like wasps in formation. Restless, Jack got up and paced, tossing the remote hand to hand. "OJ's all-time rushing record. Should we cancel the reservation?"

"Oh, come on."

"But this is *news*, Sylvie. This is Current Events. What if there's a test?" He raised his eyebrows to mock himself. I raised mine back and he pushed OFF. I could see the effort, but it's a simple trick of momentum: as soon as you let the screen go blank, you're good to go. "Anyway," he said. "I've never been one for snuff."

Was that what my workmates and I had been doing in the basement hallway of Murray Memorial Library — hoping to watch someone die in plain, mass media sight? At first there had been little to see but lawyers and the DA and the police chief speaking into a forest of microphones. We stayed in the hallway long past quitting time, reluctant to leave in case the drama was about to escalate. But the talking heads talked on. I was at my desk pulling my purse out of the lower drawer when Patrick said, "You guys, you have to see this," and there was the pursuit, in real time. The Bronco, the squad cars, the seamy creep of anticipation. It wasn't so much a car chase as a following, an escort. "Like a Hot Wheels set in slow motion," said Patrick. He put his hand on my shoulder in front of everyone. "The Deluxe Law Enforcement set."

. I slipped out from under his hand in what I would say was a smooth and assertive motion, for he and I have already had that conversation, and although I might be interested, he has a wife and I a husband. As I've said, it would be a treat to peek around door after door, but I don't want to hear the one behind me slam shut. The camera panned the crowds lining the route holding signs that told OJ to *RUN,* or *DIE*; people waving, crying, laughing. All that whirling emotion looking for a landing pad.

AT THE TAVERN the TV above the bar was on, the chase apparently the only event unspooling in the whole wide world of news. I asked for a booth near the back.

"That'll be the end of the Ford Bronco," Jack said with satisfied wisdom as we opened our heavy menus and the brass doodads at the corners landed on the table, *tap-tap.* "Sales will tank, you watch."

I *did* want to talk about it, wanted to twist in the booth and look at the screen, but I gathered my willpower. "Let's ignore it. Please."

After a moment Jack said, "Okay," and after another moment, "Let's talk about doors, then."

I slapped my menu shut, *tip-tap*. "I'm sorry I said that the other night. I'll have a chicken Caesar. I don't want to run off with, as you say, a dope fiend, I only ever wanted you."

What do couples talk about after twenty years, once they've ruled out Current Events and the Human Condition?

"I love you." I squeezed his hand across the table. It was true, is true. "Happy anniversary."

Later we walked a few blocks north to Mayhew Tower and rode up to the glitzy new Top of the Evening in what's billed as the swiftest elevator in town, glass on three sides and a one-eighty view of the city lights. Me being not so fond of heights, I faced the only solid wall as we rode up, and Jack held his hands like blinders on either side of my face. Friends had told us if you wanted a sense of occasion this was the place. Jack sees better than I do in dim light, and he led the way through the room, slow and snaking, to an empty table. My eyes still hadn't adjusted, and I had to feel my way to sitting down. I touched something — a papery tongue sticking out where the back of the chair met the seat. I took it for an upholstery tag that should have been removed. "Still working out the kinks."

The chairs were plush and low, and if we both sat back we were too far apart for conversation. We settled in, leaning forward and smiling at each other over a teardrop bowl with a squat candle inside, which lit his face from below so he looked like a character in a fright movie. How, in the long term, can a lounge succeed as a venue for wordplay-foreplay if your date looks a fright?

Jack ordered two whiskies, neat. "Canadian Club if you have it."

"We do," said my-name's-Kyle, I'll-be-your-waiter.

My jacket was bunched behind me in a bothersome way. I reached back to rearrange it and again felt that upholstery tag. Wait a minute, there was more than one, maybe five or six, and they weren't sewn in, they were loose. I could tell by feel they weren't ordinary scraps, not cashier slips or abandoned to-do lists or lost can-I-have-your-numbers. Paper money, even after it's been folded a thousand times, offers the fingertips its own unmistakable texture. It's a satisfaction.

I looked across at Jack's fright-movie face and said nothing about what I'd found. I moved my hand underneath the loose folds of my jacket, trying to hide the bills and count them at the same time.

Kyle-your-waiter set our whiskies on the table. As Jack said thanks and Kyle turned to go I slid one hand into the crevice where the back of the chair met the seat and found a stack ten or fifteen thick. While Jack looked about and rated each element of the plush décor on a scale from one to four, I slid the stack of bills underneath my bum. Then, with my secret pumping inside me, I raised my glass in honour of our twenty years. It could be enough to buy a leather jacket, hell, leather pants. Jack considered the low-loop carpet, brown as dried blood, and said, "I give them only two stars for the rug."

"I think three."

Over his shoulder on the small TV above the bar I saw dark streets lined with police cars; above, helicopters whirling; on the sidewalk, uniforms holding back onlookers; and repeated close-ups of an iron gate. I did my best to look *at* Jack rather than past him. Inside the teardrop bowl the candle struggled against invisible currents. He moved it to the side and his face softened, but now the shadow and flicker across his features aged him by a decade. I realized the effect would be the same when he looked at me.

The many ways we've seen each other over twenty years. Once, when I'd called in sick for no reason other than a person deserves an occasional reprieve from typing numbers on labels and pulling away the backing and fitting the label onto the spine of a book entitled, say, *The Elements of Social Scientific Thought,* and I was sitting in bed wearing a matched set of blue lace undies unfamiliar to Jack, with a Pepsi on the nightstand and licking the salty orange dusting from my fingers having just finished a bag of Cheezies, he happened home from work at lunchtime. Just to check in, he said.

"I thought you were sick."

"I'm recovering, is what I am."

He sat on the edge of the bed and scrunched the empty cellophane bag, and I said, "Is there any privacy in this life?" At that he walked out and closed the bedroom door behind him. I heard him leave the house. He didn't mention it again, but I'll bet that colour picture persists inside his head, ocean-blue bra, orange under my fingernails.

There are things I've never told Jack and possibly never will. He doesn't know, for instance, that over the past five years three promotions have come open at work, and I applied for only the first, and didn't succeed. Though I do take mental health breaks once in a while I'm not, in fact, unhappy typing labels nine to five. I used to be a go-getter, now I'm not. Sometimes I'm disappointed in myself, but the world needs plenty of people who are satisfied to do such work. Aunt Merry has backed me up on this in private conversation. Or, she hasn't faulted me for it.

Something else I've failed to tell him: when we lost the baby fifteen years ago, the miscarriage might have had something to do with the night that — not admitting even to myself how late my period was — I went out with the girls and drank five Depth Charges inside of two hours. Three weeks after that wasted night I deposited a small jar of morning pee at the clinic and within days received a call from Dr. Carla herself, offering congratulations. In a rush I understood what it was to have mixed feelings: I was afraid I had damaged a tiny life; also, I had decided I wasn't a good fit for marriage, this marriage at least; also, a baby for God's sake.

By then I'd even sorted through our suitcases to choose the one I could best handle if I were to load my old Meteor and head west toward the fabled opportunities of Calgary. Two weeks after the test results, I still hadn't told Jack. After a screaming row on a Saturday night I woke up exhausted and pulled out of a Sunday trip to Uncle Walter's cabin. Alone in the quiet apartment, a pair of sweatpants in hand and the suitcase open on the bed, I felt a twinge in my gut and a wetness in my underwear. When Jack walked in from his day at the lake, woozy from beer and sunstroke, I'd already been to Emerg and back, stowed the suitcase back under the bed and tucked myself in. I asked him please to bring two glasses of water. He did, and made to hand me one but I said, "Sit on the bed and drink them both, and listen." He drank the first while I told him about the pregnancy and the bleeding and the fact the doctor had ordered bed rest until further notice. While he drank the second I considered telling him about the five Depth Charges, but said nothing.

After two weeks Dr. Carla gave me the all-clear to return to work. Fine, good, take it easy. A few months on, a pain sharp and heavy like the forward edge of an axe travelled through my gut from front to back at two in the afternoon. I'd just finished lining up a spine label on a replacement copy of *The Golden Bough,* and I doubled over. My forehead landed hard on the front cover. Mixed feelings all over again. My boss called an ambulance, then called Jack, who rushed across town from the bus yards. When I woke up in the hospital I asked him if the title of the book was reverse-embossed above my eyebrows. He said he could see what I was trying to do, but it would be better right then if I didn't make jokes.

He breathed life back into me day after day until I stood on my own again, taking shape around the gift of his care. Maybe the D&C that followed the miscarriage compromised what my mother-in-law called my woman parts, or maybe the responsibility lies with simple chance, but we never had another pregnancy. It disappoints me, but that's life. Or rather the absence of it.

Here's where I might pause to ask Aunt Merry, presuming she's still listening, if she's ever noticed how rumination will pull in other things from all around the rim to think on: Is honesty a matter of either/or? Is guilt? Is *want* a river that never finds the sea?

143

The anniversary card the pharmacist found hiding in the pocket of my jacket this morning had a scroll in relief on the front: *To my one true love on our anniversary.* When I passed my hand over it I felt the slight rise of the letters, fine silver italic. It reminded me of our wedding invitations. The card was for Jack. The card was for me. We've lasted.

THIS WALK-THROUGH has rambled further than I ever meant it to. I'm no longer captive in the raised office at Andersen Drugs. No cops, no charges filed. The man with the beard of salt and rust took no action beyond confiscating what was his. Compassion, or lack of nerve? At any rate he won't see me again. Although it's right here in the neighbourhood, I rarely visit his store. Shoppers Drugs on Eighth has so much more to choose from. An emporium. And crack security, the big No.

I've managed to escape this morning's scrape, unscraped. Does this mean I wouldn't owe Aunt Merry the rest of the story? She would say, Hold on, girl. Tell me what you did with that money last night.

Literally, I sat on it while I considered my options. If I told the waiter, he would surely ask to hold it in case someone came looking. If no one came looking he'd keep it for himself and tell me otherwise, which would seem to break the law of finders keepers. I could, on the other hand, take it to the police in hopes they'd let me have it if no one claimed it after a certain period. A way to do the right thing yet hedge my bets. One possibility.

If you were to ask Jack about my honesty or lack of it, he might mention the time we stayed at the rustic lodge in the Rockies and he walked into the room when I was folding the cloud-like hotel towel into my suitcase. So precious. That morning when I'd wrapped it round my naked torso it had made me feel cared for with a special tenderness. As if he knew anything of its true value, Jack said, "It'll just show up at twice what it's worth on the Visa bill along with the room charge."

In my defense, I will say there have been numerous times I've wanted to take something and I haven't. This doesn't make me a saint, but it's a fact worth recognizing. Sometimes it seems I've spent my life specifically *not* taking things. I don't think the average person has any idea what a challenge it can be. If a person's never taken anything, but they've never been tempted either, what have they proved? I'm forever walking past a darling ring or a bottle of perfume and hearing it say, clear and sweet, *Do you love me?*

At Top of the Evening, Kyle was beside our table again. Why? – our whiskies were still half full. My left hand had once more wandered hopefully behind my back, and I'd found two more stray bills, their texture soft and strong at once. Wondering if the waiter could see this, I broke out in a sweat. I wished I hadn't chosen a blouse made from non-breathable, one hundred percent polyester just because it had a neckline that flattered my shallow cleavage, but I do try to look my best for a special occasion.

Jack told Kyle we were good, but still the waiter stood there. I managed to slip my hand into the pocket of my scrunched jacket and deposit the two bills still in hand. I pulled a tissue from the pocket and dabbed at my nose.

Finally Kyle spoke. "Did you see it? They got OJ. Cuffed him outside his house."

Jack said, "Anybody get killed?"

"Sorry." Kyle grinned. "Nobody besides Nicole Simpson and Ron Goldman."

What all this means about the murders and the chase I'm not sure, but I'm trying to tell the evening as I recall it. The allure, as if it was a movie, as if there weren't real-life children and parents and grandparents in the picture. As if it was staged for the benefit of ourselves and CNN and the people lining that California freeway with their signs that said *RUN* and *DIE* and no one knowing which they hoped for most in the caves where they never looked.

WATCHING THE SHADOWS move across Kyle's back as he walked away, I thought, suppose I do turn over the money to the police? Jack wouldn't need to know, ever. I could wad it into my pockets tonight and take it to the station in the morning and if no one claimed it I could tell him I'd saved up for the leather pants over months.

He was monitoring the goings-on at the bar, making sure the whisky going into our glasses was Canadian Club. Don't you dare try to slip an inferior second round past Jack. It hadn't even registered with me that he'd ordered fresh drinks, and now here they were. Wondering if there were more bills in danger of being lost in the crevice, I let my hand wander behind me.

"What's bothering you, hon?"

"Bothering me?"

"Do you have a sore shoulder? Or are you scratching your butt and trying to be discreet about it?"

"Just, my jacket's —"

"Anyway," he said, "show's over," and for a silly instant I thought he knew what I was up to. Until he made a hitchhiker's fist and pointed his thumb back over his shoulder toward the TV. "You should've seen at our shop this afternoon — everyone crowding in to listen on Ray's office radio. You have to wonder what the hell kind of big-Jesus empty inner trench everyone's trying so hard to fill."

I would be happier if Jack didn't have the habit of saying things like that. Trenchant things, ha. He looked at me across the candle's flicker, and I felt like I was writing an exam.

"How would I know?"

"It's just a thing worth asking."

This from the man who was reluctant to talk about doors.

"Jack —"

"Maybe not a trench. Maybe a funnel. Stuff draining out the bottom while they pour stuff in the top."

I would never go so far as to say Jack brings out the worst in me. A person can't say that. A person has to own responsibility for who she is. Suppose this, though: suppose he's so honest it makes me want to punch honesty in the gut.

"Jack, you were watching, too."

THE ELEVATOR DOOR slid open at the far end of the room, letting in a freak of light and showing the silhouettes of two slim women in short skirts and high heels. They made a beeline in the direction of our table — or it would've been a beeline except their eyes hadn't adjusted to the change in light, and they bumped, one after the other, against a low table, the big hair of the second woman floofing forward then back as she regained her balance. The woman in the lead was in tears, and Jack would say later he thought it was because she'd banged her shins, but I knew better. She stopped beside our table. "Here, this one."

Woman number two said, "Are you sure?" Her cheeks were dusted with glitter, and the candlelight set it sparkling.

"Pretty sure, pretty sure." The first woman looked at my lap and then my face, and when those two things disappointed her she stretched her neck to one side to look over my shoulder. "Did you find some money? That's where I was sitting. Earlier. I lost some money."

"Do you want to have a look?" I stood and turned and lifted my jacket, managing to drag it in such a way that it messed the neat stack of bills I'd been sitting on into the sort of scatter you might expect if a person had sat on all that cash unawares. I draped the jacket over my arm and peered at the chair as if it was hard for me to see much of anything in the dimness.

"Oh thank God! ThankGod, thankGod."

I smiled. "That's lucky." I saw, nosing up from behind the cushion, an envelope my blind fingers hadn't come across.

The woman's hands made me think of pale moths, quick creatures with hard-to-follow motions as they moved across the Ultrasuede gathering loose bills and pulling the envelope free. She knelt at the low table to count by the wavering light. The bills were almost all twenties. "Three hundred and forty . . ." She opened the envelope upside-down above the table, and a few bills fluttered down. "Three hundred and sixty . . . eighty . . . four hundred."

She turned toward her glittering friend. "Was it four, or was it four-forty?"

"Didn't you write it on the envelope?"

"No, not, no. I didn't." The kneeling woman reached her fingers into the crevice at the back of the seat, found nothing.

"Just wait." I got to my knees as if to look under the chair, still holding my jacket. I thought I might fish out the couple of bills I'd slipped into my pocket without anyone seeing, make it look as if I'd just now found them on the carpet.

"Here." Jack lifted the jacket out of the way and out of my grip. "See anything?"

"Sorry, nothing." I stood and brushed my knees and felt the silken texture of my pantyhose and imagined the feel of the leather I wouldn't be buying. I wanted to say, What's it for, this cash? The take from a fundraiser? Rent money? Are you call girls? Do you not own a decent bag that doesn't spill your valuables? "I'm glad you found it," I said.

It's true I didn't have time before the women arrived to entirely decide what to do, whether or not to take the money to the police or pocket the lot, but it's quite likely I was tilting in the direction of honesty. And the fact that, there at the end, I was considering how to slide the pair of twenties out of my jacket and hand them over, there's that.

Last night Jack and I both pretended to go straight to sleep, and this morning as we quietly drank our coffee at the little round table in the corner of the kitchen, I wondered what thoughts had deepened the typically shallow crease between his eyebrows. Was he remembering the way I'd fidgeted in my chair, and was he about to conclude I'd discovered the cash and said nothing? But maybe it wasn't — as he likes to remind me — maybe it wasn't about me. He might have been spelunking inside himself, afraid of stumbling into a trench he'd never considered was there until he found himself in the grip of that Bronco chase.

A walk might settle me. I edged past his chair and grabbed my jacket on the way out, not that it was a cold day, but I had forty dollars cash in the pocket, and my idea was to stop at the corner store for some little thing. Cinnamon buns or potato chips or a bag of pre-cooked shrimp. Something.

I said earlier that I would try to relate the simple facts, as if I were recounting them to Aunt Merry. I wonder what a simple fact would look like, I would say now to her. I would ask her, Have you ever encountered one?

The route to the corner store passes right by Andersen Drugs. Inside, I gave the display of sunglasses a slow spin. I flipped through a comic book. Then I saw the lit sign, "Greeting Cards" and it came to me that I shouldn't have let the anniversary go by without so much as buying one for Jack. Twenty *years*. It's easy enough to pay for a thing, I know. It's easy enough to take it, too. You pick it up and slip it into a pocket or a purse or a waistband, and there you have it. You just *have* it.

I don't always remember, even, what I've taken or when. I'll stash it in my separate room with everything else and close the door. Or I'll leave it in a pocket and forget. Six months will go by and I'll pull out a winter coat, and in there with a tissue and a couple of quarters will be my favourite merlot shade of lipstick, lifted last March and still in its shrink-sleeve, but in the meantime I've bought and paid for much the same shade twice over. Which means I have one for my pocket, one for my purse, and one for the drawer, in case.

May Zeus Strike You with a Lightning Bolt

THE YOUNG MAN behind the counter at the gas station had a shaved head and a Roughrider logo tattooed above his right ear. "Pump three?" His hand hovered near the cash register.

Mavis scanned the magazine rack. She ought to pick up something to serve as a distraction for Sylvie. There: *Canadian Living,* the Christmas issue, on the cover a gingerbread house and the suggestion you recruit your kids and grandkids to help you build it. A poor choice, then.

"Pump number three?"

Hold it: *House and Home.* Decorator porn. But no, not enough muscle for the mood-lifting Sylvie would need.

"Pump number *three.* Green Caravan."

"That's me."

"Are you a professor? Absent-minded?"

"Preoccupied, if you don't mind. Just in town to get my sister out of jail."

"Twenty-six thirty-five, ma'am."

"I'm joking. She isn't in jail, not really. Not yet."

"Don't forget your receipt, ma'am."

As she steered away from the pumps, Mavis checked the dash clock. She'd made good time on the highway; she could afford a detour. Let's turn right. She flicked the wipers on to chase a dusting of dry snow. Up along Broadway and across the bridge. At Midtown Plaza she found the leather store she and her sister had walked through the last time she'd visited, Sylvie mooning over "all the lovelies I can't afford." Now Mavis went to the far corner and found a rack of pants — black, brown, and a red that lost all hope of class by veering toward orange. She skimmed her palm along a top-stitched pant-leg, pale brown and butter soft. Waist 34. She took the pants to the change room, pulled them on and twisted so she could see in the three-way mirror how she filled them out in a way Sylvie with her ever-skinny butt would not. She quickened. It wasn't often Mavis still thought of herself as a woman who might look sexy, given the opportunity. She widened the angle on one arm of the mirror. My. But leather pants were not the get-up for serving burgers at the rink in Ripley or attending fraught parent-teacher interviews — the special occasions of her evenings and afternoons.

"Hell with it." She opened the change room door.

"Can I help you?"

"Uh, sorry. I'm looking for a 29 waist. They're for my sister."

A little "hair of the dog," Mavis's husband Pete might say, a folk remedy for what he'd taken to calling Sylvie's "Illegal Acquisition Condition." Mavis flung the shopping bag with its red rope handles into the back seat thinking, This is perverse. She almost threaded the seat belt through the handles to keep the pricey cargo safe. Definitely perverse. Maybe she wouldn't take the bag into the house once she got to Sylvie's. She could always return the pants day after tomorrow before heading back to Ripley.

At Sylvie's, after hugs, after "How are you really?", after tears that welled but didn't slip free, the two of them sat down at the little round kitchen table. Because the room was small, the table was shoved in a corner, which meant any two people were uncomfortably close even for immediate family. Or especially for immediate family. You had to turn either yourself or your chair to face the other person in a natural way. Maybe Sylvie and Jack were used to it. Her sister set two cups of black coffee in white mugs on the table and twisted the cap off a bottle of Bailey's to serve as cream, but Mavis went to the fridge and helped herself to milk. All right, let's tackle this. She started speaking before she got back to her chair. "When you told me that long story all those months ago about your night at Top of the Evening, the hundreds of dollars spilling out of your chair, you made it sound hilarious. As if you would never in fact have kept it, it was just something funny to think about."

"Why didn't you bring Kayla with you? I thought you were bringing Kayla."

"Can we keep to the topic?"

Her sister, looking at her lap, lifted a thin hand and tucked her limp hair behind her ear. "Kayla always likes a hit of the city." She wore no earrings, not even a stud; no makeup, not even lipstick. Under the table her leg twitched up and down, her heel tapping the lino next to a slouchy leather bag, powder blue. Mavis wanted badly to set a hand on Sylvie's pumping knee, to still it, but with one teenager still at home she knew better than to turn agitation back on itself. She managed to budge her chair back an inch and still not knock the wall. Space. When she was with Sylvie, Mavis had to work at finding space to call her own.

"Is that a new purse? Nice."

"Never mind."

"On the handle there, is that one of those inventory tags?"

"Never *mind.*"

"Sylvie. How could I bring Kayla, given she's got school, given the nature of the visit, given *court* tomorrow? Do you think I'm about to tell my kid, who loves you and who I'm pretty sure is nicking twenties from my wallet, that her aunt sauntered out of The Bay carrying a shopping bag with one pair of gym socks paid for and three necklaces not? *Three.* Do you even wear necklaces?"

"It's a teachable moment, don't you think? An aunt should be a teacher."

Mavis laughed, they both did. She landed a quick slap on Sylvie's arm and Sylvie gave her a quick slap back, their known vocabulary.

"Besides," said Mavis. "Kayla's extra busy these days." Busy was not the most accurate word. She'd taken to locking herself in her room. She would go thirty hours at a stretch, no food going in, nothing coming out either, other than she surely must sneak a trip or two to the bathroom in the dark. No school, no basketball, no babysitting for the family the next farm over and definitely no expressions of remorse. The only thing Mavis could hear through the bedroom door was music that reminded her of late seventies punk, but more cluttered. She'd stand listening for long moments, her ear to the door where Kayla had drawn a cartoon zeppelin in green permanent marker directly onto the white paint and printed the words BAD YEAR inside the airship. There was a girl in there, aching in nameless ways. Nights when Kayla was a newborn, Pete would mock Mavis when she pulled the standard parent trick of holding a mirror near the baby's nose to check for breath. Maybe she should be at the farm this minute, listening at that door.

"Sylvie-Syl. What made you think you'd get away with it?"

"*No*body pays attention to the robot voice at the exit to The Bay. It's *al*ways piping up. It makes the same announcement to every second person leaving the store." Sylvie pinched her nose. "'Apparently we failed to remove the inventory tag from your purchase.'" Her mechanical voice was funny, but Mavis managed not to laugh. "'Please return to the service desk.'" In her normal voice Sylvie said, "People stand there looking embarrassed. Nobody comes, so they keep on walking."

"Which is what you did."

"Just my luck that on *this* day a man in black with his big important, um, walkie-talkie appears from nowhere. 'If I could check your bag, ma'am.'"

"Yeah, we're *ma'am*s now."

"I know. *Ma'am*." Sylvie slapped Mavis's forearm and Mavis slapped back. Neither laughed.

She should have brought the decorator magazine, anything. A show of care. A distraction for both of them. She ran a hand through her short hair and, with a quick small motion she hoped Sylvie wouldn't notice, massaged her scalp. It was an old way she had of settling frustration before she spoke. "They'll go easy on you, it's a first offence."

Sylvie made a crooked line with her lips. "First offence on record."

"First offence on record and *outside the family.*"

Sylvie looked away.

"Joke," said Mavis.

"Laughing," said Sylvie. "But I still feel bad about raiding your little tin globe of a piggy bank. In fact."

"You didn't feel bad at the time."

"Remember how we loved the rattle? — all those nickels and dimes and quarters."

"Shake the world —" said Mavis.

" — make a little noise," said Sylvie.

"*Music,* was the way we said it. Shake the world, make a little music."

"No: *noise* is how we said it."

"Be right back." Mavis didn't really need to pee, what she needed was to be in a different space. Now here she was at the head of the hallway she'd passed through dozens of times, at the other end of it the bathroom on one side and the main bedroom opposite, and before those, the doors to the separate rooms Jack and Sylvie maintained as their private spaces. The other spouse was never to look inside, hope to die. Jack's had a plastic dollar-store sign that said *Jack's Room*, and Sylvie's had a piece of foamcore cut to look like a thundercloud and done up with markers. She'd printed on it, "May Zeus strike you with a lightning bolt." Years ago Mavis had said to Sylvie, "But they're not even properly locked. All you have to do is jimmy the door-knob and you're in." They were doors of the sort Mavis's kids had on their bedrooms. A privacy door without a key. You could lock it from the inside, or you could twist the knob into lock position and pull it closed from the outside. To unlock it from the hallway, a person had to poke something skinny through a tiny hole to release the mechanism. "You even have to jimmy your *own* doorknob to get inside your *own* room."

"Yeah, but you have to bother. That's the thing."

"I bet Jack's looked inside your private domain the odd time."

"Jack isn't one to bother."

"I bet you've looked into his."

"Boring boy stuff."

"What's in yours? Boring girl stuff?"

"Maybe."

"I guess if you don't have a teenager in the house, you get to be the teenager yourself."

"Could you maybe *think* before you say a thing like that?"

TODAY MAVIS SAW Jack's door standing open for the first time, the sign aslant on the door, the room empty but for two boxes taped shut in the corner and assorted fishing tackle lying loose under the window. Fresh vacuum tracks on the carpet. The blind was rolled all the way up, daylight reaching to the corners and into the open closet with its bare hangers. So he really had cleared out. When he'd called Mavis last night he'd said he was weary of living with crazy. For a man like Jack to reach for a word like "weary" when he could have said much worse suggested there were plenty of words he'd left unsaid.

Today as always the door to Sylvie's private room was closed, and out of long habit Mavis tried the knob on the way past. In the bathroom, while enthroned, she thought ahead to what she'd say to Pete when she called him tonight. *Weird as ever but I'm hanging in.* The last time Pete was in this house he'd made a trip to the bathroom and then come back to the living room rolling his eyes. He looked toward Mavis and mouthed the words *"The Kids in the Hall."*

Maybe she had baby clothing stashed in there from fifteen years ago, tiny yellow onesies and hooded towels still folded in tissue paper or hanging from little plastic hangers. Or maybe inside the room were leaning columns of diaries scrawled with her darkest secrets. Or stacks of hoarded magazines like their mother had kept in case she might feel good enough to sit up one day and leaf through them. Or Sylvie was having an affair, ha, and that room was where they had their fun, she and her lover, and where she kept a lacy pair of white stockings, a rose-pink garter belt, a Victoria's Secret bra and an extra-large mirror.

Still seated, still midstream, Mavis reached a hand toward the vanity — rising a little off the seat, careful now — curled a finger around the handle of the drawer next to the sink and pulled it open. From where she sat she couldn't see inside. Finish first. As she soaped her hands she looked over the drawer's contents. She needed something skinny with enough length to it. Let's see. Lipstick, lipstick, lipstick. Mascara twice over. Ah, a metal hairclip with a long beak that tapered to a point. She snapped it in two and did her best to straighten its slight curve. Worth a try. At home she'd used a barbecue skewer on Kayla's room. You just push straight in till you feel it hit the mechanism, then give a quarter turn. Kayla had started throwing things as soon as Mavis cracked open the door, but she'd walked right through the barrage – a plush penguin, an old Raffi cassette, an algebra workbook – and set a tray on the dresser. "Pot roast, potatoes and veg. Help yourself." A yo-yo landed in the gravy and tepid splatter landed on Mavis's cheek, her shirt, her forearm. No doubt Kayla had the knife from that dinner tray slotted into the door frame now.

Last week Mavis had said to young Gloria Shane when she came through her checkout at the Co-op, "Don't ever have kids." Vera, listening in from Produce and ever the supervisor had said, "Please, Mavis, that's the third time this week you've given unsolicited advice to a customer."

"They shouldn't take me seriously." The whole town knew about Kayla's current troubles, there was no percentage in pretending life was lollipops and gumdrops. Mavis swiped a box of spaghetti past the scanner and looked up at Gloria. "I don't suppose I mean it." No one would say whether it was Kayla or Jen who'd thrown the first punch, least of all Kayla or Jen. Their friends, of course, were mute, no matter the carrots and sticks old Principal Siding waved about, and good for them, good for all of them. It was the third fist fight this school year though, and only three months in. Once Gloria had left and the store was empty but for herself and Vera, Mavis said, "Everyone makes a colossal deal of it when it's girls."

"They do."

"A boy gets into a fight, he's a magnet for cheerleaders. A girl gets into a fight, she's kicked off the squad."

"Well. Either way."

IN SYLVIE'S HALLWAY, Mavis considered the lightning-spiked cloud on the door. I dare you, Zeus. She tried jabbing the half hairclip into the small hole, but its width stopped it short. She pulled it back out and pressed it against the doorframe, trying to bend it double lengthways along the shallow v already there. No dice. She put it in her mouth and the tang of tin seared a line along her tongue. She positioned it between her teeth and bit down and yelped at the sudden pain in a back molar.

"Mavis, you're pathetic," said Sylvie from the entrance to the hallway. She turned and disappeared. Mavis heard the scrabble of cutlery and shortly Sylvie reappeared waving a barbecue skewer. "If you want to see so badly."

"Sylvie, you don't have to."

"You might as well look. I think you better." She poked the skewer into the hole and gave the knob a quarter turn. Just before she swung the door in, she yanked the cloud with the bolt of lightning off the door, leaving behind three dime-sized wads of yellowed stick-up gum. Inside the dim room was a welter of slouching, knee-high piles of yard goods and clothing. In one corner, stacks of shoeboxes. A few long robes or dresses hung in the closet, but all else was in crazy piles on the floor or sliding heaps on the two club chairs under the window. Sylvie made her way along a meandering path through the mess and raised the roller blind. Mavis blinked against the new light.

Some of the clothing and fabric lay loose, some was in plastic bags, pink or white or gold, some in paper shopping bags with embossed logos.

"Sylvie, um, well. Wow." Mavis reached up and used a fingernail to pry a wad of stick-up gum from the door. "Is this all stuff you stole?"

"Most of it I paid for, but yeah, some of it I just took."

"*Syl*vie." Mavis kneaded the gum, small in her hand.

"I know. Two winters ago I brought home the same coat three different times. I forgot I already had it. Twice from Sears and once from the thrift store. Same brand, different colour, same big buttons. You'd think I'd remember the buttons."

Her sister's hunger. Go back to those weeks in June the year Sylvie was in grade eleven and Mavis about to graduate. Mom in bed again after a brief few joyous days of mobility and Dad, when he wasn't at work or watching a game or cooking soup to last a week, seated at the table counting out Aspirin rations to take the edge off their mother's arthritis. And Sylvie, hankering after something, anything new, pillaging their mother's closet while she slept, looking for dresses she didn't wear anymore, hoping to shorten or alter or cut them apart to make patterns. How glad Mavis was that she'd never given up the refuge of her paper route – her legitimate hour away from the house, something to do besides sweep the floor or clean the tub or put on the Minute Rice and pork chops. Home one day from walking her route in the rain, Mavis let her canvas carrier bag, heavy and wet, drop to the kitchen floor. She heard a sound that by now was familiar: Dad, in the hallway, shaking the Aspirin bottle slowly back and forth like a sad damn maraca.

They didn't know it then, but those were final days. Within two weeks their mother would be gone and the three of them left to puzzle through the shape of her last hours.

Sylvie stood at the table cutting out a final pattern piece, dressmaker's pins sticking out between her lips like spokes of a rimless wheel. She finished cutting, leaned forward and opened her mouth to let the pins fall on a scrap of fabric. "I'm taking this over to Auntie's to use the machine. But here, I made you something." She lifted a minidress draped across a chair and held it up to show how the gap at the front of the skirt showed off the shorts underneath. "Hotpants. I think they'll fit you."

They weren't her style — too short, too bright a blue — but Mavis wore them once or twice. The hem-stitch showed through where it shouldn't, and a close look showed lines of tiny holes around the sleeves where her sister had ripped out stitches and resewn. The practice version.

A few days later Sylvie came home with her own set. Some people could carry off that sort of look, and Sylvie with her coltish legs and brand-new breasts was one of them. Some people seemed to *need* to carry it off, and that was her as well.

Now this cache of fabric, and you could bet it would never see a pattern. A little scrap of a question that blew through Mavis's mind at intervals through the years whisked past, but she didn't reach for it. This was not the time.

"*Syl*vie." Mavis took a few steps in. Heaps everywhere, a hundred colours. "So. Most of it isn't stolen."

"Stealing isn't what it used to be. Pesky inventory tags."

"If it isn't stolen, why is it stashed away like this?"

"I couldn't let Jack see how much."

"But if you paid for it. Mostly." Mavis pulled the gum wide, then folded it small again. "God, it's too bad we're not the same size. I wonder if Kayla would be interested in any of it."

"I brace myself and I show you all this shit." Sylvie pushed a slither of pale blue fabric onto the floor to clear an arm of the nearest chair and sat down. "And that's where you go with it?"

But jokes had always worked between them. Try again. Mavis held up a tunic sweater on a hanger so flimsy the plastic bowed under the weight of the knit. "On second thought, this might not be Kayla's style." A couple of sequins drifted to the floor. There was no tag, but she pretended: "Winners. $5.99. Compare at $6.99."

"Yeah, most of it's cheap."

"I'll say." But Mavis was still thinking of Kayla; of Kayla and clothing; of Kayla and leather pants and bribery.

Sylvie's voice fell to a quivering lower register with pauses for control between her words, but the cutting tone came through. "It's not as if I have the kind of money a farmer from Ripley has."

Mavis raised a hand, slid her fingers through her hair and began with small motions to rub her scalp. She turned toward the hallway. "What have you got for rye?"

Sylvie brushed past, wiping her eyes as she went, and headed for the living room. Mavis aimed for the kitchen. A farmer from Ripley. Sylvie had never held back her unhumble opinion that there wasn't enough of the big world in their hometown. How did she think that made Mavis feel, and Mavis's kids? You make your own world, and you make it big or you make it small, and don't you dare think for a minute that a farmer from Ripley has it easier than anyone else.

Bottles clanked in the living room. "How about vodka?"

"No rye?"

"Might have, at the back. Jack took the CC."

In the kitchen they slid the coffee mugs aside and set their glasses on stylish coasters pinched from God knows where that looked like slices from unusually fat lemons. Mavis watched her sister pour Coke over Walker's Special Old. "Is Jack coming to court tomorrow?"

"I highly doubt it."

"Sylvie, don't you care that he's moved out?"

"I don't know."

Another thing Jack said on the phone last night: "Not to be insensitive, Mavis, but you lost a baby too, way back, and you're more or less normal. You weren't so far along as she was — as we were — but still. And me, in case anyone cares. I lost that baby, too, at five months and a half. Would it have made a difference if we'd had another, do you think?"

"Jack, she's always had her battles." Mavis was thinking about when they were kids and Sylvie learned how to make peanut butter fudge. The night she went to the kitchen once everyone was asleep and boiled up a batch and washed the pots and bowls and put them away so Dad wouldn't know, and then she sat on her bed in the dark with the pan in her lap eating square after square alone and Mavis lay across the room in the other bed looking at the wall and wondering how anyone could want that much of anything all at once.

"**THEFT UNDER FIVE THOUSAND,**" said Mavis. "I called a lawyer I know in Yorkton. It turns out they'll give you a fine to work off. They'll have you help out at Habitat for Humanity's Re-store or some such."

"I called a lawyer too."

"Of course you did."

"You'll meet her tomorrow. The maximum's six months, or a fine up to two thousand."

"I think it's up to five thousand."

"Christ, you're a help."

"Look, it'll be time at Habitat, no need to worry."

"You saw my room."

"Granted, there's that to worry about. But all you have to do is just stop."

"I did think I could. I thought maybe."

"But?"

"Then there was yesterday's two metres of gabardine. Silver-blue."

"Did you pay for it?"

"What do you think? Of course I did. You wouldn't have a smoke on you?"

"I don't smoke anymore. Please don't say you've started up yet again. I worry."

"I haven't, not really. And don't worry about me, ma'am, I'm not your problem or whatever."

Mavis reached a toe toward the blue purse on the floor, and Sylvie's foot rose to interrupt — not a kick, but a definite push.

"Can I — sorry — can I," said Mavis, " — can I just use your phone a sec? Check in with Pete about a thing for Kayla's school?"

Sylvie gestured at the wall phone by the fridge.

"The other one?"

Sylvie waved in the direction of the hallway and Mavis headed to the bedroom. Over her shoulder she said, "Why don't you just bloody *sew* some of it?"

"What?"

"Sew some of it. Anything. Jesus! Steer the obsession in a different direction. You know?" She closed the bedroom door and the scrappy little scrap of a question that had whisked by earlier floated down from the ceiling. What was their mother's errand that day? When they found her at the foot of the stairs, one cane beneath her and one angled to the left, it seemed as if that second cane pointed like an arrow toward a shelf that held, among an accumulation of souvenirs from healthier times, a shoebox stuffed with old dressmaking patterns. Mavis couldn't honestly say if she'd built her very precise memory of that fallen cane after the fact, in need of a pointing finger. A cane has to land at some angle or other, and its angle will be nothing more than an accident of physics.

Still, Mom was on her way to the basement to fetch *something* that day.

Go away, question, you're no help to anyone. Whatever your answer, no one's to blame. Mavis lifted the pink receiver from the phone on Sylvie's bedside table and punched in her home number.

"How's the patient?" said Pete.

"Worse than I thought. How's yours?"

"Better than I thought: she came out of the bedroom just before noon and ate a quarter bowl of Honey Nut Cheerios."

"That's great."

"No milk though. And nothing to say."

"Still," said Mavis.

"Yeah."

"Listen, I bought something for her. This gorgeous pair of leather pants. My thought was, we might use them as a, as a little, say, incentive, say. I know, I know, but nothing else was working."

"I don't know."

"Now she's out of her room, though, I guess we don't need bribery. If she's turned a corner."

"Reward, then?"

Mavis set the receiver on the bedside table and lay back on the quilt and took in the small dimensions of the room, the plain lines of the square glass light fixture. In Kayla's room a girly chandelier hung above the bed, and the dimensions were more generous, the windows taller, but still it amounted to a small place to close yourself into day after day. A cell. Was that a bad thing? Mavis thought she might like a small room of her own to close herself into. Just herself, alone, away from everyone and their weirdnesses. She spread-eagled her body on the bed, trying to claim all four corners. Reaching. Reaching.

Pete's telephone voice threaded through the air: "Mavis?"

A few days before the accident their father had come home from work one evening and noticed that all the flat surfaces in the living room and dining room had been dusted, and neither girl had done it. On a different day Mavis had come home from school to discover that her laundry, which she'd pulled from the line at noon and dumped on the couch, was folded and stacked in tidy piles. She'd shown this to Sylvie and they'd looked at each other a moment without a word, not to break the spell. Acts of care and, in the circumstances, considerable and painful effort, but neither one especially risky, not like attempting narrow basement stairs.

"Mavis?"

"Hell if I know." She brought her hands to her scalp and began to massage. She pressed hard with all her fingers, as if she could make her head smaller, along with everything inside it.

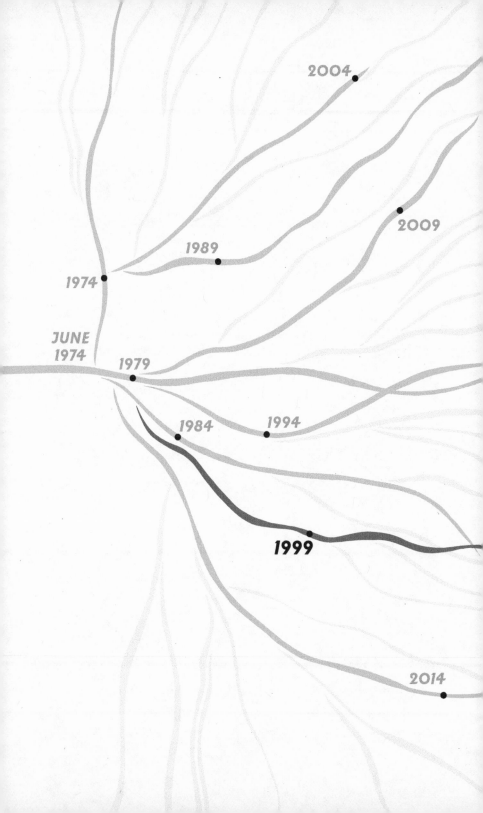

What Erik Saw

STANDING IN THE SHOWER with his eyes closed, a few days after his second surgery in as many weeks, Erik saw two bright kidney beans of light facing each other, a dark line between them. A bad sign, said his ophthalmologist. Erik and Syl made the six-hour drive to Edmonton for a second opinion, which echoed the first.

What Erik saw as he lay on the operating table for the third time, his head clamped motionless and his left eye still as stone because they'd stuck him with a needle to freeze it, was the business end of a medical instrument probing inside his eye. A small round tip of something pale and brown moving about.

"Ah," said the surgeon when Erik told her about it afterward. "Hardly anyone sees it. One percent, at the outside."

"I'll consider myself lucky then."

"I'm glad you see it that way."

"Perceptive, too," said Erik. "So to speak."

The surgeon looked him directly in the eye, the one that wasn't covered with a bandage, and set a hand on his shoulder, a light pressure, steadying. "That will depend entirely on how things heal up."

Let this be over now, please. Three weeks ago, a Tuesday morning and he was on his way to the reno in Lawson Heights, the truck box weighed down by a thousand-dollar toilet he'd just discovered was cracked, his mind working on who he could hold responsible for the damage. Sun flashed bright on the river and spikey heads of purple thistle in the ditches stood tall above the grass, the punk of posies. Forget about the crappy toilet, this was the kind of drop-dead gorgeous day this place will hand you one after another in the summertime, making the blizzards in December and the week of minus forty in February worth it. Thank you, Saskatoon. The truck phone rang beside him and he reached for the receiver. Cynthia, who was doing electrical on the Lawson Heights job, and who happened to be Syl's cousin, was calling to ask where he was. She was cooling her heels at the site without access to the house and she needed to pee and maybe this time she'd put her waiting-around time on her invoice.

"You should've gone to the other job first."

"Well I didn't."

"Julia should be there. She'll let you in."

"Julia's not."

"She will be. Right away if not sooner."

"Word is, she won't be showing up at all today."

"She what? I'll be there in fifteen."

"Make it ten, or I'll have to squat right here in the driveway."

"Twenty."

Three times he slipped past other cars on streets where it's all right so long as you don't get caught, and ten minutes later he was within a block of the job. He rounded the final corner and was suddenly driving through a storm of black flecks. He stopped in the driveway and blinked and blinked again. You get one set of eyes. Blink. One set. Cynthia was knocking on the side window and Erik was reaching for the phone again. He lowered the window and handed her the receiver and the mini-Yellow Pages with the tiny print that he kept under the seat.

"Look up an eye doctor, any eye doctor." He could see the steering wheel, the dash, the gearshift, the control for the wipers, the stick for the signal lights, but between himself and all those was a storm of black.

"What the hell, Erik?" Cynthia was flipping through the book; he was in good hands, but still: one set of eyes.

"I'm inside a snow globe and all the flakes are black." A pair. Two in total. He closed his left eye and all was clear again. He saw the steering wheel, the dash, the sticks, the gearshift plain as day. This calmed him. He closed his right and opened his left and the black was back. He cupped a palm over the bad eye.

She shoved the receiver back through the window. "Found one. Second Avenue. She says come right away."

"Glorious fucking day. You drive."

"I need a toilet."

"Just hold it!"

"Okay, okay."

173

He edged his ass to the right, lifted his legs one at a time past the bulk of the phone, slid carefully to the passenger side, took the mini–Yellow Pages from Cynthia and clutched it to his chest.

"Erik?" Cynthia shifted, shoulder-checked and backed out of the driveway. "I told Syl."

"What are you talking about?"

"I called the house this morning looking for you and she didn't know where you were either, and then I told her how last Friday I saw you and Julia coming out of your office, her hair messed into a haystack at the back and why did you have the venetians closed, I wondered. So I just told her. This morning on the phone. She said she was going to call Julia right pronto and have a conversation."

"Glorious fucking, fucking day."

BUT SYL HAD BEEN with him at the hospital through operations one, two and three. A few days of rage and shock, and then she'd taken Erik's hand as he lay in bed between surgeries one and two and told him they had too many years together to let it ruin them. "This sort of thing happens all the time. People get past it." The drive to Edmonton and back had been a tonic, all those miles of music, all those hours of talk about anything but the affair. A truce, like living inside brackets.

When he told her that during the final operation he'd watched the instrument moving "inside my very eye," she said, "Stop. Just stop."

His friends were squeamish too. But where was their appreciation for mechanics? Where was their fascination for how things worked? The job of the tiny instrument, he told them, was to suck the vitreous jelly out from his eye because it was drying up and tugging at the retina.

"Must you use the word 'suck'?" said Calum, the designer he was working with now.

After the surgeon had drawn out the jelly and injected the gas bubble in its place and sent him home he was determined to follow orders, heal properly, resist the temptation to look up.

"Keeping my head down," he told Syl. "Ha."

"Good idea. Keep the other thing down too."

"You said you didn't want to talk about that."

"I don't."

While he waited, neck bent, at the table that first evening, his view was of the placemat. He was allowed to raise his head for five minutes or so at a time, and only once in a while. He would save those minutes for swallowing. He tried to admire the placemat while he waited for Syl to slide a dinner plate onto it. It filled almost his entire field of vision, yellow flowers bright against lime green. Syl had bought it a couple of years ago during her everything-sixties phase, around about the time she sewed a mini dress in paisley print and walked around the house singing about buying the world a Coke and keeping it company. "No," he'd said to her one day, "you'd like the world to buy *you* a Coke."

"That would work too."

I would like to buy her a Coke, he thought now. Truly. She was soldiering on, sticking around, slipping only rarely into punishing sarcasm. Yes, a Coke with a wedge of lime, the way the waiter brought it that time in Orlando. Such a small thing, but she said she'd never seen that sort of flourish with a plain old glass of pop, and she loved it, didn't he? Yes, he did. People do get past this sort of trouble, don't they? He stared at the yellow flowers. Often, yes, they do. Here was dinner now: ham steak, kernel corn and fried potatoes. And beyond the plate of comfort food and the placemat and the table's edge, a glimpse of Syl's legs, clad in jeans, which was about the most he'd seen of her all day, given his angle of vision. There would come a day when he'd see those legs unwrapped again, the curve of her calf, her slim ankles, her soft inner thighs.

A FEW DAYS IN, Syl said, "You've been walking around looking at the floor for half an hour." She came close, stood on tiptoe and kissed the top of his head. "Calum brought by the elevations for the Casa Rio kitchen reno. I can lay them out on the floor for you." Syl would do that — extend an olive branch. Sometimes she'd yank the branch away as soon as she'd offered it. You had to watch the tone of your reply.

"Thank you, babe. That would be great." He sat on the couch, his knees wide, and looked down at the drawings. With the patch covering one eye, his world had been two-dimensional for days now, and he had a jolt of recognition when he saw the elevations, a kitchen wide and high but not deep. The drawings looked competent, if uninspired, proportions well thought out, appropriate to the space. This new designer would work out, but he was no Julia. Julia had a talent for adding something unexpected, yet right, in every room.

"No jarring," the surgeon had said. "I can't tell you how important that is." She'd waggled her finger like a teacher when he asked about snowmobiling. "Not this coming winter. Preferably not ever."

"And sex?" he'd said.

"You'll know."

His movements careful, Erik got down on the carpet on all fours, gathered up the elevations, rolled them and slid them into the tube. To his left was the low bookshelf where Syl's long-forgotten correspondence binders leaned in on each other. Discouragement under a layer of dust, and after that failure she'd tried retail. When Brycie and Adam were in high school Syl would come home Thursdays after her evening shift at The Bay and hide in the basement with the TV on, as if her years inside the four walls of family had made her go rusty with the world outside those walls, those few people. Once, when he went downstairs to visit her — not to talk, she was typically out of sorts for conversation after work — but just to sit side by side a while on the comfy red couch, he'd caught the beginning of a rerun of Hill Street Blues, the part where, before he sends them out into the streets, the sergeant says to the officers, "Let's be careful out there." That's what I should say to her every day, Erik had thought, show her I'm thinking of her in her world. But when he did say it the next morning she replied with a defensive glare, "Let's be careful in here, too."

He lived with a different Syl now: since taking on the book-keeping for the business she'd recovered confidence aplenty, in here, out there, every-which-where. She would form her lips into a little curve that made her less attractive than she really was, and he'd ready himself for whatever she might be about to say or do.

"COVER YOUR GOOD EYE," Dr. Patel had said after the final operation, and Erik, standing beside his hospital bed, cupped a palm over his right eye and looked at her raised hand. He felt a little nauseated, and with his good eye in darkness his balance was off. He slid his feet apart to steady himself and reached for Syl, who guided his hand onto her forearm.

"How many fingers?" Dr. Patel said.

"Three. Three fingers."

"Good. Lie back down and get some rest now. I'm going to ask you to stay the night."

"Effing right I will. Make sure it's in working order, finally."

Dr. Patel leaned in over the bed and reattached the bandage she'd removed a few minutes earlier. With gentle hands she smoothed the tape into place on Erik's forehead and along his cheekbone. "I understand your frustration."

"You might think you do."

"Sometimes things don't go quite the way we hope."

"No shit."

"I'll check back with you later. Try to relax."

The woman didn't see the simplest things. Like the fact that telling a person to relax would do the opposite. Erik would never say to a client, "Try to relax." He would say, "I will make this right." He heard the surgeon's shoes on their way to the door, and he heard them pause when Syl said, "Wait, please, I have a question."

"Certainly."

"He got the right answer, three fingers, but he was looking way to the right and down. Not at your fingers, but over at the baseboard, so?"

178

"This last operation left things a little out of alignment."

"So he'll have a wonky eye from here on in? He'll be looking off to the side just to see what's in front of him?"

"We'll put a prism in his glasses to bring things back in line. Bend his sight, if you will."

"Erik," Syl said after the doctor left the room. He didn't open his good eye; he couldn't manage the sight of anyone or anything. He heard her stifle a giggle. "Erik, you can't even see straight."

"Is that supposed to be funny?"

"You always say there's a way."

"I don't *always* say it."

"Well my way right now is to make a joke."

"I say it when I'm in a better mood."

"Which is almost always."

"Can you please stop talking?"

"Okay, Erik. I'll go down and get myself a coffee. You relax."

AN EYE PATIENT goes early to bed. Following doctor's orders, he slept on his belly with his forehead resting on a bolster, so the gas bubble holding his retina in place would keep on trying to rise out the back of his head. Syl had helped him arrange pillows under his chest and shoulders to save his neck. It was early September still, and there was enough light even at nine-thirty that with his good eye he could make out the fragility of the cornflowers on the sheets. They looked as if they'd blow right off the fabric if he breathed too hard. Wedding sheets from the seventies, a present from Syl's Uncle Davis and Aunt Viv. The better linens, the five-hundred-count Egyptian cotton that Syl said she'd found on sale, were now on the bed in Adam's old room, where a few days ago she'd moved her book and lamp and the small amber bottle of sleeping pills she resorted to on occasion. She wouldn't want to disturb his eyes, she'd said, and it was like she'd chosen that particular phrasing for the sake of irony.

"You'll sleep better," she'd said then, softening.

"I appreciate the care."

"It's the thing to do, right? If there's one thing I learned from my dad."

"True. Legendary, the way he looked after your mom. Let's hope this will be weeks, not years."

The early days of cornflower sheets, no one ever gets those back. It was going to be a long night. And a long haul. Twenty-five years, and suppose we have that many again. As long as he wasn't in the same physical space as Julia, he could almost believe the affair hadn't happened. He was – they were – both forgivable; they'd done the hard thing, they'd left each other behind. The very hard thing. When he told Julia she didn't have to quit, and she said, As if, and, There's plenty of work out there, I'll be fine, he'd made a gesture of protest, but he hadn't argued. He could put her out of mind if she was out of sight – sometimes he went hours without even thinking of her – but he couldn't guarantee his behaviour if he found himself in the same room. Physical presence, it's a power. Twenty-five years ago Syl would have gone through with marrying that other guy, count on it, if Erik hadn't made the trip to Saskatoon as soon as he heard and asked what the hell and put his own physical presence undeniably in the way.

ERIK'S EYE PATCH was frosty pink, a shallow cup of hard plastic. He waited for the day he could take it off. He wondered how much sight he might recover in the bad eye, and how much depth perception. But the brain has its ways, the doctor said, its workarounds and compensations.

"You could be a pirate for Hallowe'en," Syl said one morning. She reached across the breakfast table and with a fingernail she tapped his glasses lens in front of the patch. He felt the same red jolt he'd felt that day in July when the stupid damn neighbour's stupid fucking parakeet had landed on his shoulder and clamped the arm of his glasses in its beak.

He took a moment to recover before saying, "I'll be long done with the patch by the time Hallowe'en comes."

"You'll still have it, though."

"Stowed in a drawer where it belongs. Besides, I'll have my newfangled specs. I don't think a pirate would wear both."

"You're right, honey. We'll come up with something else."

Honey. That small word flowed deep into him. It was the first time she'd used it since her cousin Cynthia had blown his secret open. "Something else would be great, babe." From where he sat he could see their two cereal bowls, their two cups of coffee, their hands. He raised his head, as allowed, to eat his bowl of Just Right. Syl was busy with the crossword. She looked up briefly and smiled in a quick and ordinary way before she looked down again.

Game Face

SYL LED ERIK to the bedroom to show him the elements of his Hallowe'en costume laid out in a tidy lineup, black against the yellow bedspread: turtleneck (men's large), pants, leather gloves, a stocking cap. Thrown across the turtleneck, a coil of rope, spanking white, for contrast.

"Suits me fine, pun intended." He settled a warm hand on her lower back. "But before we put clothes *on* let's take some off."

"You're on." She reached for his zipper.

Fresh from the shower afterward, his cock relaxed, he sorted through the tangle of covers and clothing their lovemaking had sent to the floor. He sat on the edge of the bed, the unnatural angle of his left leg more pronounced than usual as he lifted his foot to pull on a black sock. Bent since birth, that's me, he sometimes said.

"That's anti-sexy," she said, "a man in nothing but socks."

"Even when the man is me?"

"Okay, maybe."

Earlier that afternoon she'd hauled out the box of Christmas decorations and dug through it for a downy white bird to go with her own costume. She played with it now as Erik proceeded upward from his socks, item by item to the stocking cap, and finished by sliding an arm through the coil of rope and settling it on his shoulder. On the bedside table, talk radio was talking about the millennial catastrophe the Y2K bug was sure to bring on in two months' time: *Give us a call and tell us if you're laying in a supply of canned tuna and bottled water to get you through till the world's computers come back up. If they come back up, ha ha.*

Syl reached for the off switch. "Shotguns and baseball bats too. Stock up on those, why not?"

"Don't laugh. I had a guy call me yesterday, wanted to know if I could build a bunker in his backyard by December 31."

"What did you tell him?"

"Told him where he could buy a shovel."

She led him back to the bathroom, removed her black glove from her right hand and her white glove from her left hand, and dabbed cold cream below his eyes. Since the third operation, there'd been a sag in his left lid that made her think of old burlap. With a thumb against his temple she lifted the eyelid taut for a moment, then let it droop again. This was how they were now, altered.

"You're my joy," she said. Saying it could make it so.

"You're mine."

She massaged cold cream into his skin, playing against the resistance of his cheekbones, opened her box of face paints and brushed heavy black marks below his eyes, like in the photo

on the dresser that showed him suited up for high school football decades ago. Syl wasn't sure why a cat burglar would have
such marks, but she liked the way they underscored the look.
Calum and Mitch had billed their party as a masquerade, heavy
on the first syllable, and so Erik ought to show at least a token
gesture toward a mask. A game face.

"You'll hardly see those for my spectacles."

Syl shrugged. "You could have told him just to have a little
faith."

"Who, the guy that wants the bunker?"

"Yeah." Faith was what she herself was leaning on.

Working blind behind her back, she pinned a length of
black boa to her leggings, a flowing tail. She settled an Alice
band with glued-on velvet ears on her head, leaned toward the
mirror and painted feline whiskers fanning across her cheeks.
An inverted yellow triangle of nose at the tip of her own. With
sufficient makeup she could manage kittenish at forty-four,
just. She struggled to fix the white bird to her shoulder, slipping the wire claws through the loose knit of her sweater. They
scratched at her skin. The bird flopped forward and buried its
beak in black angora. Erik managed — "Hold still, this'll *work,
baby*" — to pass the claws through the sweater in a new place
and cinch them around her bra strap.

They stood side by side and faced the couple in the mirror,
the cat burglar and the cat. "We don't even look like ourselves,"
he said. They hoped to meet new people at Calum and Mitch's
tonight, clean-slate people, but in a city this size the renovation
and design trades amounted to their own small town. Odds
were they'd see familiar faces.

Syl felt the claws against her skin and coaxed the bird forward a smidgen. The old joke about the guy with the spear through his middle: Only when I laugh.

They'd done well together the past couple of months, and you couldn't even say they were doing it for the kids, because the kids were off and gone. Brycie had switched to UVic for the final year of her commerce degree and moved out of the basement in August none the wiser. Adam had begun a masters in set design in Edmonton. Syl and Erik made a great parenting team; they often told each other so; the evidence was there in Adam and Brycie. Through the years of soccer and swim and elementary teacher wars, they'd sometimes referred to the kids as a unit: Trial and Joy. Which was which? the kids wanted to know. Depends on the day, you understand? Most days they understood well enough to laugh about it. Most days Syl and Erik did too. A rough beginning, though, with Adam's tantrums the winter he was closing in on two, and Erik, the nerve of him, packing the car for a weekend in Ripley snowmobiling with his brother. "Try out that new machine."

"You can't leave me alone with a cranky kid all weekend."

Adam banged a yellow dump truck on the fake wood of the coffee table again and again.

"That's twice this month," she said.

"But the snow's going, babe."

"So's my sanity."

"Just one night then."

"*No!* You'll kill yourself out there. Drunk and dark and hazards in the ditches. I know that brother of yours."

"Are you worried about me flipping in a ditch or are you worried about yourself flipping out?"

"Does it matter?"

Erik dropped his duffel bag, snatched the dump truck from his son's fierce grip and hucked it at the door. The child wailed, red in the face.

"I get scared," said Syl.

"I know." Erik pulled on his heavy snow boots and said, "I'm going for cigarettes." He didn't smoke; it was what either of them said when they were desperate for a breather. He'd stayed in town that weekend, for Adam and for her.

They'd been through that and how much more.

Now they were footloose in their forties, playing Californication loud enough that James from the next house over had knocked one day and asked could they turn it down, he had three dozen first-year philosophy essays to mark. Syl felt so young in fact that once of a late afternoon, Erik being off with his buddies on their annual BMW ride through the BC interior and she sitting on the front step toking up, anxious as always that Erik would come back dead one year from that damn bike trip, she'd called out to James, who was on his own front step with a glass of wine. "Do you want a hit, Jimmy?"

"Name's James," he'd said, lifting his glass to show he was fine. From then on, he'd been *Name's James* in her mind. If Name's James hadn't declined — all that first-year marking, you've no idea — if he hadn't declined, who knew? And he *had* suggested she ask again once summer session was over. Syl remained aware of this slim crack in the wall of her rebuilt marriage, and once in a while she tried peeking through it, hoping to catch sight of herself and wondering how she'd feel if she did.

The bird flopped forward again on her shoulder. "I got it," Erik said, and he bent its wire legs to keep it standing. "In this life there are *ways*." It was a phrase he used often, in varied form; a motto, you could say.

"In this life are many options," he'd said all those years ago when the distance course that would have made her a CTC, a Certified Travel Consultant, hadn't worked out. Followed by the course that would have made her a Certified Public Accountant, ditto.

"You can't just give up," he'd said as yet another binder gathered dust. "Any day of the week, with the business, I could up and say it's too much, but where's the fun in that?"

"I didn't *say* it's fun."

"Look, there's always a way. For me, it's lay someone off or find a new supplier, put in longer hours. You figure it out."

"It's not like you think."

"Then what *is* it like?"

"I take out the binder, I stare at the pages, I freeze. In the face of it, I just freeze. If I want to start breathing again, I have to go do something else."

"But you're way smarter than the next person. Be logical."

"You want a world where logic applies to everything."

"Do not fret." He held her close and cradled her head against his chest in the way they had back then. With relief, she'd stacked and stowed the binders of unfinished worksheets and put in a couple of years in front-line retail. The biggest trial had been the fondling of so many hats and scarves and gloves for seven-odd hours, only to fight the temptation to slip a soft little something into her purse at the end of shift. When the impulse to do that surged to the level where it frightened her, she told Erik she was murdered with standing on the store's ceramic floors all day.

"It's okay, sweetie," he said. "We've got options we haven't even sniffed at yet." He sat with her at the computer in the den and trained her to do the books for the reno business. "It's simple. The debits go by the window. Can you at least smile? You won't even have to change out of your pyjamas." In high school she'd excelled at math, and accounting wasn't even math, only arithmetic with a particular set of rules. The salary she and Erik settled on was half as much again as they would have paid a pro. Her part-time hours showed up as full-time on the record, and *voilà*: income splitting with paper trail enough to satisfy what Erik called the bureau cats.

Last week a woman on the radio had recited a stat that was supposed to represent the number of women in Canada who appeared to be well off, but who might be described more accurately as "one man away from poverty." Hearing this, Syl had felt a tiny sharp needle in her temple. How did they come up with such a number, anyway? Don't think about that right now; go for a walk and maybe Name's James will be out front on his step with his glass of afternoon red.

No such luck.

ERIK DROVE, and Syl sat holding her jacket away from her shoulder so she wouldn't crush the white bird as the truck bumped along the potholed streets. At Calum and Mitch's they rang the bell and waited on the verandah, Erik cradling his two-litre bottle of ginger ale. Syl was giddy, thinking in a save-it-for-later way of the black silk undies only she and Erik knew she wore underneath her costume. A Rapunzel they weren't acquainted with opened the door and disappeared back into the party, her braid wrapped twice around her neck and trailing down her back. Syl was startled by an urge to yank hard at the braid. She had to still the muscles in her arm that wanted to reach for it. In the living room they saw a brick in conversation with a bricklayer, and an undertaker – or was he a necrophiliac? – kissing the hand of a corpse. The dead woman wore an artful mask of papier-mâché flesh falling away from papier-mâché bone. Syl hadn't been to a costume party in years, hadn't realized these tandem get-ups were so common. She turned to Erik. "There's nothing so original about us."

On a bookshelf they found a stack of plastic glasses and eased two off the top for their ginger ale. So far they recognized no one aside from their hosts, who were Doctor Frankenstein and his creation. Mitch had an extra ear attached to his neck, and a spare eye dangled against his cheek, attached with theatrical putty. He reached to pet Syl's hair. "Pussy, pussy."

Calum was plain and scrubbed and wearing a white lab coat, spectacles in the pocket. He proffered a Melmac tray with brie-filled dates, squishy bundles that made Syl think of the organs of small animals. She turned her face away. "No, thank you."

Mitch dipped a finger into his wine glass and held it above his extra eyeball, where it dripped bloody looking drops.

"This little touch," he said, "was inspired by true events in the life of you, my man Erik. Why would you go and get a detached retina?"

"It isn't as if I ordered it."

"I can think of only one way they could have gotten at your eyeball, and that's to pop it right out."

"Can you please not?" said Syl. "Why do people have to talk about the gory details of every little thing?"

"Wow. Okay. Relax, wee pussy."

THE DINING ROOM TABLE was draped in deep purple and strewn with iridescent stars. Dry ice smoldered around the punch bowl so it looked to be levitating. Syl and Erik stood in the mist. Close by was a man with a Bill Clinton mask, and next to him Rapunzel. Clinton reached for her long braid, uncoiled it from her neck, wrapped it around his own and mimed a hanging. Rapunzel feigned lack of interest and moved the stars about on the tablecloth.

"Make a constellation," Syl said to either or both of them.

Rapunzel smiled, at the table rather than at Syl. "Okay. Orion." She gave the hunter a heroic build, small at the waist, the stars for the shoulders wide apart. Lining up two stars below the belt, she said, "Does Orion's dagger point left or right?"

Clinton laughed. "You think that's a dagger, do you?" The two of them moved off, linked by the braid and by Clinton's hand on Rapunzel's bustle.

ERIK'S EYE CRISIS had gone through three stages. The first was, Don't worry, this happens all the time; a simple procedure, time to heal, and you'll be good as new. Tick-tack with a laser, and the retina was back in place. In a matter of days it tore again, clear across the top, and slumped inside his eye. At City Hospital the surgeon sewed a silicone cinch around his eyeball to give the retina a little slack. If it didn't have to stretch so far it might stay put. Syl fetched and carried for several days while Erik rested, but the coddled eye refused to heal. Syl could hardly bear to hear the particulars of the third surgery and the gas bubble the surgeon injected into his eye. Yet more fetching and carrying while Erik walked with a forward lean, sat with a forward lean, cogitated on who knew what while he studied his knees, so the upward pressure of the bubble would hold steady while the tissues knit themselves back together.

Syl angled a mirror against the foot of the couch to reflect the TV screen in a way that allowed him to watch. He sat on a straight-back chair with his back to the television, neck bent, and looked down into the mirror. He watched the news; he watched Law & Order; he said, "Rent me a movie, sweetie, please." She brought home *Blue*, because he liked Juliette Binoche so much and he'd only ever seen *The English Patient*. She slid the videotape in, and when it began to play Erik said, "I'm supposed to read subtitles, babe? In the mirror?"

"Oops." She handed him the remote. He flipped through the channels, bouncing the signal off the mirror, settling on *Mad about You*. Apparently if you couldn't have Juliette Binoche, Helen Hunt would do. She knelt to eject the videotape and caught herself in the mirror. In the past few weeks her looks had become a worry out of all proportion. But her hair was better with the new cut; the length suited her. And the jeans fit well enough. Fine, she would never be a stunner. Fine. "Have a nice evening," she said, "you and your mirror." She pretended that last was a joke. It was outrageous the way he'd one-upped her with this eye trouble.

GOOD OLD, BAD OLD Miles from On the Level Flooring walked into the dining room wearing a wizard's gown and cap, drugstore vinyl. He was carrying a nose made of soft, flesh-coloured plastic, warts and all, which he set down to ladle himself a drink.

"Good All Saints' Eve," he said.

"Hello Miles," said Syl, because one of the ideas about a party was to avoid being rude for the space of a full evening.

"Miles from Nowhere," Erik said.

"You two don't even look like yourselves."

Syl wished for a proper mask. "You recognized us easily enough."

Mist moved in shreds across the stars on the purple tablecloth. Miles looked down at the stars. "Is that supposed to be Orion?"

"Ten points for you," Syl said. Erik gathered a fold of tablecloth in his fingers and twisted it.

Miles said, "It looks like Orion's, um, dagger is . . . disoriented." He picked up his plastic nose and used it to nudge the stars below the belt so they angled toward the hunter's right thigh rather than his left. "It's important, which direction a guy's dagger leans."

193

Syl looked at the empty vodka bottle beside the punch-bowl. Erik hadn't had a drink in over three months now, and his sponsor just last week had rewarded him with a "clean and serene" keychain, and good for him but his weaknesses were not hers and she'd had it with ginger ale. She ladled vodka punch to top up what was left in her glass.

"Why not just say what you mean?" Syl looked Miles in the eye.

He pumped the nose in his hand so it made air farts. He raised the ladle and looked at Erik. "Punch?"

Erik raised his half-full glass to show what he was drinking. His face was expressive in its inexpressiveness.

"Right. Slipped my mind." Miles turned and left the room, saying over his shoulder, "Don't forget to party like it's 1999."

Syl picked up the plastic nose he'd left behind and plunked it some distance from Orion. "It ruins the look."

"The look of what?" The corpse they'd seen earlier in the living room was approaching the table, her mask tilted back above her forehead, visor-like, exposing her face. Julia. Trust a professional designer to craft such an elaborate disguise from papier-mâché. The man in the midnight suit, who was under-taker or necrophiliac or both, followed her, his top hat dark above the painted pallor of his face, his red lips wearing the smile a person puts on when they know they're in a situation but they don't know what it is. His eyes were on Julia as she doled out small nods, first to Syl, then to Erik.

Julia raised a hand and tapped the mask above her fore-head. "My plan was to remain incognito, but I lost my straw, and I can't drink through this thing." The elastic strap of the mask had pulled her silver wig askew, and a curl of her own hair, coppery and shining, escaped at one side. Erik's hand rose just slightly in the direction of that curl. The hand stopped in mid-air and fell back to his side, but the ghost of the unfinished gesture hovered.

For this I wore my new silk underwear.

Julia looked toward Syl. "I thought you two would be at Rhonda's.

"Ditto." Syl drained her punch, confiscated Erik's unfinished pop, and set both glasses on the table close to the man with the top hat. They searched their jackets out from the heap in the entranceway. Syl zipped hers shut without a thought to the bird or the dig of its claws. She would drive. As they waited for the truck to warm up she brushed with her white glove across the fog inside the windshield. Erik sat hunched in the passenger seat, his hands tucked under his thighs.

"Give me details," she said. "Tell me everything. Did you screw her in the master bedroom at the reno in Lawson Heights, or was it always the office at the back of the showroom, like Cynthia said? Did you do it in the chair, or on the throw rug? Up against the desk?" He'd just seen Julia, which meant he'd just been back in that chair, or on that rug, or bracing his feet on that office floor.

"We don't need to talk about this."

"What did you use to wipe up afterward? Your shirttail? Kleenex? The Calvin Klein boxers I put in your Christmas stocking?"

"You said you didn't want to know these things. And they don't matter."

"Did you watch her fall asleep?"

He was still sitting on his hands, which she wanted to yank from under him, but then what?

"Tell me every goddamn thing."

"Oh, Syl." He turned toward her. "Everything?" The black marks she'd painted below his eyes, shadowed by his glasses, were darker than anything else in the car. "Here's something I can tell you, for instance: you need attention every second, baby, and nobody, nowhere, has that much attention circling around looking for a place to land."

A hole opened low in Syl's gut, and her idea of who they were fell through it.

"What else? You come out to a job site and you rant about Joseph's sick days until *I'm* sick of hearing it, and poor old Joseph — hell, Syl!"

"But he —"

"And you've been toking on the sly, and you know that messes me up when I'm working so hard not to. What else? Last month you expensed a pair of boots to the company and those were no workboots, they were from Aldo, and yes I look at the receipts, of *course* I look at the receipts!"

"Those were for —"

"If you want new boots, baby, just take real money and buy new boots. Buy whatever you need, whenever you need it."

Syl pulled her fingers and thumbs back inside her gloves and made two fists and pushed them together in her lap. Her knuckles knocked against each other, and the empty fingers of her one black glove and her one white glove collapsed in a stalemate.

"Look," he said quietly, "this isn't necessary. Everything does *not* need to be said. Some things never need to be said. We're together, just like always."

"Just like always."

"*Almost* always," he said with a shrug and a smile. He laid a hand, a gentle pressure, over the place where her two fists came together. "I thought we were past this."

"What if I have more to say?"

"All right, Syl, you have more to say." He squeezed harder now across her fists. "Say it." He leaned in, his warm breath blasting her face, the sweet of the ginger ale gone sour. "Say it!"

"No!" she shouted. She would not put words to the un-finished gesture, his hand rising toward that lock of Julia's hair as if to take it between thumb and finger and give it a tender twist. It was years since he'd raised his hand in such an unthought way to her own stray locks. "No." If she were to give words to how he'd reached before he hesitated, there would be no setting that moment aside.

"Come on, Syl. How do I know what *you're* up to when I'm away? I don't. But I know we're *us*."

"Jesus, Erik."

Revelers ran by, mummies and vampires on the way from one party to the next. Syl half-expected them, *wanted* them, to rock the car and press their gruesome faces against the windshield, bounce on the hood, leer in at the windows, give her an excuse to burn away from the curb and send them screaming in their sweaty masks and their ripped up sheets. But they scurried on past. Hell anyway! She shifted

197

into gear and stomped the accelerator, and the tires spun and caught. She managed a crazy right turn at the end of the block, almost in control, but then the wheels jumped the curb and the headlights shone on the rough grey bark of an elm and the right front grill crunched hard against it. Erik's head whacked against the side window and Syl's slapped back onto the headrest.

"What the Jesus hell, Syl!"

The moment the truck slammed into the tree was the moment she realized she'd had every intention of crashing into something. Either then, or it was hours ago, as she'd rummaged through the Christmas box looking for the bird, letting tin snowflakes and coloured lights and plexiglass icicles clatter on the hardwood.

"My *truck*." He raised a hand and she shrank from it, but he wasn't preparing to strike, he was only groping into emptiness.

What did he mean with his *Jesus hell?* Why should he be surprised? It had to end in a wreck, and this was the sort of wreck that was available just now.

"My *truck*."

She got out and leaned against the tree. One side of her back blazed with pain, shoulder to hip.

He came around to her. "Get back in. Come on."

"No. I'll spend the night here."

"Where? With Calum and Mitch?"

"Everyone's got a couch."

"Okay, sleep on someone's couch. Better yet, don't sleep. Better yet, lie there and try to decide who it is makes you the madder: me, or yourself."

Standing clear, she waited as he backed and turned, as the wheels thumped off the boulevard and he drove away, one headlight out, bumper thunking. She sat down on the grass beside the scattered fragments of the broken headlamp, sweating cold into her bra, damp silk chilly against her breasts. She let out a giggle of loss and looked to the sky. She would have liked to catch sight of a constellation, any constellation, but there were clouds and there were streetlights, and her gaze found only a couple of pallid pinpricks. Ah well, she'd never really had a handle on the stars. Inherited myths. "Make your own," she said out loud. "Make your own myth." She said the next bit out loud too: "I wonder how that's done." She was wearing a little smile she sometimes put on to fool herself into confidence. Erik's truck was a couple of blocks away now, two small taillights, dwindling.

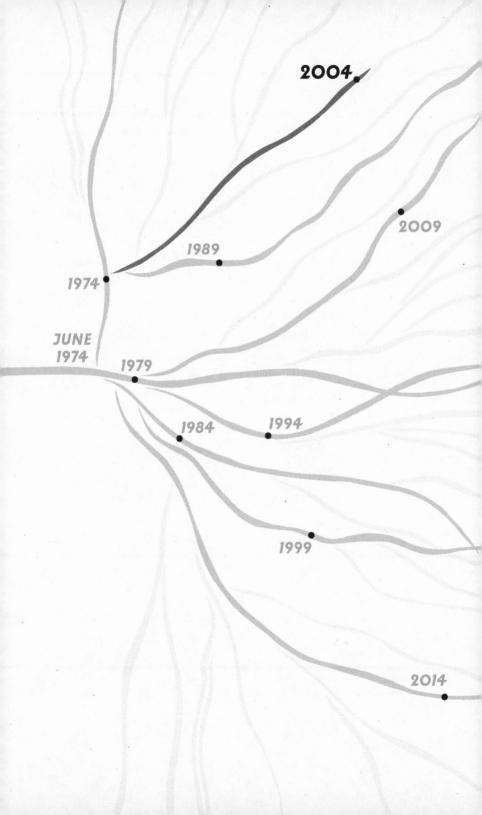

Nekyia

OUTSIDE THE GATES OF HELL Sylvie bought a swingy green
beach dress with swirls of tiny silver beads, a fling of bling to
match her mood. Two full days of skipping out in northern
Greece. Yesterday she'd been one of three academics on a panel
of mentors, sharing mid-career wisdom with scholars so fresh
you could make a salad of them and watch to see who'd wilt
when the vinegar rained down. Day after tomorrow she would
lecture on the use of the mask in classical theatre. But these
two days between were all about holiday, and Will was here.
"Where there's a Will . . ." he'd said yesterday when she asked
if they might drive off in his little red rental.

As legend had it, the journeys of both Odysseus and Pindar
had brought them here to the Nekromanteion to consult the
Oracle of the Dead. Glory days. Of late, the site was apparently
little visited; Sylvie and Will had seen only one other seeker
as they wandered between the massive cyclopean walls wondering at the puzzle of polygon masonry. In the cavern below
ground, where twice Will knocked his head on the low arches,

Sylvie whispered, "Anyone home?" and Will whispered, "Not on your life."

They climbed back up the steep iron stairs into sunlight and went down the slope to the parking lot below the ruins. At the edge of the lot a lone outpost of enterprise shimmered in the heat — a thatch-roofed stall where beach dresses hung limp on plastic hangers; T-shirts, too, in four colours with flames rising from block letters: *I HAVE BEEN TO THE GATES OF HELL.*

"A shame, such pandering."

"Don't blame the vendor," Will said. Sunlight silvered his curls, what was left of them. "He has to buy groceries too." He lifted his sunglasses for a moment, the watered blue of his eyes familiar from all those years ago, and lovely to see. The rest of his face was, well, years older, and somehow less than itself. "Blame the people who buy that shit." He gestured toward the rack where Sylvie had found her dress. His sunglasses settled back into place.

She stuck her tongue out at him, feeling like a teenager — uncertainty, ache, squirming joy. She folded the bead-spangled dress, wrapped it around the black ceramic sheep, raku-fired and fragile, the size of her closed fist, that she'd carried across two continents and an ocean, and stowed the bundle in her shoulder bag. She'd meant to sit on the hillside near the ruins, alone and quiet, and break the sheep open. Leave the shining fragments in the grass, an offering to the oracle in exchange for guidance. That had been her plan when she packed her shoulder bag in Vancouver, but this morning when she'd woken at Villa Stavros, with Will in the next room, the urgency had ebbed. She knew, now, the answer to her question, had known since yesterday when he'd appeared, looking up at her from third row centre in the lecture hall, waiting for her to recognize him. The past made physical.

———

Athena Rocks: Women Mentoring Women.
Panel at the 63rd gathering of the International Association for Studies in Classics. University of Ioannina, 2004.

Graduate-student moderator: This panel, Dr. Fletcher, is meant to give students like me the chance to gain practical wisdom from women like yourself, who've achieved a measure of, um, staying power. I'll begin with a question most of us can relate to: How do you keep at it, when, on occasion, things get tough?

Sylvie: Yoga every morning, without fail.

[Polite laughter]

Sylvie: It's good that you laugh. A sense of humour is essential. [*There are at least five men in the audience. What are they doing at a panel for women mentoring women? Looking to get laid?*] But about the yoga: I'm serious. Patience. Practice.

Student: Good point, Dr. Fletcher. But can you tell us what made you decide on an academic career?

Sylvie: I had a job, just out of high school, in the basement of a university library. [*That face — third row — no, it can't be.*] It was not all that interesting, this job. A way to get by, was all.

Student [clearing her throat]: So you worked to put yourself through your undergrad —

Sylvie: Wait, now. I was at that job five years before I even *enrolled*. I had several, um, delays. [*Time off without pay. Self-loathing.*] At lunchtime I would pick up one of the journals from the stack on my desk and read while I ate my sandwich. The Humanities, mostly. Within that, Classics. Day after day for years. The more I read, the more I began to believe, finally, that I could do this too, study these things and have my own ideas about them.

Student [hesitating]: Uh-huh, and —

Sylvie: Which had used to seem impossible. [Pauses.] I advise you to take a much more direct approach. My, uh, detours didn't really — [*A certain person I disliked and even feared but went ahead and fucked anyway*] — what I want to say is, get down to it: grad studies, post docs, those first positions. Keep at it. Avoid the sort of delay I let myself fall into. [*Aunt Merry, her face gone so pale that the small vein at her cheekbone stood out, a lace of red, saying, What did you expect, dearie?*]

———

SYLVIE BOUGHT A passion fruit pop from the vendor's ice-lined camp cooler. She held the sweating bottle against her cheek and let a chill drop of condensation slide into the crease under her chin. He dropped her change into her open hand and she said, *Efharisto*. She was somewhat familiar with the language, though not, as she'd explained to her host at the university yesterday, "on speaking terms"; a reader, not a speaker. All those years of picking her way through passages of Homer and the tragedies in Ancient Greek, earning fleeting epiphanies as the ambiguities of language swelled before her and she saw how the texts had been — were still being — reinterpreted, misinterpreted, overinterpreted; and this must be true of all of life as well, and wasn't that a worry and a wonder and a joy? What, for instance, did πάθος, *pathos*, really mean? Press the word like a plum and meanings burst the sides.

As Will made his own transaction with the vendor in rudimentary English, Sylvie lifted the strap of her bag from her left shoulder, swung it around and settled it on her right. She was certain, and she wasn't. It would wait for another day, but she would still have her visit with the oracle, if only to lock in a decision already made. Any scholar worth her parchment will triangulate.

They walked in the heat across the stony lot. "Your little red Hyundai looks like a hard candy on wheels." Not an easy car to take seriously, but a good fit for the narrow roads. Sylvie looked again toward the ruins. She didn't give a blue fart that scholars had come round to saying this wasn't the site of the legends after all — more likely a large farm holding with walls to keep the barbarians out. Where was the fun in that? Where was the use? Better to imagine the ancients and their pilgrimages to what they took to be the entrance to Hades' Underworld, home of Demeter's lost girl. She'd hoped against logic to trick herself into seeing a flash of white, a fleeting glimpse of Persephone's pale arm or ankle in the vaulted hall below, a hint of a daughter lost, then found. But no, just condensation on the walls and the smell of mould.

Once past the village, Will turned off the main road. "Let's explore."

"I'll have to come back."

"To Greece?"

"To the gates of Hell." In a drawstring pouch inside her carry-all was a do-it-yourself ritual kit that, along with the raku sheep, would bide its time: two small stones that once in a while Sylvie heard tap against each other; a plastic bottle with a screw-top lid; and a bubble pack of Gravol — a couple of tablets might be enough to get her half-stoned, now that the strongest drug she did on a regular basis was Alberta rye.

Will slowed and shifted for a sharp left. "You told *me* not to call it the gates of Hell. Cheapens it, didn't you say?"

As the car swung through the turn, Sylvie's head bumped the passenger window. "Yikes, it's like a maze here. Anything could come around the curve."

He shrugged. "I've always had a sixth sense for driving."

"But this is *Greece*."

Will made a raspberry, loud and wet. Spittle shone on his lower lip.

Oleander bloomed tall and pink and powdered along the roadside. Their wheels raised a silver dust to coat the spear-like leaves with yet another layer. Now a sharp right, and Sylvie's stomach swirled.

"Why do you need to come back?" he said.

"The same reason Odysseus came. The living ask for guidance from the dead." She thought he might smirk, but he nodded.

"Oh, look left!" she said. A whitewashed box on spindly legs at the side of the road; a small blue dome of a roof with a cross atop; a tiny arched doorway and a picture of a saint looking out. "Pretty little shrine."

"Oh God, somebody died right here."

"Or someone wants to thank a saint for saving them."

"Sylvie the mentor. Say some other wise things."

She fished in her carry-all, fingered open the drawstring pouch, worked a Gravol free of its bubble-card. "I'm not *wise*, wise guy, I'm knowledgeable."

"Say some knowledge, then. Some of your ancient Greek what-have-you. I could use it."

The tablet lodged at the back of Sylvie's throat, and she swallowed twice. "Yeah, sure."

"Suit yourself, then."

Thirty years ago hardly a week went by that they didn't know each other's movements; now these shy failures of conversation. A burp rose past the lodged Gravol. "Okay, no, listen," she said. "Tragedies. In classical tragedy you never saw death on stage. Blood, death, mutilation – it all happened out of sight."

"Drama without drama."

"No, no. Oedipus stabs out his own eyes – that happens off stage but then here he comes wearing his gory mask, blood running out the eye sockets. It's the *result* you have to deal with. Which is so much more affecting than today's big-screen violence."

"Did I just catch you practising for your presentation?"

"I'm always practising for my presentation."

"Say some character actually *dies* off stage, then. How's the audience supposed to know?"

"Hue and cry. Wailing and gnashing of teeth among the loved ones."

They rounded a shrubbery-obscured curve to see two cars coming at them side by side with not a metre between them. Sylvie landed her right foot hard against the mat. As she tromped her ghost brake, Will tromped the gas. He made it, barely, to a break in the roadside bush and stopped there while the two cars blurred past. Sylvie and Will sat staring ahead, taming their trembles. Oleander was plastered flat against the glass on the passenger side like a painting in pink and green. Sylvie slid the window open and a fragrant branch of leaves and blossoms spilled in.

"It's gorgeous!" said Will. "*You're* gorgeous. Look at you."

"I'm alive. That makes me at least *feel* gorgeous." She bent her head to sniff a blossom.

"You'll get a bug up your nose. You can die that way."

She saw how he wanted her to laugh, so she did.

He laughed too. "I'd have to build a pretty little shrine."

———

Student: Academic work, Dr. Fletcher, calls for a measure of confidence. Have you always been a naturally confident person?

Sylvie [laughs out loud]: Think about that young woman dropping sandwich crumbs onto scholarly journals and trying to imagine being bold enough to write her own words. [*These young women in the lecture hall, they have the world by the tail.*]

Listen: I built my career the same way I built myself, the only way I knew how. [Looks toward the third row.] Little by little by little and mistake by mistake, and each mistake a lesson.

Student: For instance?

Sylvie: For instance, I once offered an honest critique of the department head's presentation at an international conference. He had, after all, asked me to please be frank and he even bought me a goodwill latté after I'd said my piece. That sort of honesty, I learned, will erase your chance at a merit increase even though — [laughs just enough to show this is no laughing matter] — even though you've had two articles accepted for publication within the year, and a revise-and-resubmit for a third. [*For a further instance: doing your roommate's fiancé can leave you royally fucked for nine months at least and somewhat fucked over for a lifetime after that.*] [Clears throat.] Know who your friends are. Know who is not your friend. Chances are you'll find more of the second than the first. All of you, I'm sure, will be more swift about it than I managed to be. [*Will they? Do they, in fact, have the world by the tail?*]

———

SYLVIE AND WILL ate lunch on a terrace overlooking the Ionian Sea, side by side on a loveseat so both would have the panorama of the bay and the half-dozen white-sailed boats. Yogurt, fruit, walnuts, bread, Greek coffee. He turned his head to the side and popped something into his mouth. When Sylvie raised her eyebrows he said, "Vitamins." Wind played across their faces. The sweat and stink of near-miss driving had soaked Will's blue button-down, and he'd changed in the restaurant washroom to a black T-shirt, which he wore inside-out the way some of Sylvie's students wore theirs.

Beyond the basic catching up, including his dozen-plus years of working for a small press in Edmonton and her long clamber over the boulders of academe to arrive, finally, on what seemed a fine plateau to rest awhile, they'd found little to say, which seemed not right. They hadn't touched on personal relationships or lack thereof, an avoidance between them like a balloon and neither one with the nerve to wield a pin. She nudged his arm with her elbow the way she used to do when she was nineteen. "You haven't said what made you Google me? Fess up. Sorting through the past in the wake of a breakup?"

"Ouch, but that's a tired old trope to accuse me of. Cusack in *High Fidelity*. Besides, we never —"

"Tell me about it."

"*I'm* doing the *new* trope. Searching out persons of note from my past, the nice and the nasty, so I'll know whether to be gleeful or envious."

"What was it, then, when you saw I'd landed at UBC?"

"Suppose I say astonished."

"You could be accused of stalking, you know, showing up without warning so far from home."

"I thought you might like the surprise."

"Oh, I do."

"Man!" Will said, looking at the sun-spangled sea. "What could be more beautiful?" He wrung his thick white napkin in his hands as if answers, not to that question but to others, might drip out of the fabric and onto his lap.

Kalos, Sylvie thought. Would that be the word? The waiter stopped to top up their water. Sylvie shaded her eyes with her hand. "Can you tell me something?"

He remained motionless, bottle in hand.

"Can you tell me the Greek word for *beautiful?*"

"In what sense do you mean?" He widened his arms. "Beautiful like mass on Sunday? Beautiful like watching your child who is sleeping? It depends."

She lifted a hand to indicate the play of sun on the waves, the silver-green of the olive trees nearby. "This. I mean all this."

"And then, your mood when you are seeing it. I cannot know from the outside what you are feeling." He walked away, softly singing.

Sylvie saw how Will's hands had slackened around the napkin he'd been wringing. *Skeletal,* was the word she lit on. Those strange but familiar hands had a skeletal beauty. She sensed a ticking down inside the man.

"I wanted to see you, that's all," he said. "Friend of my youth. It's grounding."

"I'm glad it's that. I'm glad you stalked me here." His thin arms, motionless. She smiled to coax a smile from him. It worked. "Will you take me to Hell again?"

"Yes, tomorrow. Today, the beach."

They followed their instincts along a bumpy road. Not knowing the name of the beach they found, they christened it Paradise. Like Hell, it was populated only sparsely. A middle-aged couple were getting it on in the shade of the cliff that rose to one side of the cove. An extended family had scattered blankets, wide-brimmed hats and flapping towels across the sand. A naked baby crawled toward the surf. A woman Sylvie guessed to be roughly her own age slathered a toddler with sunblock. Grandchild? She imagined the smooth feel of the young skin under the woman's hand. Sylvie was not, to her knowledge, a grandmother.

She and Will took turns changing into swimsuits between a bush and a held towel. They left their things in a heap, took a quick dip in the calm water of the cove and then stood, feet burrowed to find the coolness underneath the hot surface of the sand. A cypress that had taken root on a ledge partway up the cliff leaned out in profile against the blue sky. Sylvie pulled the sparkling dress from her shoulder bag, careful to leave the ceramic sheep nestled there next to the drawstring pouch. She shook the dress once and slipped it on. At forty-nine she was still happy to wear a brief bikini, but only briefly. The dress turned a darker green where wetness plastered it slick against her suit, showing, she hoped, the results of thirty years of fidelity to yoga and other salutary practices. Let the mentor-seeking young scholars take note. *Jug feathers!* Aunt Merry would say if she were to hear that thought. Aunt Merry, Sylvie's own mentor since childhood, though neither of them had ever used that word.

Will's wet body as he stood on the beach was doughy around the middle. Grey curls in a patchy pattern between his shivered nipples. Only that single time had he taken her in his arms when they were young, just the one occasion on the landing at the top of her outside staircase. Pulled her to him, held her ass in his warm hands for a couple of seconds, then

214

let her go and said good night. Afterward they'd carried on as if it hadn't happened. She'd never lost that moment. Over the years she'd coaxed it into the present with a frequency that would surely surprise him.

He pulled his T-shirt on, still inside out. Rubbed a hand across his chest. "Itching me," he said, and he took it off and turned it right-side out. *I HAVE BEEN TO THE GATES OF HELL,* it read. "Whatever kind of plastic transfer they used. Irritating. We'll go back tomorrow, you can buy your own."

"Land of the dead."

"Sylvie, I have to tell you." He was looking down, watching the slither of sand as he wiggled a big toe. "I lost so many friends in the early years, before the drugs got better." He tightened his starfish beach towel round his waist.

Sylvie swallowed. She looked at his profile, thinking again how he looked less than himself. "Oh, Will." Taking the hem of her dress in her hands, she twisted the fabric hard, wringing a drop or two of seawater onto the sand. "Will, I'm sorry." She wove her fingers through his, used her other hand to stroke his forearm, elbow to wrist, in a soothing motion.

"I'm positive," he said.

"How long have you known?"

"July 21, 1995."

"That's nine years, almost."

"But who's counting?" He leaned toward her, and she held him. "So-far-so-good." He said it rapidly, as if to get it out before the facts would change.

"Oh, Will."

"So many funerals. I stopped counting years ago."

MORNING. Breakfast at Villa Stavros was served outdoors on a high terrace. They looked over the tops of cedars toward the patch of beach where earlier they'd spent forty-five minutes practising asanas, alone together. The wind blew their paper napkins off the table. In keeping with the rites of purification and preparation before a pilgrimage to an oracle, Sylvie ate nothing. "Good decision," said Will. "Best not to have anything in your stomach. It would only come back up once the nausea sets in, which it's bound to do once you drink my special tea."

He ate his yogurt and avocado, his white bread, swallowed three pills and chased them with bottled water. They'd lain together all night on the narrow bed in Will's room fully clothed — talking, sleeping, singing a little, intimate but not — and woken side by side and calm. He peeled an orange and the scent burst toward her. A drop of juice landed on her wrist and sparkled, then itched. She licked away the drop, tasting sweet and salt. "Breakfast." She was nervous, waiting.

"I wonder what sort of person your girl's turned out to be."

"I wonder too." She liked to imagine a face that resembled the young Aunt Merry in black and white photos from the fifties, her wide smile tilted with mischief. "If not for you, she'd never have been born."

"You can't be sure."

"If I hadn't picked up that copy of *The Prophet* you left behind at my place, if I hadn't used it as an excuse to find you at yoga and return it, I don't think I would have —"

"I'm glad you came that day, but I won't take credit for your decision."

"You should. You were there for me." Then, trying on the

idea of active motherhood, something she'd been taking tentative steps toward for weeks now, she said, "For her and me." She stared at the sea and counted four small boats, whitesailed. Which sort of beauty was this? Heartbreaking? Joyful? Either way, it was powerful enough she had to look away for a moment. She reached a hand and touched Will's temple, fingered his hair. "I've always loved your curls. So handsome, the way they're silvering."

"You're sweet. Sweeter than you used to be."

———

Sylvie: Look: you apply yourself. You do everything in your power to make your work exceptional, and with a little luck the work will get noticed. Sometimes the validation will come only from inside yourself. *You* will know when you measure up. And you'll know when you don't. If you're honest. [Silence.]

Student: Thank you, Dr. Fletcher, for some very, um, helpful thoughts. Now [turning to her left], let's hear from Dr. Yiannakis.

———

THE PARKING LOT at the Nekromanteion was mercifully deserted. Inside the walls they passed a terracotta pot reconstituted from dozens of shards glued back together and placed in a metal stand. Sylvie pointed as they passed it. "Reunited." Will smiled.

As soon as the conference organizers had invited her to Ioannina, she had begun to imagine this side-trip. She'd done her homework and she was ready with a mix of milk and honey she'd coaxed after breakfast from the cook at Villa Stavros and poured into the plastic bottle she'd brought from home. She had two small stones from the courtyard outside her condo in Vancouver to throw at hostile spirits should any appear. Now, thanks to Will and his mushroom tea, she wouldn't have to resort to a dubious Gravol high. The ancient pilgrims were granted their audience with the dead only after extended preparations and purification — sensory deprivation, fasting, exhaustion, hallucinatory concoctions made from beans and lupin seeds. They stood on a patch of grass on the rocky hillside and Will handed her the thermos. "Anything lupins do, this can do better."

She nearly dropped it. She hadn't indulged in so much as a toke in twenty years.

"Second thoughts?"

"Those ancients went through days and days of rites."

He laughed and touched the thermos with a fingertip. "Trust me, this will *feel* like days. Go now, find a spot. I'll stay close by. Don't worry, this is a good place. For me too. I have many friends here." He made a half smile and slid a bottle of water into her free hand, then bowed and backed away. She found a grassy space further along the hillside and sat cross-legged among the dandelions and daisies. Looked back at Will, who sat with his back to a cyclopean wall. She drank. Took the shiny raku sheep from her shoulder bag and set it on a stone to her right, at the ready. The small photograph of Aunt Merry, too, at the ready, tucked under the sheep. She drank again.

THE GRASS ALL AROUND was a softly rolling sea, and Sylvie afloat. Despite Will's effort to mask the flavour by adding a bag of orange spice from Celestial Seasonings, the tea in his thermos – she'd downed more than half of it – carried a lingering tang akin to sour dirt. She swallowed water past a swell in her throat and used what yoga had taught her about breath to quell the nausea. Her bones felt small inside her body but heavy too, in a pleasant way, as if they'd found their way home from a four-day walk and were settling back in. She felt watched over and at the same time stomach-sick. *Mixed feelings,* she thought, and she would've giggled but giggling seemed redundant.

Was she worried about something? No, but her body seemed to think so. Tightness in her chest, and then a gradual softening. She watched the waves of the rolling sea around her. She'd been afloat for hours now, or minutes. She slipped the photo from where she'd tucked it underneath the sheep. Looking into Aunt Merry's eyes she saw that she didn't have to ask out loud, she just had to look at her aunt's face, which was moving a little but not in the way a face moves when a person speaks. It was simply alive in a lovely way, more physically lovely than Merry ever had been in her time on Earth. Sylvie knew, then, that her aunt lived inside her. As all of Earth lived inside her, and all of her own life past and to come, and the unknown life of her lost daughter. All of these together, there was no separation. She set the photo down and weighted it with the lid from the thermos, opened the plastic bottle, spilled milk and honey in an arc around Aunt Merry and watched as it dripped through the weave of grass and sank into the ground.

Journey to the Underworld. Tired old trope. She laughed, and the commotion the laughter caused made her want to vomit. She heard Aunt Merry inside her: What is it, then, dear? I haven't got all day.

I should look for her. Should I?

If you're ready.

Maybe she's registered. To say she's willing. Has she registered, Aunt Merry?

You don't need an oracle to answer that, all you need's a telephone.

Should I do this, then?

Aunt Merry sighed an exasperated sigh, clouds of steamy breath rising from the shimmering photograph. You already know the answer. A breeze tugged at the photo, threatened to free it from the slight hold of the thermos lid.

Sylvie nodded, and tears of relief dropped into the green ocean around her. You've always helped me decide what to do.

I've been your sounding board, that's all. I've never told you a single thing you haven't already sorted out.

Aunt Merry? What I really want to know is . . . could you tell me what's ahead? Only just a little? A clue?

That's not my job, honey. I will say this: It's a tragedy how late you've left it.

Yes. Her daughter would be twenty-nine. Sylvie looked at her hands and saw that she was cradling the sheep. She ran her thumb over the rough raku. How long had she been holding that bit of fragility? She faced toward the stone on the hillside and raised the sheep above it.

Saint Peter in a puddle, Sylvie, what the hell are you about to do?

Odysseus – when he came he slaughtered a black lamb and a black ewe. A sacrifice.

Aunt Merry laughed. That's a perfectly good tchotchke, my girl. Have you got a present for her?

Not yet.

Well?

With this final question Aunt Merry's photo escaped the small weight of the lid. Sylvie rocked the sheep in her hands and watched the picture skip away, thought how Merry would enjoy the dance across the ocean of grass and into the blue sky. She watched until it disappeared in the direction of Corfu. The hillside was empty, eerie. Will's here, she thought. Behind me, leaning against the wall. He needs me. He needs me, and she needs me. Sylvie tried – thought she tried – to turn to see Will, but her body, when she checked, had failed to move.

LATER, IN THE CAR, she held the sheep in her lap along with the pebbles she'd brought in case of hostile spirits. They made small clinks against each other as the car jiggled along the rough road. She tried to tell Will how Merry was still and always inside her, lobbing Sylvie's own answers back in response to her questions. As she had always done. Was that some form of wisdom, what she managed with her dead aunt?

"Jeez, Sylvie, don't *study* it, just let it be. You're still bemush-roomed, and it's such a fine day, and this is a stunning place."

"Why are we taking the long way back? I need to get to Ioannina."

"Because *you're* taking the long way back. You won't land for hours yet, not fully. We'll drive a little, find the shore, watch the sun go down."

"What about you, will you visit the dead? Will you, Will?" She found her own phrasing hilarious.

"Yes, in fact, tomorrow while you cavort with scholars. We'll compare notes afterward, over dinner."

"I've said too much already." She winked. "If you talk about your visit to the Underworld, Hades demands your own life in exchange."

"You think I'm scared to mess with *Him?*"

They took a curve and screeched to a stop to avoid driving into a herd of sheep milling on the road. Sylvie opened the door and vomited a pale wet thread onto the gravel.

"That's my girl."

The last of the bleating sheep left the road. As Will put the car in gear Sylvie pulled her door shut and opened her window all the way for air. "How will you find the shore?"

"Drive toward the sun till the land runs out. But let's talk about what's important here. Let's talk about how you'll find her."

"Yes, yes!" Never until this moment had Sylvie found a use for the word *rapture*. That was the word for what she felt now. Rapture with a silver dusting of anxiety. Would she be welcomed or spurned?

"Look left," said Will. "Pretty little shrine."

Another curve obscured by oleander and sunlit dust and now a truck coming their way, high speed and almost as wide as the road itself. Sylvie thought, *Will I ever know what she looks like?* and then impact. The two small pebbles fell through her fingers. The ceramic sheep flew out the window and tumbled through oleander striking leaf after flower after leaf.

SHE WAS ON HER BACK on pebbled ground, lying in a long cold shadow cast by . . . what? Her body was small and heavy at the same time. The air was silent but for the ting and tick of metal settling. She was far from home. Where? Someone called her name. Again. She would answer, soon. He was saying something else now. She turned her head and saw a shiny object the size of her closed fist, cradled on a tuft of wild grass.

Things He Will Not
Tell Her Daughter

NO DOUBT Mavis will have her own ideas about what to tell Sylvie's daughter, should they ever track her down. What those ideas might be, Will can't begin to guess — he's known Mavis only three days now. Her mere existence had come as a surprise, and her features a witching, so familiar but in a squarish face and framed by hair brassy with highlights. A sister Sylvie had never once mentioned. Of course not. Their friendship happened back when both were shedding themselves of family, hometowns, high school.

"We were always close," Mavis said after she introduced herself, meaning, he supposed, that a person of any importance would know of her.

That encounter was days ago, but its keen point still digs. "Ah," he'd managed, "I'm so sorry for your loss. How hard this must be." His impulse to reach his arms around this person so similar to Sylvie in height, gesture, even the askew angle of the eyetooth on the left. To grasp the life of her and hold it. "I am so, so sorry, Mavis." Her flinch, though, under even the light touch of his palm on her shoulder, the little nub of bone under the seam of her blouse a small declaration.

He won't see those almost-Sylvie eyes again until the funeral. Mavis isn't on this plane, she'll catch a later flight, the one that will bring the body home to Canada. That weight, at least, he's out from under. He uncrosses his legs and flexes an ankle to relieve the numbness, often there but worse on planes. The mp3 player that's been lying forgotten on his lap slips off and dangles. Its small jerk at the end of the cord tugs at his headphones, and the muscles in the back of his neck jump. He pulls the player up and lets it drop back onto his thigh. He hasn't even turned his music on, wears the phones only to discourage the young girl in the next seat from asking why is his arm in a sling and what about the bandage on the side of his head. Though he's not without experience in deciding what to say and what to leave out — in the early years especially. It's just a rash; it's only a cold; a little flu, it'll pass. Incomplete. As is he, by now. There was a time, in his Seattle years, when he'd attended a funeral every week for two months running. With each, another swathe of his personal history thinned out for lack of a person to share memories with. Who was he, anymore?

WHEN HE RECONNECTED WITH SYLVIE in Greece, wanting to impress this woman who had somehow become a prof in the decades since he'd last seen her, he'd let her believe he had a primarily editorial role at the micro enterprise that was Moonlit Publishers, but in fact his tasks are humdrum — sometimes proofreader, hard-drive troubleshooter, invoicer/shipper, window washer even. One true thing he told her, late in the night to the sound of the sea, was that from time to time he writes the copy that goes on the website and the backs of the books. "Bumf, it's called. People don't know where that word came from. Bet you don't." She didn't. "Short for bum fodder. Toilet paper." She let out a scoffing little laugh that called back to the time when they were close. There she was: Sylvie – a new version of her, but the girl he'd known still there to glimpse, and to offer glimpses of himself.

"It's the bumf that sells the story," he said. "Promise tears and laughter, promise audacity and wit. Tightly framed, two hundred words or fewer. Consider using the verb *to limn*," he said, to make her laugh again, and she did. "What might the story of your life so far, Sylvie, limn?"

"How to be happy in spite of yourself."

"Because of."

"As you wish."

HAPPY IN SPITE OF HERSELF. He will not tell her daughter, supposing they find her, how Sylvie appeared so easy with the lie as she walked the aisle in her bridesmaid dress those many years ago. A hot day in late summer and Will, wearing the navy sportcoat he'd worn to his high school grad the year before, slipped in and took a seat at the back. "You have to stay for the whole entire ceremony," she'd said that morning. "I might need you." Okay but still, a person needs air.

Forty-odd guests clotted in pairs and singles under the vaulted ceiling. Sylvie did enjoy playing to the crowd, such as it was, and the pale apricot satin brought the brightest tones of summer to her skin. Glossed lips and her hair just long enough for salon-set ringlets that grazed her chin on either side. She performed a pretty, measured march, pausing with every step before swinging the next foot through. Behind her another bridesmaid draped in apricot, then a third. The church had a wide centre aisle, picturesque in the traditional way. Now here came the bride, and Will remembers wondering if she, at least, was actively practising birth control.

Best he not say much to Sylvie's daughter about her biological father. Best he not say that, sitting in the back pew, Will had studied the cleavages, the tanned arms, the postures of bridesmaids two and three and wondered if the groom had been in them as well. He'd stepped out, then, taken off his jacket, slung it over his shoulder and waited in the shade of a ragged maple till Lisa and Dave emerged through the double doors under showers of confetti and lashings of rice. Did he think about how he would never do that, duck that white rain? He doesn't remember.

He drove Sylvie back to her suite for a beer break after the ceremony and before the reception. Shed of her dress for the moment but still in her full-length slip with Will's sportcoat overtop, still wearing her white pantyhose, her ivory shoes kicked off, she told him she'd been running to the bathroom again and again all day to check, it could still happen, she was only three weeks late.

"Only," he said.

At the dance that night at the Ukrainian Hall on G, she disappeared yet again into the Ladies for a few minutes, then came out and sat beside him smoothing her yards of brides-maid skirt, brushing at the grey creep of floor dust that rimmed the hem. "Nothing." A couple of months earlier she'd told Will that she'd tossed her dial pack of pills because they gave her an extra jiggle around the middle.

"What'll you do though?"

"I'll just hold back at a certain time of the month."

"And you know that time for sure."

"I can count," she'd said.

"Can you count on not being horny?"

"I can *count*."

His question a week before the wedding when she modeled the satin dress for him and told him of her worries was, "I still don't understand — he's a grade-A jerk. Why?"

"Curiosity. Come *on*. I held back for a long time."

"Alice went through the looking glass and there she saw a sign that said Drink Me and so she did."

"This bodice is *tight*. If it isn't a baby then I still have to solve the jiggle." She even laughed. So young. Nothing serious could happen to them, nothing that would last.

FINAL WORDS that Will has had the privilege of hearing:

Seth: "We sure did laugh that time, didn't we?"

Drew: "I love you a thousand miles wide."

Doug: "God damn it all to fucking hell."

Trent: "Is it spring yet?"

Sylvie: "Can you reach —?"

"I PROMISED SYLVIE I'd find her daughter," Will said to Mavis the day she landed in Ioannina after the accident. "It was the last thing I said to her."

"No, but it's best I be the one to do that. Isn't it." Not a question.

Certainly, yes. The sister is the one with the chance of gaining access to official channels, adoption records, registries. If she succeeds, will she let Will know? But maybe the young woman won't care to meet an ersatz uncle when she has an aunt by blood. Maybe he's redundant.

You weren't there, Will thought as he stood with Mavis in the lobby of the Hotel Politia, both of them looking down at the marble floor, his scuffed loafers, her patent sandals. You weren't in the car. The lowering sun, the dust, the curve, the narrow road they were following in search of the sea. It might have happened to anyone. The tail of the truck swinging round when the driver tried to miss them, the leftways skid of Will's little rental with his sudden stomp to the brake.

This morning at the Politia, as he swirled the dregs in his cup and stood to leave the small table he'd claimed in the corner of the noisy breakfast room, Mavis had come through the doorway, spotted him and looked away, as if she had to shift her emotions a few degrees before she could bear to acknowledge him, bandaged but walking and breathing. You don't know, he wanted to tell her. He wished her good morning and offered his table. "I'm just on my way."

"Well, then," Mavis said, her fingers fidgeting through her highlighted hair. "It's Edmonton, you said? I suppose I'll have to —"

"I have your number."

The cab ride to the airport was startle after startle, thighs tensing at near miss after near miss, each of which the cabbie managed with swerve and horn and equanimity. Once, braking hard, he looked over at Will with an uneven grin: such a jumpy creature, this foreigner.

THE KID FROM THE SEAT next to Will's sways her way back along the aisle of the plane after a trip to the toilet, squeezes in and plunks her lanky self down with a thump. Will traces his thumb around the ring on his mp3 player, pretending concentration. To meet the eyes of anyone, even a half-grown stranger, would leave him raw. The bones at his temples feel steeped in ache. He clicks to call up the CSNY album from the summer they listened to music together, the year this one came out on vinyl. A haunted hollowness in the sound, a signature of longing. Sylvie's sister blames him, sure. She's right to.

SYLVIE HAD RETURNED his question the other night: "And you? The story of your life, so far?"

He had to take a moment to invent a word: "Vanishment."

"You're very much here."

"Every time someone close died, something of me vanished."

"I'm here, Will." The soothing *swoosh* of the sea through the open window.

"Yes. I'm so glad."

BACK-COVER BUMF. Promise love and sorrow, promise struggle and redemption. Consider using the adjective *resilient*. Professor Sylvia Fletcher, from library clerk at University of Saskatchewan to tenured professor at UBC. An authority on ancient classical theatre. Refer to defining character traits — be they heroic or flawed or both at once — curiosity, for instance.

He pauses his player, then starts it again. Stephen Stills with a mournful lyric about four and twenty years ago. It's more years than that since Will bought *Déja Vu* upstairs at Eaton's. *Rolling Stone* savaged the album, the song. So little at stake, the reviewer said, it's hard to care. Will and Sylvie sat on her outside stairs in the summer dusk and he held the magazine in the light coming through the open door and read the choicest parts aloud.

Sylvie held her lighter to the curling corner of the front page. "Tell you what *I* don't care about. I don't fucking care about that obnox and his opinions." Will loved her for that and wished he could say the same. There: that's something he might tell her daughter about.

He will not tell her how Sylvie made a joke of blaming the pregnancy on him: "If you would've let me seduce you, I wouldn't have resorted to the grade-A jerk." She used to pretend that much of what she said was a joke, but he didn't find it funny, the idea that the existence of a child was a fault to be pinned somewhere.

"Yes but Sylvie, you know I don't feel that way about you." It was rote by then, a joke in itself, and Sylvie nudged him sideways on the stairs so his shoulder knocked the wall.

THE TRUCK DRIVER — gesticulating and spitting — raged above Will after the accident as he cradled Sylvie's bloodied head with his left arm, his right arm askew and flaming with pain. It's been a week now, but still he hears the tirade in a language he doesn't understand, still lives out the moment before the accident repeatedly, wishing he could wrench the steering wheel fast enough to swerve time in a new direction. Why Sylvie and not him? Why all those others?

"SOMETIMES YOU ACT like you're some kind of homo," she said once when he told her he didn't feel that way about her. Exactly that. She made a lot of homo jokes in those days, everyone did. Will certainly had. The one how, if you drop your keys on the street in San Francisco, don't bend over, just kick them all the way back to your hotel and get the doorman to pick them up. He told that one over and over, as if at nineteen he'd known anyone who had the means or the nerve to get to San Francisco.

Both his feet are numb now. He flips his seat belt undone and negotiates his way past the girl next to him to walk the aisle up and down, lugging his right foot, then his left; right, left. All these faces, and every one a someone and behind their features a labyrinth of thoughts and half-thoughts, memory and certainty and puzzlement. The plane skids over a quick series of bumps and he gets his good arm up and clamps his hand over a seat back to steady himself, accidentally pulling a woman's long brown hair. She turns, wincing, then musters a half smile to show it's all right. About thirty, is she?

What will she look like, this girl of Sylvie's out there in the world?

He will not tell her — he'd never even told Sylvie until they reconnected — that sometimes in those young moments when she brushed his hand with hers in invitation he very nearly clenched her fingers and pulled her hard against him. That what made him want to do so was in some part bodywant but also this: If he slid onto her mattress, slid into her, could he dissolve and reappear in an alternate world, or nowhere?

The girl angles her knees to allow him to step past and fold back into his seat. His good arm is next to the window. The shade sticks, but with patience he coaxes it up. He wants to see the tops of the clouds, what can't be seen from earth. Sunlight sears in. The kid, distracted from her Game Boy, flashes him a look. She's right, the brightness is eye-watering. Will works the shade back down till only a narrow knife of light cuts in below it. He leans his head, the side without the bandage, against the cabin wall, and the firm curve above the window presses hard into his skull. It'll be eighteen hours and two more airports before he's home.

ANOTHER THING he certainly can't mention: how he's bounding up those rickety outside stairs and thinking that what Sylvie needs is to come back with him to yoga, the quieting of it, the slowing; and what Will needs is a friend to come along, to help him open the door at Animesh and Satya's little bungalow and walk in, get to that space of empty mind, the body reaching away from itself, and a drawn-out chant, wave after wave, to wash fear off the edge of the world. He's bounding up those stairs, the startling bit of give when his foot lands on the rotting step third from the top, the one they used to say they should knock right out so they wouldn't forget to skip it. Her door wide open in the heat, her roommate away on the Greyhound to see her folks in Langenburg, and on the couch Sylvie's flushed face visible past Dave's shoulder, her heels bouncing against his naked ass.

THE KID IN THE NEXT SEAT fell asleep a while ago, and now her torso lists and her head comes to rest on Will's shoulder above the sling that cradles his elbow. He sits forward, "Hey," but she doesn't wake, just shifts in her sleep. She looks even younger now, open-mouthed, her fingers slack around her Game Boy. She's just a kid, this kid. Will eases quietly back, resettles her lolling head into a position that doesn't annoy so much.

When he landed in Ioannina what he wanted most was to rediscover a single friend from long ago who hadn't gone and died. And then she did, and it's he who made it so. He will find her daughter because he promised. He'll find her because as soon as he found Sylvie again, he lost her. Careful now, don't hope to put the daughter in that empty space. Careful. Now you think you need her, need someone, anyone, more than ever.

"Take pains with tone," he said to Sylvie, riffing a week ago at Villa Stavros. "Consider echoing the author's style. Wry like Dali with an eyebrow raised; sharp like a paper cut; blurred, as if through a lens smeared with Vaseline." Sylvie's tone could be any of those at different times.

"Consider silence," she said then, closing her eyes and turning on her side. "Consider getting some sleep."

He is not redundant. A life is large, with many rooms, and people in every one. There are things that only he knows.

The night before the accident, their chaste but intimate hours on a twin bed, dozing and waking and dozing again, separately and together, and when the sunrise roused them they sang all the words they could remember to the melancholy tune from that young summer, filling in lost half lines with humming. He broke off partway through, remembering her response to the critic's review. "I don't fucking care about that obnox and his opinions," he said, to make her laugh, and she did. The lyrics were beside the point; they could have been anything; the power of the song was the amount of ache you could soak into every note. Will and Sylvie did their best. When he broke down in tears before they finished, she said, "Oh, honey, my honey," and stroked his arm in a tender way. Might he, one day, tell her daughter that?

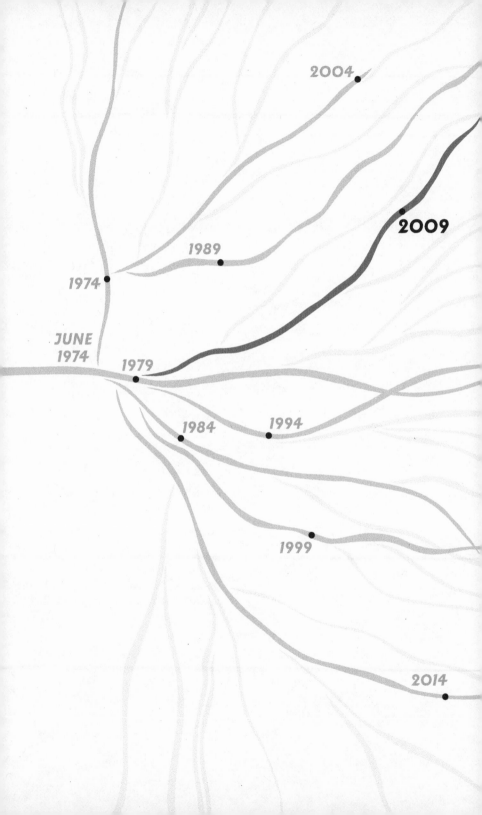

Philosophies

STAN'S GANGLY TEENAGE FRAME was hunched over a cereal bowl, spoon clanking on crockery as he shoveled his breakfast at the counter of what passed for a kitchen in the cramped quarters of the Sleep Well Hotel. Sylvie sat down on the stool next to him, the vinyl upholstery giving off a fabulous fart as it took her weight. She laid a light hand on her grandson's shoulder and took in a side view of the downy beginnings of whiskers, the sprinkle of under-ripe pimples on his chin, the oily sheen on his face from the nonstop pump of teen-juice. Thirteen and ahead of himself in more ways than one. "Could you. Possibly. Crunch your Harvest Crunch less crunchily?"

Sylvie, her daughter, and her daughter's two kids had scored what was generously called a suite at the Sleep Well. The counter where they perched acted as room divider, separating the sink and the microwave and the itty bitty fridge from the living room with its perpetually pulled out pull-out couch. There *was* a separate bedroom with a door that closed, small mercy, where toddler Sooze was sleeping now. Some among the two dozen displaced families had to make do with single rooms.

"And might you please fold back your bed before you leave for school?"

"Love you too, Gran. I'll miss my bus." Stan kissed the top of her head, lifted her coffee cup right out of her hand to take a slurp and handed it back. Shouldering his backpack, he made for the door. Hand on the doorknob, he stopped. Dropped his pack, slouched across to the window that looked onto the parking lot and knelt in front of it. Sylvie's gaze rested on his bent knee where the denim folded into shadows. She thought of his long-gone grandfather, skinny legs like that with the jeans slumping loose around them, running shoes he rarely used for running. May Stan be safe in this world.

"Lookie, Gran, Thomas showed me this thing." Stan pressed his left cheek, the entire side of his head, really, ear and all, against the window, then slowly rolled so that now his face squished hard against the glass, his slick forehead, nose, lips, and chin, flattened. He rolled further, pressing his right cheek and temple, his right ear, to the pane. He backed away then, leaving a wavy fun-house mask translucent on the glass, an oily ribbon extra wide from ear to ear, with a stretched grin a person could read just about anything into.

"You be home in good time," Sylvie said as he got up to leave. "Court tomorrow."

When he opened the door the noise of the soccer game going on in the long hotel corridor, already in swing at this time of the morning, rabbled in. Then he was gone. A whimper floated out from the bedroom, but Sooze had a pattern of falling back to sleep after stirring for a moment when her brother left. Sylvie thought of folding up the sofa bed, but no: she pulled the blanket over the smell of teenage sheets and lay down. The truth was, he was a good kid.

A PRESENCE IN THE ROOM. She opened her eyes, hefted herself onto her elbow. Stan stood by the door, about to exit. "Sorry, Gran, missed my bus."

"Where did you get that Pop-Tart?"

"Itty bitty freezer."

"You bought Pop Tarts. With what for money?"

He chewed, grinned.

"And why are you *always* putting something in your mouth?"

"I get hungry." He flashed his tongue, covered in bits of goo.

"Well, deny yourself a little for once."

"Gran, you are preachy. Preachy, preachy, preachy."

SOOZE IN HER ARMS, Sylvie waited in the parking lot at the housing complex for the insurance investigator. A ragged watermark a metre high ran along the fences and the outside walls of the row houses. Sooze wanted down. She arched her back in a way that, if Sylvie weren't hyper-alert, would have landed the child on the asphalt with a broken head. What the girl wanted was to go exploring in the filthy heap by the bins. Of course she did. Among the trash were a baby-blue baby swing, two kitchen stoves, boxes of whatnot soaked in shit. A Christmas wreath, a basket of Easter eggs, a child-sized Big Bird with a brown stain across his yellow belly.

They waited. They waited so the inspector could see for herself, take pictures for the record of the warped floors, stairs, window frames, the filth in the carpets. The swollen section of kitchen wall where, over her daughter Catherine's objections, Sylvie had given Sooze and her crayons free range. She'd promised to paint over the doodles herself once a month. Two times at least she'd followed through.

The row house had been pristine when Catherine moved in with the kids, bright white walls, fresh pages. Then the first flood a year ago, and the cleanup. Then the second flood this past June. Catherine had cashed the insurance cheque for that one only seven days before the late August deluge that sent them packing to the Sleep Well. Sears Canada had installed the replacement washer, dryer, furnace and water heater just in time for all four to drown. Too much water in her daughter's life, going all the way back to an afternoon at the beach in 1979 when Catherine was the size of a bean sprout curled inside Sylvie's own warm lake of womb and her father, dancing under a hot disco ball of a sun, hadn't even suspected her existence.

———

TWINKLE, TWINKLE LITTLE STARS

River Crossings, Your Community Newspaper Supplement,
September 6, 2009

Families from a flooded west-side housing complex, living tem-
porarily at the Sleep Well Hotel, will stage a pageant based on
nursery rhymes and fairy tales, and they have a clown to thank.
The pageant is the inspiration of Mrs. Sylvie Callaghan, grand-
mother to two of the displaced children, and a mainstay of the
local amateur theatre scene. I stand with Mrs. Callaghan beside
a row of cardboard boxes lining one wall of a banquet room
the hotel has given over to be used as a playroom. She wears a
pinch-on clown's nose, a bright plaid shirt with a ruffled collar,
and loose pants with a lively print, the ensemble she'll wear when
she takes the stage as mistress of ceremonies for the pageant.

The boxes are filled with toys and necessities donated by
members of the congregation of nearby St. Bride's Anglican
Church. Mrs. Callaghan shows me shoes, plush animals, diapers,
T-shirts in sizes that range from infant to adult. Many of the
families lost toys and clothing in the floods. "Mould and con-
tamination," says Mrs. Callaghan. "We had to bag it and toss it."

She wants to show me the contents of one donation box in
particular. It's full of Hallowe'en costumes. "When I saw this
dress that surely was meant for Little Bo Peep, bows and frilly
bloomers, that's when the idea came to me. Somewhere in all
this —" she gestures at the cartons — "we can find white shirts,
make a few sheep. Something for a Red Riding Hood, faux fur to
make a wolf, a plaid shirt for a **Please see Stars, p.6**

243

IN THE BANQUET ROOM Sylvie used her pocket knife to slit the tape along the top of a box. Little Sooze was a warm weight wrapped around her lower leg. "Gran, Gran." She folded back the box's flaps. Aprons. Not even a useful kind, but tea aprons, the sort her mother's generation tied over their skirts after a wedding or a funeral to set out butter tarts and brownies. She put a hand to her granddaughter's hair, so fine in her fingers it might melt. "Sweetie, sweetie."

All this passel of displaced kids running in the hallways with their giggles and screams, their flying soccer balls, the dramas of their shifting anger, love and jealousy. She'd whirl at least some of that verve into a different sort of drama. She would need a Bo Peep and willing sheep. A Miss Muffet, how about seven dwarfs? Could she put Snow White in a tea apron?

She glanced at James, a volunteer from St. Bride's. He was gently balding and wore glasses so strong they distorted his face, though the lenses looked expensively thin. She'd heard he was a grandfather of six. He'd begun by delivering boxes; now he showed up every day, sometimes with more, sometimes to help sort and distribute the contents. But there were so many children, and so many among them whose most urgent need was for a willing grown-up to simply spend time with them, and Sylvie often saw James cross-legged on the floor, listening to a child.

Now here was Logan, delivering his two to Sylvie. They were next-door neighbours both at the hotel and back at the waterlogged complex. She would watch his little ones this afternoon, as she did every Monday, while he put in a few hours at the food bank. On Wednesday morning he would look after Sooze while Sylvie did her own shift. Toddler Cody, squeezed into a too-small onesie, rubbed an eye with his fist as Sylvie reached up to take him from his dad and sling him onto her hip. Preschooler Desirée stood beside her father, swaying side to side and punching his leg, her black curls long and loose and bouncing. Logan looked toward James, who was holding a striped shirt to his chest as if to guess the fit, then looked at Sylvie and rolled his eyes. "Do-gooder." He didn't bother to lower his voice.

Sylvie was a do-gooder herself, she supposed. When Catherine quit work at the ShopEasy and started classes for her education degree in hopes of one day moving her kids to a house less vulnerable to flooding, Sylvie had found a renter for her own place and moved over to help with the kids. She diverted the rental income toward tuition, groceries, the rent on Catherine's unit. Her three separate pensions from sequential, lower-rung jobs at the university, the school board, and the public library added up to just enough to allow her to retire early. The job of full-time grandma hadn't been how she'd expected to fill her days at this stage of life, but the responsibility grounded her. Living in as housekeeper/nanny was more than grounding, in fact — it felt fair and just. The sense of a debt outstanding had eddied around her all of Catherine's life.

"Who is that joker, anyway?" Logan was tall enough to point with his chin.

"Retired professor, I've heard."

"What's he want with our mess?"

"Like you said. Do some good."

"No thanks."

"The kids like him." Little Sooze had grabbed Desirée by her chubby hand and was pulling her toward James. "Tell me, Logan, do you think your girl would be our Bo Peep?"

"Long as the dress is pretty."

Sooze was on her way back already, legs churning. She charged Sylvie's calf, slammed into it, raised her arms, "Uppie!" Sylvie took her up and the girl buried her face, her sweat and tears and snot, in the hollow between her gran's neck and shoulder. Sylvie's shirts were damply sweet and sour in several places morning to night.

"Get the do-gooder to find something for Cody to wear."

"Will do. Bye."

Sylvie slid her knife through the tape on another box. "James, hi."

"Afternoon. How are you?"

"I heard a rumour you're a prof."

"*Was* a prof. Philosophy."

"I have a few of those. Philosophies."

"Yes?"

"Here's one: It never rains but it pours."

"That's apt. On the other hand, It's an ill wind that blows no good."

"So they say." She pulled from the box the first thing that came to hand, a hoodie, deep red, man-sized. She laughed and shook it out. "You might just be our Red Riding Hood."

He held it to his chest, and he laughed too. "Are you serious?"

"Actions speak louder than words — that's something else they say."

"Fools rush in."

Stars, continued from p. 1 *wood-cutter and, well, all those fairy tale characters."*

Older children will read the narration, and Mrs. Callaghan will direct the younger ones through enactments. "Or maybe acting will be too complicated," she says with a wry smile. "We might just have them stand up front in their costumes."

Mrs. Callaghan introduces me to her daughter, Catherine, who tells me about the flood. "I was in the basement when it started. First it came down the dryer vent and into the dryer. Full load of my son's T-shirts and underwear. The water came in the basement windows at the same time, and the cracks in the walls. Then I hear the gurgle, and I turn around and it's [sewer] coming up the floor drain and soaking the pile of jeans that's waiting to be washed. So I run up to the main floor. The smell, it was just overpowering. That filth came up and up."

———

SYLVIE AND JAMES SAT cross-legged on the floor at some distance from the other parents and volunteers, taking a break. Logan's little Cody, now wearing a Superman costume, slept with his head at the crook of Sylvie's hip.

"How's your house?" James asked. "Inspection done?"

"Yeah. A mess. It isn't my place, it's my daughter's. My own house is elsewhere. It's fine, rented out."

"Ah."

Desirée and Sooze sat close by, building walls out of plastic blocks. Sometimes they couldn't wait past six or seven in a stack before they knocked them down, squealing. Sylvie looked at James, his classy glasses, his face framed by the red hoodie he'd been wearing since she pulled it out of the box. She would have liked to lean her head for a moment against the soft red fabric on his chest.

Without forethought, she blurted, "I bought my own place decades ago when houses were cheap enough that the payout on a working-class life insurance policy plus a couple years' savings could land a three-storey in City Park."

"Ah."

That was all. *Ah.* Did she wish he would ask about the why of the insurance payout? Yes, because it was a tangible mass in the air between them now, where earlier there had been only breathing space. No, because she was embarrassed to have hung it there. There was more that she wanted to say, and not to say — both those things at once. Inside herself was another Sylvie, and the two of them had been in a wearying wrestling match for decades. Maybe she hoped professor James would mediate a truce. Don't: there were so many strays already that he felt obliged to listen to. Do: she swallowed and spoke past her hesitation. "I wonder if everyone's done something they can't forgive themselves for." He sat completely still. An open stillness. Her cheeks burned with heat. In an airy voice that asked not to be taken seriously, she said, "Nor should they."

James turned his head and looked directly at her.

A wall of plastic blocks came crashing down and Cody woke and pushed himself to standing, bracing his little hand on a toy cash register.

"Do you need to talk?" said James.

The cash register swayed under Cody's weight. He swayed too, then fell smack on his bum, whimpering. "We are talking." Sylvie held James's look. "We are. It's fine." She turned away and raised a hand for an instant to her hot cheek, then took a charity apron from the pile beside her on the floor and wiped drool from the baby's chin. She patted his saturated diaper and pulled the boy onto her lap. Wet. Everything was wet.

The little girls approached, each with a tea apron on her head and draped in front of her eyes, weaving blindly, giggling. Pretending not to see James, they fell onto his crossed legs. He almost swore — she could see the *F* in the press of his teeth to his lower lip — but he stopped himself. He grasped the hems of both aprons and looked at Cody, eyebrows raised. "What could be under here?" He lifted the fabric away with a magician's flourish. Cody laughed and threw his arms wide. James reached and gave Sylvie's hand a light squeeze, which she returned.

The truth was, she had never succeeded, after the fact, in piecing together the specifics of that afternoon thirty years ago. A sense that the lake was so cold it slowed her limbs and even her thoughts as she did her best to tread water. But no, it was July, it couldn't have been that cold. Still: her muscles remembered a chill that left her without heartbeat enough to move, without will enough to call the other four away from their antics. She remembered — or did she? — the sense that not a soul was watching to see what she might do or not do in that moment.

———

Our city has a reputation for generosity, and donations have poured in, so many that, for the time being, Mrs. Callaghan has asked that people hold off until the families' remaining needs have been better assessed.

———

STAN CLANKED HIS CEREAL BOWL into the sink.

"Ten o'clock at the courthouse," Sylvie told him. "Wait for your mother before you go in."

He opened the door onto the racket of the hallway soccer game.

"And be polite!"

"Gran, you take everything so *seriously*."

The door closed behind him and the noise cut to a muffle. Sooze was curled over the coffee table concentrating with her crayons and paper. The soccer ball thudded against the door. Enough, already! Sylvie yanked the door open, looked for the ball and went after it, but a kid almost her height won it away with superior footwork.

"Don't you have school?" she shouted. She slammed back into the suite, looked for Sooze, found her on the floor in the bedroom scribbling a bird's nest of red squiggles low on the wall and burbling her joy. Sylvie grabbed the crayon. Sooze's mouth made an *O*, but she had a crayon in her other hand too, and she started making left-handed zigzags further along the wall. Sylvie dropped the red crayon and gripped Sooze's wrist, tried to pry her stubborn fingers. The child screamed her grief, and the noise set off a strident pulse in Sylvie's temples. She fetched the other crayons, spilled them onto the floor beside her granddaughter. "Knock yourself out, Picasso." Sooze laughed, still with the shine of tears on her pink cheeks. Jack's grandchild.

THE BANQUET ROOM *cum* playroom was quiet this morning, school agers off to school, preschoolers not yet tumbling in. James was there with a dozen gaping boxes, puddles of clothing on the floor, angular stacks of unsorted toys. He wore an apron over his jeans, extra-long tie-strings wound around his back and knotted in front, dangling. Sylvie held back from making an obvious joke.

He said, "I'll tidy this. Never fear."

"Don't worry, be happy." Sylvie set Sooze down near a plastic post with a rainbow of rings a child was meant to slide onto it. She pulled her clown nose from the pocket of her sweatpants and hooked it into her nostrils.

James tweaked the nose. "Become the change you want to see."

Sooze picked up a red ring and a purple ring and banged them together. She bit into one then the other. Sylvie bent forward to touch her limp curls. "'Most of life is choices," she said, "and the rest is pure dumb luck.'"

"Are you working up your stage patter, Ms. Clown?"

"I worry about that. I don't know a single joke suitable for a family audience."

"You don't need jokes. Go for the style where the clown's the only one on stage who gets to tell the truth."

"*Commedia dell'arte.* Is that what you're getting at?"

He widened his eyes.

"Stock characters. Italy some number of centuries ago, I forget. Don't look so surprised. I worked in libraries all my life."

He blushed.

Upper-middle-class do-gooder. "Anyway — telling the truth ... doesn't that require that the truth —" She held out a hand, palm up. A person didn't even need to finish that sentence, the empty hand seemed to say — the ending was obvious; but Sylvie herself wasn't sure how to fill in the blank. That the truth was out there waiting to be uncovered? That it didn't change from minute to minute, person to person? That the truth was even useful?

James took up the apron strings hanging from his waist and pulled them lightly across her open hand. "Spoken like a true clown."

SYLVIE LAY IN THE DOUBLE BED cuddling a sleeping Sooze. Stan was on the fold-out in the main room, *Survivor* playing on the TV. Her mind went soft and dark. She drifted, then startled, her legs twitching to save her from some half-dreamed stumble. She drifted again. Twenty people were seated at a dinner table, Jack among them, but Sylvie had nothing to offer. She checked the microwave, the hollow oven, the empty pots on the stove. She must do something. Wait, she tried to say, but no voice came. She jolted awake. "Shush, Sooze, Gran didn't mean to."

The dreams full of expectant guests would come and go in cycles that lasted weeks or months, but fewer and less often with the years. Now they were back, as if washed in by the flood.

"Shush, shush."

There they were in her own backyard — though not a backyard she'd ever seen — Margo, Penny, Benj and a grinning Alex — the other four who'd been at the lake with Sylvie and Jack — all of them holding up their glasses, and her with nothing to pour.

The opening and closing of the door to the suite woke her. Catherine, home on the last bus from campus, because how could she study here? Her backpack made a soft thump as it hit the floor. The itty bitty fridge out there opened and closed, and Sylvie heard the spill of cereal into bowls and the mother-son music as their voices ranged from soft to tense to soft again. Catherine was a kid herself when she had him, nursed him in the back row of English class and toted him along the hall to and from the in-school daycare. TV light flickered across Sylvie's face as Catherine came into the bedroom. Dark, then, and the soft rustles of her daughter undressing and pulling on her T-shirt. Catherine slid in on the other side of the bed, her day's-end breath coming closer as she kissed Sooze's head.

"Night, Cat."

"Night, Mom."

Sleep.

Catherine's legs scissored under the sheets. She whimpered. She flung an arm, hitting Sooze, who let out an unwoken wail. Sylvie pulled the child toward her, out of range, and reached a hand to touch her daughter's shoulder. Philosophies, sure: She who fails to save a life may yet save a moment.

AT THE FOOD BANK, Sylvie sorted soup to the soup bin, beans to the protein bin, dented cans to the box in the middle aisle. Mac and cheese had its very own container, as big as all the others. Next week Stan would be sorting too, later in the day after high school was out, putting in community service to work off his fine.

People did experiments where rats would press the reward lever over and over for a sweet treat until they died. Nothing was enough. Could a child inherit a craving disposition from two generations back? Was it fused right into the genes, the compulsion to take and take? At the food bank, Stan would discover he could pocket chocolate bars left and right, atone for his sins and repeat them all at once. The organization was there to supply people with real food, not candy, which never went into the food boxes but into a catchall the volunteers raided on their breaks.

Sylvie worked her way through a waist-high carton of food-stuffs, and there in the bottom rested a twenty-four-deck of beer. More accurately, it was a twenty-three-deck: someone had pilfered a single can and closed off that corner with a criss-cross of packing tape. She looked at the signs above the bins, as if, somewhere to the left of *Protein, Soup, Vegetables* and *Miscellaneous Dry,* she might find *Booze.* Dean, a volunteer who seemed always to be there — Sylvie suspected he often had fines to work off — stood close by puzzling out expiry dates on canned goods.

"What am I supposed to do with this?"

"What you got?" He bent at the waist and leaned close over the open carton in the way of a person who would be better off with glasses. "Yeah. They use it for gas."

"How's that?"

"Drain it. They get the deposit on the cans and use the money to fuel the van. Big sink in the back."

"Want one for your pocket first?"

He shook his head but not before a moment's hesitation during which he inspected and then reknotted the tie at the waist of his sweatpants.

The sink was two feet deep, two feet wide and four feet long. It had a slight, unfortunate tilt, with the drain at the higher end. Sylvie popped the tabs on two cans and held them upside down close to the drain. The beer foamed and swirled, a pesky trickle running off to the low end. Jack used to make beer. One night when he was out and she was alone in the basement suite she'd heard a bang, loud and close, and feared it was a gun going off out on the street. It spooked her, but she'd settled back in. Another shot, and she pulled her pyjama top tight around herself. The upstairs people were away in Regina at a football game. When she heard the third bang, it came to her that Jack's new batch of brew was exploding one bottle at a time in the laundry room. She wasn't about to peek in, risk a blast of slivered glass. She read her book and counted explosions, reporting thirteen to Jack when he got home around midnight.

Too much sugar, he said. The yeast had gone, as he put it, logarithmic. He was in the laundry room in his rain jacket and safety goggles till three, uncapping brew and pouring it down the floor drain, no doubt sliding his mouth over the bottle-tops to suck up the rise of foam. She could hear his laughter through the door. When he crawled into bed he was soaked inside and out in under-ripe beer. That had been the first time she'd left him to sleep on the couch. The slippery cushion she tried to use as a pillow kept sliding onto the living room floor, and she'd gone back to the bedroom to fetch her real pillow, found Jack hugging it and tried to slide it gently out of his grip. He held it close and mumbled into it, "Come on back, my sweet, sweet love, to your intrepid chemist."

"Not tonight, honey."

"But I'm full of yeast, and rising."

"You're full of something."

IN THE BACK ROOM Sylvie slid a can of beer into the left-hand pocket of her fleece vest. Its weight sent the vest off-kilter, and she slid another into the right-hand pocket for balance. She finished emptying the others and tossed them into the recycling bin. On her way out she slipped into the office of the warehouse manager, empty at the moment, and left a loonie on the corner of the desk to make up for the lost deposit on the cans she'd pocketed. She was no thief, anymore.

After Jack drowned, the throb of want that had always lived within her changed its nature and became an amorphous longing, not centred on things. It was no easier to tame than her earlier yearnings. Just as she'd never been able to satisfy herself with a liberated T-shirt when she was twenty-four, she couldn't satisfy herself by *not* taking one now; nor by volunteering with community theatre; nor by sitting at the big oak table in the library helping adults who'd never learned to read decipher prescription instructions or household bills or the provincial driving handbook. Nor by nor by nor by.

SOOZE WAS A WARM WEIGHT against her chest, her belly, her thighs as she leaned back in an armchair in what passed for a lobby at the Sleep Well. The ersatz leather chair was hardly meant for grandmothering in but Sylvie's own soft body, more ample with the years, made a comfy bed for a toddler's nap, Sooze's head on one slack breast and her small hand clutching the fabric above the other. Before sitting down, Sylvie had taken a complimentary newspaper from the stack on the check-in desk. She had it open now to the editorial page, folded back on itself and back yet again so she could hold it one-handed and read the letters to the editor Logan had been griping about.

I would like for those people from the flooded housing complex to stop their whining. My taxes subsidize that housing. If they would smarten up and stand on their own two feet, just maybe they'd find a better place to live.

So Logan had a point.

These people are sucking the system dry. Now we're putting them up in hotels. Hotels! They're on vacation at my expense and still they complain. God, I hate whiners!

God, Sylvie hated whiners. She let the newspaper drop to the floor. The best advice to Logan would be to stop reading the letters. Better yet, write his own:

Dear fellow taxpayer, I cannot go home. The housing you are so unhappy to subsidize — so that I can get a break so as to stand on my own two part-time jobs, neither of which I can go to since the daycare has flooded as well — that housing was built on low ground, unfit, and all the water that might otherwise flood your house, in these times of extreme weather events, has

257

flooded mine. Dear fellow taxpayer, my daughter is running at both ends, vomit and diarrhea for days now because she walked through sewer water to get to the bus to get to the hotel while I carried the baby. Dear fellow taxpayer, it is impossible to police a child's hands, pants, shoes, whathaveyou, enough to keep the germs from spreading. Dear —

Maybe don't bother. You had to laugh or else you'd cry.

Cradling the sleeping child, Sylvie walked her butt cheeks forward on the vinyl upholstery. Life with a little one, lurch, lurch. The friction raised rude noises from the vinyl, and she laughed. The clerk looked across the desk, his face backlit and bearing a slight scowl. Then he laughed too.

The corridor soccer game was once more in swing, pre-schoolers now. The ball rolled slowly along the carpet toward Sylvie. Holding the still-asleep Sooze close to her chest, she bent forward and kicked it gently toward an eager, black-haired girl in a pink T-shirt that said *Playgirl* in silver glitter. The little Playgirl wound up and kicked hard, her straight black hair swinging forward with her effort. The ball smacked into Sooze's head.

Searching inside the freezer of the itty bitty fridge as little Sooze screamed and screamed, Sylvie found a single, empty ice cube tray underneath the Pop-Tarts. The bump above Sooze's temple rose. Ice bucket, where? She grabbed a cereal bowl, opened the door and shouted, "Stop with that soccer ball! Hear me?" She made for the ice machine, the child hot and screaming in her arms. The ice cubes melted in Sylvie's fingers, melted into Sooze's hair. A trickle ran into her ear. Water ran down Sylvie's wrist and streamed along her forearm inside her sleeve.

SHE WASN'T LIFESAVER MATERIAL, hardly kept her own head above water, but any one of the others horsing around in the water might have managed it, would have, surely, if Sylvie had shouted, "Help him! He can't swim!"

To Jack's funeral she'd worn an A-line shift, pale green, that she'd chosen because among all her home-sewn wardrobe it was the item with a cut generous enough to hang loose over her thickening belly. The colour was inappropriate for the occasion, but that was Sylvie for you, or so she was certain she heard Margo whisper to Penny over tea and dainties in the church annex. You had to wonder about Sylvie, didn't you?

Yes, you did. Uncertain guilt leaves a person up for grabs. She could be this, she could be that. Had she willed things to come to a bad end? The truth was, she didn't remember exactly the events of the afternoon — Alex tossing Jack off the dock in what he assumed was harmless play, what she herself tried or hadn't tried to shout to the others, what she might have wished for in whatever inner reach.

The uneasy dreams were with her almost nightly now, never to do with the day at the lake, always to do with finding herself unready, inadequate. They spun a mist of anxiety that circled the rim of her consciousness through the day. What did they serve, that they wouldn't go away? How would they help her daughter, her grandkids? How would they help Jack? The years had taught Sylvie a strategy: lose herself in something, anything, whatever might be handy at the time. It hardly worked and it hardly worked for long, but it was a relief, of sorts. Thus, the pageant. But leading the children through rhymes and fairy tales had failed, so far, to conjure the magic.

LOGAN'S DAUGHTER DESIRÉE left the stage leading her herd of seven sheep, who shuffled on all fours, the oversized white shirts that served as costumes hanging low under their bellies, shirttails draping their little bums. Sylvie the clown took up her mic. "That marks the end. Or" — she made a show of counting the receding bottoms — "that makes seven ends."

Could someone please laugh? So many faces out there expecting more from her, the little ones on the floor up front, the grown-ups and the older kids behind, looking imprisoned in their rows of chairs. James was off in the wings, sheep milling around him behind a portable room divider. The full-grown man skipping on as Red Riding Hood singing *tra-la* had been the one gag that earned an unforced laugh. As resident clown, was Sylvie now supposed to come up with an appropriate truth, as James had suggested the other day?

Everyone in the room had already swallowed an overdose of truth. Even the children — the adorable little ones in their fairy tale costumes, the older ones with their practised readings — had taken the occasion too seriously, every gesture hesitant, and even wearing this pinchy damn red bulb on her nose Sylvie had coaxed only a trickle or two of laughter from all the tight throats out there.

She gestured toward the room divider. "Let's get our do-gooder out here."

James came out to a scatter of applause, and bowed. He'd taken off his hoodie and put on one of the big white shirts. "Feeling kind of sheepish," he said. So easily, he could call forth laughter. He made for the wings again, but Sylvie grabbed his arm.

"I need a volunteer. You're one of those, aren't you? We're going to have a wheelbarrow race." She took off her red nose and held it high like a badge of authority. "Yes, everyone! Not just the little ones." A vivid image of Jack flashed through her mind: sunburned in his swim trunks, clapping out a beat, playing emcee and coaxing their lolling friends onto the dock to dance the Hustle. "Everyone!" She clipped her nose back on, adjusted it to minimize the pinch. "And you, James, will help me organize it. See all that empty space at the back?"

The younger kids were up already and scrambling over each other, but the grown-ups and teenagers shifted in their chairs. Fine for the children, said their bent heads, their thigh-tapping hands, but I'll stay put. The kids paired off and made themselves into human wheelbarrows without urging or instruction, the kid in back holding up the ankles of the one in front while the forward end of the barrow hand-walked across the room. They started across the carpet, not a race but a free-for-all. They collapsed and recovered, laughing so hard Sylvie was sure some had peed their pants already. She implored her own Catherine with a look, Logan as well, and Stan. Logan lifted his baseball cap and resettled it. Catherine looked at her lap. Others in the audience performed variations on those same gestures. Oh, my girl, my heart, if you knew your father's talent for getting folks to loosen their lacings, for a moment at least.

Well, she wouldn't plead. They could be their own worst enemies. She made for the back of the room, where the kids were falling over each other, and James followed close behind. His arms in their white shirtsleeves, cuffs undone and flopping, came from behind and grabbed her around the waist. He pulled back and she swung forward, and before she knew it he'd lifted her parallel to the floor, so that she landed on all fours when he lowered her. She planted her hands, felt her knees touch down. He took hold of her ankles, and her weight shifted as he lifted her legs off the carpet. She slapped a hand forward, fast, so she wouldn't fall on her face.

Laughing, sucking a string of drool back in through her lips, Sylvie walked forward with her hands, James following, holding her ankles, letting her set the pace. The posture tipped her forward, and she fought the feeling she might land on her forehead. They skirted the mêlée of raucous children, heading back toward the rows of reluctant adults solid in their seats. The carpet's pattern of whirls dizzied her, and she bent her neck to look up, toward the people she wanted to shake loose. She saw their shifting expressions as she and James barreled toward them — embarrassment, laughter, resistance. One skinny woman wore the face a person makes when someone close by has let one rip. Forget it, let them sit. The kids are having a whale of a time. They were always the best reason to go to this trouble anyway.

Looking up was a strain. She needed to swallow and could only manage a choke. She lowered her head again, reaching further with each step of her hands. James was slower to change pace, and she felt the drag on her legs. Then he sped up and her elbow buckled and she fell, laughing. A pain shot through her shoulder and then it was gone. James lurched and landed heavily on top of her. She felt her bladder let go, relief both sweet and searing. Heat rose to her face, and sweat trickled into an eye. Oh, she could make her own window mask now, like the one Stan had made, couldn't she? — a grimace you could read anything into, stretched across the pane. She could be this, she could be that. A person really can laugh and cry at the same time. Maybe once she stood up and all those stifled folks saw the places where the wet had deepened the colours on her clown pants, maybe something would let loose inside them, too. Her red nose had come off in the fall, and it rolled across the carpet. A little dark-haired girl wearing a baggy white sheep shirt scooped it up and peered inside. In just a moment Sylvie would stand up and make her way over and show her how to put it on.

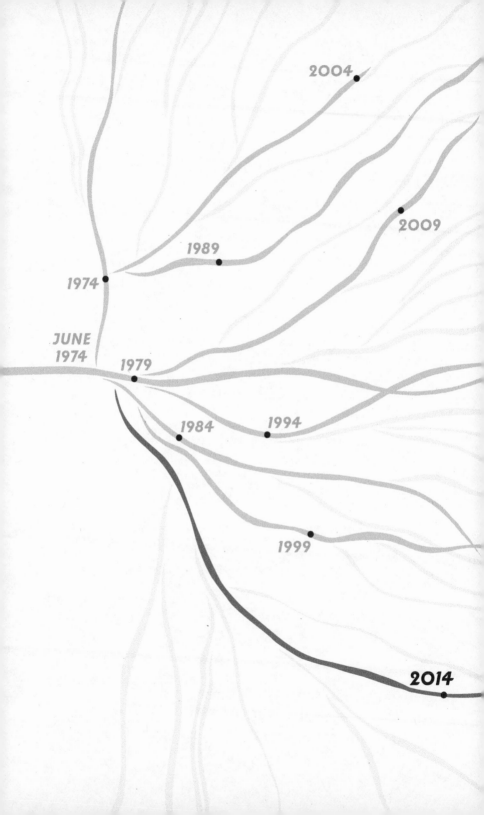

Blueberry Hill

SPEEDING DOWN the wickedest stretch of Blueberry Hill their skis scrape through yesterday's two fresh centimetres of snow to a layer of week-old ice. "Stay loose!" Syl shouts ahead. "Stay low, use your edges!" It's all she can do to keep from falling, and she's no novice on cross-country skis. Lolly, well, she's just audacious. Syl's lost sight of the girl in her bright yellow jacket. There's a final long turn to negotiate before the grade will level out. Rain should not fall at this altitude in the Rockies at this time of year, or not in the amount it fell last week. A "rain-on-snow event" is the term she and the others on the research crew use. The new normal, Brian is fond of saying, is that when it comes to weather there's no such thing as normal. He's the expert, the lead scientist.

Syl manages the treacherous turn and there's Lolly, stepped to one side of the track and waiting.

"Relax, Granny S."

The other two grandmas, Lolly's grandmothers by blood, are Gran and Nan. Syl would have preferred her plain first name, but never mind, just don't break some part of yourself on this hill, precious girl.

To calm her jittery knees she snaps out of her bindings, stretches one leg and then the other, knocks the snow off her boots and snaps back in. She could wallop her fellow grad student Kirby, who said, "Take her up Blueberry, she'll love it! Stop somewhere on the way down, listen to the birds."

"What sort of birds?"

"Dunno. The sort that sing."

Syl doesn't hear birdsong as well as she used to. "Lolly, do you hear birds?"

"Yeah, I guess."

"What sort?"

"Dunno."

"The sort that sing?"

EARLY MORNING, and it's time to get out there. Don't keep the reporter waiting in the cold. Syl dresses in the dark so as not to wake Lolly. She hopes this guy won't be a nuisance. None of them make the climb to the Petrina Ridge sites alone, they buddy up, but yesterday Brian asked if she'd be all right with a different sort of buddy. Could she take this person from the newspaper along? It'll be good for the project, he said. Probably some cub making his newsman's bones at the local weekly. Well, he'd better be fit. These mountains will lob something new at you on any given day. Up on the slopes you're only as strong as your weakest link. *Your leakest wink,* her first husband used to say. With a wink.

Last year's floods were catastrophic, and now TV and the

papers and the news blogs want to know what Syl and the others on Brian's team hope to accomplish with their high-altitude weather stations, their windspeeds, their sounding of snow.

Groping through a drawer in the dark to find her socks, Syl stubs her toe on the dresser. "Shit!"

Lolly stirs.

"Sorry." A whisper. The young, so vulnerable with their defenses given over to sleep. Last night Syl came in late from revisiting the lab after supper. Getting undressed in the wedge of light from the main room, watching the girl breathing through open lips, she thought what a child she looked, closer to eleven than fourteen. She remembers her own Adam at that age, fatherless, breakable, how many times she risked waking him because she couldn't stop herself from tucking his long hair behind his ear and setting a wrist to his forehead to feel for health or fever. Adam's daughter Em, an indoors girl with drama club commitments and a burning need for down-time to balance the drama, showed no interest in the fact that her grandmother was living in a motel suite near the mountains for three months. Lolly, however, begged to come for the week of her high school break.

"I can look after myself when you're busy. Promise and hope to die." Lolly's mom and dad, Steven's daughter and her husband, are on a beach in Costa Rica this week trying to reheat their marriage.

"I love you to pieces. Of course you can come."

She eases the bedroom door shut, flicks on the light in the larger room, hears the first hollow sputter of the coffee pot and catches the wake-up smell of it. She eats porridge, toast, an egg. A person needs a strong start for such a day. Into her backpack she stows a thermos of hot broth, two peanut butter sandwiches, granola bars, toolkit, and a down jacket stuffed into a compression sack. Laptop at the back. First aid kit, check. She straps her snowshoes to either side of the pack. Steven was the one who taught her to snowshoe, their first vacation together, Christmas fifteen years ago.

"You know how to show a woman a good time," she said, laughing as she changed her blister pads at the end of the first day.

"You'll find," he said, "I'm not one for engine-powered amusements. I'm more about hiking boots, sails, pedals. Human locomotions."

"I can get used to that." Neither she nor he referred in that moment to the obvious — that it was a fast night ride on a snowmobile that killed her first husband — but the knowledge freighted their silence as she gathered up her socks.

HER BLACK TOQUE isn't on the hook, so she borrows one of Lolly's, pale blue with a dance of yellow snowflakes around the band, and snugs it over her short hair. Funny how wearing a young girl's hat can make a person feel she's shed ten years. One last pee and out the door, poles in hand. The reporter's there ahead of her, waiting at the trailhead. It isn't yet light, but she can see that the hair that curls out from under his toque is grey. He must be as old as she is, older even. Trim enough, though.

"I'm Syl." She shakes his hand.

270

"I'm Robin. Hi."

"Does your editor often send you on day-long, back-country treks?"

"Just this once, so far." His teeth are white in the dimness, a confident smile.

"It's no walk in the park, this." She settles her headlamp over her hat and clicks it on.

"I expect not."

The start of the trail is a noisy crunch over a few metres of wet gravel with dirty patches of snow that last week's rain didn't finish off. Syl's hiking boots are well seasoned but his show years' more wear. "Old dogs," he says. "Faithful." Up a short, pebbly slope and they're into more snow, slidey, like porridge underfoot. Very soon the cover deepens. When they stop to strap on snowshoes Robin's quick into his bindings, she'll grant him that. Syl leads, setting a good pace as they enter the forest, headlamps lighting the way, their route a white path through spruce and bony winter larch.

"I like your snowflakes." The closeness of his voice behind her is startling. So he's having no trouble keeping up.

"Oh, the toque. Thanks."

"I'll take these trails in winter over summer any day, wouldn't you? The sound of the shoes."

"It's a good sound."

They say little for the next hour, their effort spent on advancing one foot ahead of the other. It's comfortable, their silence. Robin keeps pace, stopping occasionally to take a photo as the sun lights the tops of the trees. He closes the distance afterward without difficulty. Realizing she's been testing him at her own expense, not pacing herself for the distance yet to come, Syl relaxes. She turns to wait as he catches up after one of his pauses. He's a natural, with a flowing stride she'll never master.

"I see you're no amateur."

He smiles. "I've lived in one set of mountains or another all my life."

Now comes the toughest stretch, switchback after switchback to make the ascent manageable, but still it's a test. Syl and the other grad students have christened this bit the TFS, Too Fucking Steep. They still say that, but they don't mean it any more. It's a wonder what training will do. Once past the TFS they're into fresh snow, deep and unexpected. Syl sinks halfway to her knees with every step.

Behind her Robin says, "I can go first, break trail."

She shrugs, physically shedding his offer. "There's no need."

"Of course."

She turns to look at him.

"Sorry." His white teeth again, a nicely lopsided smile. "My father's idea of what makes a gentleman still travels with me."

"No problem."

The look they've exchanged leaves her unsteady, and she pulls an antidote to mind, an image of Steven back in Saskatoon, tending home fires. Taking advantage of temporary bachelorhood, keeping the heated garage lit late into the night while he works on his wooden sailboat, his two-person Enterprise, gouging out dry-rot and mixing resin and hardener with filler to patch the wounds; drawing down over an evening in his measured way on two scant fingers of premium scotch.

Syl pounds out a path, covering a respectable distance before stopping. "Let's take five." The forest is still. The spruce boughs are laden. White scarves of snow, long and soft, lie on the fallen logs to either side of the trail. The silence is as thick as the snow. "Listen."

"Yes."

She begins again, one step, another, another. Just when she's about to suggest taking turns after all, the depth lessens. The band of fresh snow's behind them, as if it was the work of a single cloud crossing through on its way to town. Syl and Robin have breath enough for conversation. He begins to ask his reporter's questions about last year's floods, about weather patterns and predictions of long-term drought. Having become something of an evangelist studying under Brian for the past two years, Syl has plenty to say. The days for debating climate change are years past. It's here, and has been for some time now. The proper question, she tells Robin, is how to cope. She gives him facts, figures, guesses about when the dry times will arrive on the plains.

"You bring a lot of energy to your work."

"So do you."

THEY'VE BEEN OUT more than three hours by the time they reach the first station, a tall, three-sided metal skeleton that resembles an obelisk in shape though not in mass, anchored to the mountain not far above the treeline. She and Robin exchange a smile of congratulations. He slips his thermos free of its webbing. "Tea?"

"Thanks, no." Syl shucks her pack, sets it at the station's

273

base, and immediately feels the chill on her back in the place where it rested. Standing on tiptoe she checks a gauge. Minus twenty. Humidity forty percent. The body cools fast up here, the sweat from the climb a wet liability. Wicking fabric, sure, but there's a rivulet of sweat running down her spine and a trickle between her breasts. She faces away from Robin, strips to her sports bra and, covered in goose flesh, pulls on the fresh base layer she carried up in a warm inside pocket of her jacket. Now her soft-shell again, and now the down jacket from her pack. The grad students change in front of each other all the time, and Syl, older by decades than the others and not plagued with all they have at stake in the realms of appearance and competition, has felt separate and not even that embarrassed, for they do not look her way. They could be her grandchildren, she's told herself, and don't they know it. But now here's Robin. She's proud her body's fit, but still she's aware of the way the skin on her back creases above the waist no matter how slim she is, how muscled. She turns to see him facing the other way and putting on a layer of down as well.

"So." He turns and zips his jacket. "This is the measuring gear, all this?"

Syl nods. "We measure snow, rain, wind. We look up the mountain and down the valley and, based on all these observations, we make our best guess of what we'll have on our hands come April. Come May, June." With bare fingers she fishes for the safety clip sewn into her pocket and frees the key to the metal cabinet that houses the datalogger.

"The floods in Calgary," he says. "Whole neighbourhoods underwater. People want to know what they're in for this year."

"Of course. Yes." She unlocks the cabinet. "We need the best numbers we can gather." Her hand trembles a little as she opens the laptop she carried up, connects it by cable to the datalogger and starts the download. The best thing is to keep talking. She doesn't look at Robin directly. "That's why all this new equipment. So we can say to the folks in their spanking new houses that should never have been built in such a place, Watch out, people, the flood plain is going to, um, *flood*."

"I see you've thought about this."

Now she does look at him. "It's my job."

"Sorry again."

"Never mind. We all have preconceptions. I do."

He picks up his thermos again, opens it. "Tea now?"

"Not fond of tea. Thanks." She wishes maybe she were. He holds the steaming thermos lid under his chin a moment, eyes not quite closed, and she can see this small performance even though she's turned to check her laptop.

But Steven. She visited him one evening in the garage, his sailboat overturned on blanketed sawhorses. He was using a small rectangle of beveled wood to press a gooey compound into a gash in the hull. Under the light from the unshaded ceiling bulb, the wedge of his brow cast shadows over his deep-set eyes.

"Fairing," he said. "Isn't that just the perfect word for this?" He alternately pressed the filler into the gash and then scraped it flush with the hull, pushed and scraped. He took great care, and she could see the honest pleasure in the slow motion of his wrist.

"Faring?" she said, thinking it was a word well suited for something to do with a boat, but hard to make sense of. "Like seafaring?"

"No, silly, *fairing*. Making it fair to look at, to touch."

"It *is* the perfect word."

ROBIN SNAPS A PHOTO of the open cabinet. "What does that give you?"

"Soil temperature, soil moisture, snow temperature. Ultrasonic measures of snow depth."

He leans in closer to look at the nest of wires and cables. His breath warms her cheek.

"You didn't say it was chai you had in that thermos."

When he shifts away, the warm scent of spices leaves with him, all but a hint of vapour. She straightens and points. "The cylinder hanging over there sends a chirp down through the snow and counts the time before it bounces back up. And those are radiometers. I'll give you an info sheet once we're back down."

He follows along as she cuts and weighs core samples, his camera busy but not intrusive, focused on her gloved hands, her tools. He shoots another photo of the datalogger, then does a slow half-turn. "What a view." He steps back for a long shot of the station. "Say cheese." Rather than look into the camera, and aware that she's posing, Syl looks up at the lines of the aluminum frame against the clear sky, a stark and striking geometry.

"Found art," Robin says.

She nods. "We have to move on, though." She sets her gloves and her sunglasses on top of the cabinet and bends to organize her pack. Finally, she checks that the cabinet is well latched and locked. Her fingers are cold and not so steady. The key slides out of her grip and into the snowbank, slicing its way in near a guy wire, leaving only a tiny slit of shadow to show its track. "Damn!" The surface of the snow blasts her with white light. A sudden, sharp ache in her eyes, and she shuts them tight, feeling for the key with an ungloved hand. Snow bites her wrist. Damn, where is it?

"Let me know if I can help."

"Got it." Eyes still closed, she fishes in her pocket for the safety fob and clips the key onto it. She feels an unexpected touch at her temples, and her nerves jump. Robin is gently sliding the arms of her sunglasses back through her hair, settling them in place. Her hands are freezing. She reaches for her gloves.

"Wait, Syl, let me." Her own name sounds new to her, longer than its three letters, almost musical. He sets his gloves on top of hers on the cabinet and takes her hands between his warm palms. She begins to pull back, a reflex, but then she relaxes. It's a comfort the way his skin draws the cold burn off her knuckles.

"Better?"

"Yes. Good of you." She pulls out of his hands. "So."

"So."

"We need to get going."

They visit two more stations close by. At the last, standing in the snow, they wolf down a sandwich each with their gloves still on, laughing at the awkwardness. He touches his tongue to a glove to pick off a last crumb. She does the same and they giggle like kids. A drink of tea, a drink of broth to warm their insides, and they start back down. Her movements are steady but inside she quivers. Her skin underneath her clothing feels awake in a way it hasn't since she can't remember when, not only in the warm and wet places, but everywhere — where her sleeves hug her biceps, where her socks encircle her ankles, where her pants glide over her long johns as she takes a step.

Once back on the gentle grade that follows the steeper descent, she asks, "Have I answered your questions, then?"

"I'd love a single sentence to tell the people what the end result of all this data gathering will be."

"As I said. We're refining models that help us understand the physics of snow and make predictions about water events. What will happen in the spring. Trends over time. The possibility of drought."

"But in a sentence."

"You're the writer." She means to open a distance with that remark, so it surprises her to understand, once she's said it, that it sounded flirtatious.

"Fair enough. And what about you. What's your story, Syl?"

"I have any number of stories. I'm not sure they'd be much help to you." She smiles at him over her shoulder. "In terms of your article."

THE STORY OF THE PRESENT is Steven. Faring, fairing, fairness. A man committed to doing what's right. Last summer he put in four weeks of unpaid consulting for a small contractor keen on rammed-earth construction and the optimal angle for solar panels in latitudes above fifty degrees north. If it weren't for Steven's support she might not be on this mountain trail. It's he who's taught her the most important things in life. The value of hope. Lasting love. The rewards of good work. Sometimes it's hard to measure up.

Vows. Do you take this man? I do, yes. And this one, and?

THE STORY FROM LONG AGO is Erik. Syl was twenty-two, their son Adam toddling toward his second birthday one tantrum at a time, and Erik had his duffel bag packed for yet another weekend of snowmobiling out in Ripley.

"You can't leave me alone with a cranky kid all weekend."

Adam banged a yellow dump truck on the fake wood of the coffee table again and again.

"That's twice this month."

"But the snow's going, babe."

"So's my sanity."

"Just one night, then."

Teetering at the edge of her own tantrum, Syl stamped her foot three times, much the way Adam had done a day earlier when she'd tried to scoop him back into his stroller at the mall. "Will you look at your kid?!"

Adam let go of his truck and it clattered on the tabletop. "Stop Mommy, please."

It was his very first sentence. His parents knelt on either side of him. Erik patted his back and Syl kissed his light brown curls. Erik tickled his neck. "Congratulations, my son!"

Adam laughed.

"That's one for the baby book."

"You know what, Erik?"

"Mmm?"

"You go ahead."

"Are you sure?"

"Yeah, the snow's going. We'll be fine."

On Saturday night he stayed later than the others at the Ripley bar. At closing time he mounted a borrowed snowmobile and went roaring along snow-filled country ditches on the way to his brother's farm, a route he knew well. Whether disarmed by its familiarity or by too many beer in quick succession, he crashed into the rise where the side road to old Gary Panchuck's place joined the main road. He flew off and landed on a rock pile.

Not long after, Syl moved from Saskatoon back to Ripley. Both her parents were buried by then, but Uncle Davis invited her in to help around the farmstead. Room and board, salary too. They put up with each other, Syl, Adam, and Uncle Davis, shouting and laughing in love and exasperation, for over a year. *Room and bored,* she told her sister one Saturday morning as she poured coffee and Baileys. A few weeks later over Sunday pancakes and bacon, Davis, who'd done a vocational certificate at the College of Agriculture as a returning veteran in the forties, said, "If you were thinking of university, something along those lines, dear, I would help."

Syl had not been thinking along those lines. She hardly knew anyone who'd even been to tech, let alone university. Higher education wasn't a common destiny for graduates of Ripley High.

"The College of Ag, Sylvia, that's the place. There's no healthier industry in the province. Diversification, good crops year after year. If you could find it in yourself to do an Ag degree, you with such good marks as a kid, I would stand you the tuition."

"*Pfft.* Me a farmer."

"Oh, honey, no. I'm talking about those other jobs. I'm saying study animals, study soil, study genes and breed a new strain of wheat. Professional type."

"But there's Adam."

"I'll pay for daycare." He spread his arms to gesture at the square farm kitchen, and it seemed he meant to indicate much more, for he said, "I've got no kids of my own. Do you have any idea what this place is worth?"

"No, Uncle Davis. No, I don't."

She majored in soil science, led there by her childhood fascination, long hours crouched in the vegetable patch doing a kid's experiments: the run of soil through her hands, the rivers of movement she could create by scooping together a hill of dirt and then starting a flow with a finger. The way she could change the course of that free-running river of dirt by setting a stone here, wiggling a twig there. At school she discovered the flow that's truly of interest to a soil scientist is not that of dirt but of water. She grew to love that, too. Studying felt good, the way it had in early high school before she'd grown more interested in back roads at night, a cold beer, a hot joint. In the course of her four years of study in Saskatoon, the ag boom went bust. She graduated *cum laude* with what she called her dirt degree and never landed a job in her field. She parlayed her volunteer shift at Adam's grade two classroom into a position as a teacher's aid and bounced for years from school to school. At forty-four she married Steven Martins, architect for the renovations at her current school, and took early retirement at fifty.

"Congratulations," Steven said when he toasted her at the goodbye gathering in the school gymnasium. "I predict you'll be bored." She remembered trying to guess at hidden meanings. He was, she suspected, voicing an expectation and hoping she'd live up to it.

She tells Robin hardly any of this on the way down the mountain. What she does tell him is that retirement suited her, until it didn't. Until she read too many in-depth articles in *Harper's* and *The Walrus* and *Maclean's* and couldn't stop thinking how the world would look by the time her own grand-daughter and Lolly got to be her age. And so she's once again a student and once again preoccupied with water. Water is where the questions most in need of answers are in Western Canada. "You can't live here and ignore it."

They reach a break in the trees, Robin leading now. His movements on the descent over the snow are fluid, sinuous, while Syl does a less speedy but competent sidestep, mindful of her thinning bones, using her poles to steady herself. Time and experience have quelled the fear of falling that dogged her as a young woman, an internal lurch at the crest of a hill or the top of a flight of stairs. Her caution now has more to do with the practical fact a broken arm or ankle could set her research back months.

"Well done," Robin says when she catches up.

"And you, you're like a cat."

"It's just I've more experience."

Syl heads toward a piece of deadfall, bench height, at the edge of the clearing. They brush away snow and sit. To avoid meeting Robin's eyes, Syl takes a long time finding her second sandwich in her pack. "What are you looking at?"

"Nothing. Just, I thought I'd be making this trek with a graduate student."

"Which I am."

"Just, you aren't what I expected."

"Likewise, cub reporter."

"That's *mister* cub reporter."

Syl shapes a tiny snowball and throws it soft against his cheek. There's nothing to it, a spray of melt. If she were to raise her hand and wipe it away for him, she would feel the beginnings of afternoon stubble that show more salt than pepper in the sunlight.

He brushes his face lightly with a glove, in no hurry, and says, apparently to the sky, "Truly, what a rare day. We could have run into any kind of weather."

Syl looks up. A feathering jet streak softens the blue. She thinks of the passenger flight that went missing a week ago. "That lost plane. There's nothing yet, not a trace."

Robin bends toward his pack to pull his thermos free of its webbing, and when he resettles he's closer to Syl than before. "All those souls."

"The people on board — that's who I thought about, too, when it happened. But it's the families I think of now. Waiting for the worst." She's glad he's moved closer. "Not certain, but certain. Not knowing why or how."

"And here we are. The lucky ones. In near paradise."

"A compromised paradise."

"Granted."

BACK ON THE TRAIL Robin continues with his questions, less about her work and more about Syl the person. She makes sure to refer to Steven in several of her answers. She mentions Lolly, wonderful girl. She mustn't be late, for she's promised to take her out for pizza.

When it's time to take their snowshoes off they crouch side by side and take turns, using each other as props at wobbly moments.

"What was it drew you to this research?"

She's glad he didn't add "at this stage of life." "A person has to *do* something. This is what I can do." And it beats Netflix binges with a pan of apple cake on the end table.

"I admire you for it."

"I don't know. We're greedy creatures, human beings. I'm as bad as anyone." She's talking too much. She meets his look. "This article you're writing, I hope you're not turning it into 'Sylvia Salverson-Martins, graduate student at fifty-nine.' Aren't you supposed to be writing about the science, the climate modeling, the dire straits?"

"You have to add the human side."

She sees how filaments of green run through his brown eyes close to the iris. I will not let this in, she thinks.

On the final shallow grade before the pebbly slope above the parking lot, Syl puts her poles to good use while Robin, ahead of her, does without. He turns to look over his shoulder. "Honestly, then: let's say I'm getting to know you because I wan —"

— and he's tumbling.

Syl feels that old lurch of fear inside. "Oh!"

His pack stops him from rolling far, and he manages to sit. "Talk about clumsy!" His pants and his long johns are torn, his knee skinned, blood trickling.

She's beside him, poles on the ground. "You're all right?"

"Of course I'm all right. I feel like a bloody fool."

Syl pulls out her first aid kit.

"Really, you don't need to bother with that."

She considers the hole in his long johns and uses her scissors to widen it.

He puts a hand over hers. "It's fine."

She slips her hand away and finds the Poly-To-Go in her kit. "Bear with me."

"Syl, can you meet me later? After pizza with your granddaughter. Tie up some loose ends?"

"Hold on now." She triggers the spray. Antiseptic trickles across his broken skin, and he winces. "Stings a little, I know," she says, swabbing, "but it numbs in a second or two."

"Syl?"

"I'll have to see when I can manage it." Let it settle. She'll be here another month gathering data on the mountain, running it through computers, wrestling with refinements to her model. Long enough to take the measure of this man. Long enough to take her own.

Before she and little Adam drove off to Saskatoon to start anew, the old boat of a Meteor packed to the roof and riding low on the road, her sister had hosted a goodbye lunch with everyone Syl still had within reach for family: Mavis and her husband with little Chad and baby Kayla, Aunt Merry from their dad's side and Uncle Davis from their mom's, all there to wish them well. "Go now," Aunt Merry said as she gave her a final hug. "Go and find yourself. Is that what you kids say?"

Syl slides her fingers inside the hole at Robin's knee and fixes a gauze pad over the wound, feeling the warmth of his skin as she presses the edges of the tape. "I'll be in touch."

SYL AND LOLLY have watched an episode from the boxed set of *Gilmore Girls* that came with the motel suite; Lolly's conquered the KenKen in today's *Globe* and four Sudoku on her phone and texted three girlfriends and one boyfriend. Now they're reading side by side in bed like old marrieds.

Lolly sets *The Hunger Games* face down on the duvet. "Granny S?"

"Yes, Loll?"

"I want to study water too. Like you."

"That's terrific." Oh, to know so early what you want to be when you grow up. "Maybe I can help you get started."

"Not your kind of water, Granny, no offence. I'll do oceans."

"Ah. Good choice."

"I read in the paper about that search."

"The lost plane?"

"They say the wreckage — if, you know, if they ever find it — they say it'll be scattered maybe in the Indian Ocean. Or maybe way, way south, far away from anywhere, even Australia."

"Those poor families."

"Yeah no, but it's so interesting, Granny S. The currents down there are totally iffy. And even if they find one piece of something, it doesn't mean they'll find anything else. They give this example, like if you had two things, like a purse and a backpack that belonged to the very same passenger, and they fall into that ocean, they'd be separated right away. By the time they get waterlogged and sink, they wind up hundreds of kilometres apart. Even if they start out exactly side by side."

"I can see how that could make a girl want to study oceans."

"Know what I'd do if I was at a university like you? I'd go there in a helicopter and drop a couple of, I don't know, kayaks on the water and I'd watch what happens. How far they get from each other how fast."

Syl doesn't tell her that universities don't write blank cheques. She doesn't tell her that in the real world of science the fascination and the beauty are wonderful and welcome, but grunt work is your life. She certainly doesn't tell her that she has the same questions about life that Lolly has about the sea. You could be swept into a current and find yourself miles from where you left your backpack. Your pack and whatever of yourself you'd stowed inside it.

"Something like that."

"What's that, Granny S?"

"Lolly, that would be a fascinating thing to work on."

OVER SKYPE a couple of nights later she tells Steven, "Lolly wants to ski Blueberry again."

"That's great. She aced it the other day, you said."

"But that under-layer of ice. I —"

"There's new snow again, you said."

"Here and there, but hardly at all on Blueberry."

"Lolly's the kind of kid that needs a challenge." He gives her his most winning expression, the slight tilt of his head, crinkles at the corners of his pale blue eyes, and the curve of mouth that manages to transmit both understanding and expectation. "And she's a natural athlete."

It's settled then.

"Goodbye, sweet," he says.

"You're my perfect man, man," says Syl, a rush to get that in before he disappears.

"And you," he says, with some surprise, "you're my perfect woman," sounding reflexive, but she knows he means it.

TWO YEARS AGO, when Syl sat in Brian's office at the university lobbying him to take her on as a graduate student, Brian had held his reading glasses between thumb and forefinger, swinging them so they tapped the inside of his arm repeatedly. She would later come to know this as body language for "you must be joking."

"Your degree is three decades old, and it's in soils, not hydrology, and you want me to find a spot for you."

She gestured toward his computer screen where he'd called up their correspondence.

He said, "Suppose I ask you one final question, then, and your answer will settle mine."

"I'm ready."

"What was your mark in first-year physics?"

"Ninety."

He folded his glasses and set them on his desk. "I'm always looking for talent. File your application. Maybe we can catch you up."

When she presented her good news that evening Steven made a run to the liquor vendor close to home and returned with an approximation of champagne. "I was rooting for you all the way, sweet. Something to get your teeth into." He poured a scant two ounces each and handed her a flute. "Congratulations. You're my perfect woman, woman."

SHE ISN'T CERTAIN about taking Lolly back to Blueberry. Steven isn't here, he doesn't know the conditions. It's more than that. It still surprises her sometimes, the things he doesn't get, and maybe it's the same in the other direction. You have to move out of each other's way. He spends whole mornings rustling up someone to crew for him in his two-person Enterprise, for Syl has tried and failed to love sailing with him. It is, after all, his boat, and when you have a main and a jib and a rudder in play, one of you has got to be the boss, and always it must be him, and, frankly, Syl has a more natural feel for the physics of it than he ever will. That, and the damn Enterprise has a faulty gasket around the centreboard and when she's out there with him she's the one who bails and bails.

"Is this supposed to be fun? All those hours with your epoxy and your shiny wooden finish, but what about where the water gets in?"

"Heaven's *sake*, Syl, don't stop. Look, already."

"Fuck's *sake*, Steven, promise me I'll never have to get in this rig again."

DOZENS OF SKIERS have been over this hill already today, plowing the thin skiff of new snow to the sides, leaving ice exposed. There's no stopping to rest on the steeper grades. Lolly and Syl score their way up herringbone style, Syl coaching herself silently the way Steven taught her, One more step, one more, one more, pressing her weight forward over the insides of her skis. Seven coats of wax in the kick. Every time they ascend an especially challenging stretch her thought is, We'll have to get back down somehow.

"She's a natural athlete," Steven said last night. That's true. They crest another rise and step off the track to rest. Around the bend above comes a skier in a careful descent. He plows to a stop and raises his iridescent sun-shield. Robin.

"Good day! Think twice before you go further."

"Yeah?"

"There's still that final slope. If I'd known how dicey coming down would be, I wouldn't have gone up. And I do this hill twice a week."

"I'm sure you do," she says. "After all, you've lived in one set or another of mountains all —"

" — all my life, yes."

They laugh, and Lolly looks from one to the other.

"Sorry," says Syl. "Robin, Lolly."

She's spent time with him twice now since their climb to the stations, once for lunch and once for drinks in the evening while Lolly was at the pool. She's learned he's in semi-retirement, left the editor's chair two years ago; that he's been divorced now seven years; no children. They've heard by this time a few of each other's stories, the content less important than the ease of the telling and receiving, the accidental bumping of knees or elbows or shoes. Something about his manner of speech after a couple of beers feels comfortingly familiar, as if he grew up in a small town and never quite left it behind.

"Sure, yeah, Coleman," Robin said the other night. "Not so awful far from here. I drove down a couple of weeks ago and went snowmobiling with my brother. Yeah. The speed." Was he sheepish about that reference to speed, or proud of it?

Both, she decided. He described his brother's new tattoo of a banana eating a monkey, and she burst into loud giggles and teared up. He took her hand and held it tight. "Settle down," he joked, trying to keep a straight face. He kissed her knuckles as if this were the usual first aid for someone laughing too hard. The giggles travelled through her hand and into him and soon it was the two of them wiping tears and reaching over to wipe each other's.

His phone buzzed then, and he checked it and looked up in apology. "I'm sorry, dear Syl. Work. A cub reporter needs me." He looked directly into her eyes for a quick moment. "We'll do this again, yes?"

"Yes." She watched him wind away through the crowded bar. Chilly, she pulled her fleece close around herself. She felt something she couldn't name leaving her, a twisting filament that followed him toward the door. He knows that's happening, she thought.

ROBIN LIFTS ONE of his ski poles and sets it down so the tip lands close to the tip of Syl's. Hello on the snow. She feels Lolly's eyes on her, on Robin. Lolly stamps her skis, her yellow jacket bright against the forest. Syl squints toward the bend that Robin came around.

"Don't be scared, Granny S."

"Thanks for the read on that," Syl says to Robin by way of goodbye. Not that she wants to be rid of him; she wants to coax another laugh; she wants to tap his ski pole with her own and hear the click. We just *clicked*. But she and Lolly will settle their argument to better satisfaction once he's gone.

"I'll be out of your way, then. Take care." As he slides away, he says, "About that wrap-up interview?"

"Yes, let's." She swishes her skis forward and back in the tracks to prevent them icing up. "Time to turn around, Lolly."

"I'm not scared."

"We'll be lucky to make it down even now without a spectacular crash."

"Mom and Dad would let me."

"I won't."

Lolly takes a few smooth strides forward, then angles her skis and starts uphill.

"We're not going up."

"I am."

"It isn't you I'm afraid for, dear girl, it's me." Lolly stops, her skis braced in a V. She digs a pole in and flicks snow to the side. Her shoulders rise and fall. Slowly she lifts one ski and brings it around and sidesteps down. She pushes off and flies past on her way downhill.

"Stay low!" Syl says, turning, sliding, still seeing that thread of green in Robin's brown eyes. "Stay loose." But the yellow jacket's out of sight. Syl's left ski has a mind of its own, and she flexes her ankle to get more edge. *Watch yourself,* Erik used to say. It was a joke they had, those many years ago. *Why?* she'd say, and he'd say, *Someone has to.* She's giddy through and through. But I didn't *ask* for this, she thinks. I wasn't looking. Since meeting Steven, she's known who she'll grow old with. She's living in Briarwood, even — not that she's ever laughed out loud at a neighbourhood block party, not that she feels at home shopping in All for Women, with its repeated racks

292

of black and white and the single new shade for fall, or for winter, or spring. But costume jewellery's so easy there — you just leave your own rings at home, try on two from the open display and make a show of putting one back but only the one. *Voilà*. She shifts more weight to her stuttering left ski, wondering just when it will happen that she'll fly out of a turn, smack into a tree, break an arm, a leg, a hip. Her neck. She must not, must not fall.

She hears a shout from below: "Shit!" She's never heard Lolly swear, but that's her voice. "Fuck!" Syl hears, and then a shout of straight-up fright.

She narrows her snowplow to get there faster, loses her edge, shoots into a snowbank, jars her back when she falls. One of her skis points to the sky, the other points right at sixty degrees. Pain flashes through a wrist, then disappears. "Are you all right?" she calls to Lolly, and she hears "No," thin and soft. Her back throbs. From where she lies she looks across the track and down a little and sees a bright yellow heap that is Lolly, one red ski pointing high.

"I'm here, sweetie, I'm coming." Syl strains forward, reaching for the binding on her own skyward ski. Why can't her arm be just one inch longer? She rests a second and then uses all she has to swing forward. She grasps the binding barely long enough to pull it open, and kicks herself free. The second ski's a simpler matter.

"Granny, help me!"

On her feet now, Syl looks up the hill, runs across the track when she ought to have waited and hears a skier curse as he speeds past. "Get ski patrol!" she calls after him, not knowing if he hears. The next skier stops long enough to shed a jacket and drape it over Lolly. She pulls out a phone and tries it while Syl snaps Lolly's boots free of her skis.

"Just one bar, no luck. I'm on it, though!" *Swish,* and she's gone. Syl tugs at Lolly's hat to bring it lower at the back of her neck, then takes off her own and snugs it overtop of Lolly's.

"My shoulder hurts so bad."

"I know, my girl." Syl takes off a mitt and wipes tears from Lolly's cheeks. "But you'll be all right. You will." She is prickly hot with relief.

"Owwwww!"

"I know. I know." She unzips her fanny pack, pulls out her tiny bottle of Grand Marnier and brings it to Lolly's lips.

"World's best granny."

Syl takes a shot herself, rubs her lower back, wipes sweat from the back of her own neck. She puts a tender hand to Lolly's forehead. "Someone will be here soon."

A LITTLE AFTER NINE, Steven rushes into Lolly's room at Canmore General, his jacket smelling of cold air and coffee, waves of body warmth floating out the front where it's un-zipped. "Made the drive in just over five."

Syl and Lolly have been through much by now — the excruciating moments as the doctor set Lolly's shoulder back into its socket, the positioning of the sling, the tears and frus-tration and ice packs. The girl's half-stoned on pain killers now. The two of them hold hands like sisters, a female sort of club, watching the end of an episode of *Gilmore Girls* on the laptop Syl rushed home for during one of Lolly's dozes. Steven leans between them to hug his granddaughter. Lolly and Syl both shrink.

He backs off, slips out of his jacket and holds it clasped at his waist. "Sorry. Bit of an ambush?"

"It's okay. Here, sit here. It's tough to make that drive nonstop." Syl reaches a hand underneath her chair for the tiny, almost empty Grand Marnier bottle and slips it into her purse. She kisses Steven's cheek, then circles to the other side of Lolly's bed and strokes her forehead. "We're so lucky, Lolly and me." The girl is drifting off again.

Steven looks across at Syl. "This, today – this adventure, shall we call it – are you all right? You must have been almost as shaken up as Lolly."

"I'm okay."

He reaches over, takes her hand, holds it high so not to bother Lolly. "Because I know how –"

Syl feels a strain in her shoulder and takes her hand back. "I'm fine." Setting a spare key to the motel suite on the bedside table, she says, "I should stop in at the lab. I'll leave you two."

"How long will you be?"

"Good question. I have some catch-up."

"See you in a bit. Love you."

Syl's inner thighs as she walks the corridor are weak and shaking, as if they're made of elastic and have been stretched to the limit, then let go. For all these hours she has smiled and hugged, held hands and made small jokes. Rearranged pillows and puzzled out the workings of the bed to achieve a satisfactory tilt, but she is angry. With Lolly. For falling. Not angry a lot, angry a little. But stop: a person takes a fall, it's not their

fault. Or not *necessarily* their fault. For most of Syl's life, she's
wondered about exactly that. About fault. Intention. About
why her mother, twisted and half-lame, tried to negotiate the
narrow basement stairs that long-ago June day. Syl had three
theories, and she gave them even odds: some forever unknown
errand; the wish for an exit after years of despair; or surrender — to set out on an errand and let the stairway itself decide
her success or failure.

How dare life be so arbitrary? Who does it think it is,
sending you this way or that in the blur of a moment?

Yes, she's a little angry with Lolly.

Watch yourself, Syl, you're taking aim at the handiest
target.

All right, it's her mother she's angry with.

Watch, now, you set that to rest years ago.

Who does that leave?

IN THE PARKING LOT, one hand braced against the door of her
Jeep, she doubles over with a quiver in her stomach. Looking
up, she sees the lit white ellipse of a Tim Hortons sign. For a
moment it's as if she floats a little above her body, watching,
waiting to see what she'll do next, as if she doesn't know for
certain she's about to take out her phone and tap on Robin's
name. Human beings, she thinks as she lights the screen: is
there no stopping us from squandering what we have? Rivers
drying, glaciers disappearing, and that's not the half of it. Then
there's me. Isn't that the problem, though: me me me? No matter
how much, how many, the human animal is not satisfied. She
drains the final few drops of Grand Marnier. Sugar and oranges.

Tim's, then, because it's a family restaurant, noisy and neutral. A place to answer his further questions about her research. Who do you think you're fooling, Syl? You're my perfect man, man, she heard herself say last night on Skype to convince herself she didn't need this fresh attention Robin gives her, when in fact she could drink it till she drowned. But you can't have everything, all at once. Everyone knows the heat of the beginning fades. Everyone knows you take what's left and fold it into something that will keep. There's no sense starting over only to end up miles away a year from now in a place the same but different.

Fault, intention, surrender.

An extended family group has colonized one corner of the restaurant, a couple about the same age as Syl surrounded by adult children along with grandkids ranging from babes-in-arms to teens. Fourteen or so, and they've pulled two long tables together and strewn ketchup-bloodied napkins and remnants of garlic toast on the floor. The elder man, the grandfather/dad, reminds Syl of the long-ago fiancé she took a powder on not forty-eight hours before the wedding. Jack might be bald by now in much the way this man is, a tonsured look. The elder woman, the grandmother/mom, is greying at the temples just as Syl is, though her hair is shoulder-length while Syl keeps hers short and easy. They even share the same body type, though Syl is more trim. It's as if she's looking at another version of herself. She has the urge to wave a greeting. Across the table from this grandmother/mother, a boy of about ten is using a comic book to hit a girl a few years younger over the head. The grandmother reaches long and takes the boy's arm. "I do wish you would act your age." The boy shakes free and leaves his chair and stomps over to the condiment counter, where he fills a tiny white paper cup with ketchup and stands there swirling his tongue into it, letting it smear his nose, his chin.

Robin, just arrived, slides onto the bench beside Syl. "What's this?" He nods toward the ketchup lover.

"He's acting his age."

"No kidding." He touches her arm, a hesitant touch, then takes his hand back. "So. Um, thank you for the call, Syl, but why in God's name Tim's? Why not the Cave, where it's quiet?"

"Close to the hospital." She cannot steady her hands. She holds them in prayer position between her knees a moment, then unclasps them and rests her warm palms on her thighs and feels her own heat through the denim. A surge of arousal.

Robin lays his hand on her forearm again and leaves it there. "Syl?"

"What's happening here?"

"Something out of the ordinary."

"Suppose it isn't." She takes his hand. "Suppose all it is, is new. That old story. Middle-age itch."

He laughs gently. "We're both past middle age."

"Sixty's the new fifty."

Sometimes, like now, she's felt as if he looks straight into her. She isn't sure what's in there to see; things that used to be certain have shifted. If it isn't this man, now, how long before it's another? When does a person's final chance come around to taste someone, something, new?

"What I'm saying, Syl, I'm saying this feels good." He lifts their joined hands then lets them rest on his leg. "It feels *right*, not wrong."

She allows herself a nod. "It's true that —" What? — that she likes the shiver at her centre when those eyes of his take her in? That when he says her name it's like a drug? This woken thirst. She says, "If this were real life you wouldn't be saying things like that."

"This isn't real life for you? Because it is for me."

"I have a husband. I love him. This isn't happening."

"It already has."

She isn't sure when she let go, but they aren't holding hands anymore.

"Can we at least get out of Tim's? Get a drink at the Cave?"

"Yes. Okay." She pulls her jacket on, picks up her purse. As she passes the condiment stand she palms two packets of pepper and one of salt and slides them into her pocket, where her fingers meet the pleasant surprise of a forgotten pair of pewter wishbone earrings still fastened to their plastic card. Outside, their elbows touch, a jolt of current between them before they head for their separate cars. "Meet you there," they say at the same time.

She buckles in. The unlikely power of that touch, just one elbow to another through layers of jacket. She slides her window partway down and calls to him, "Robin, wait."

He stops, turns.

It's wrong, and impossible. "Where do you live?" she says.

"Not so far. Follow me."

"This is bound to end badly."

"You don't know that."

No, she doesn't. What she does know is that Lolly is lying not far away in a hospital bed, her grandpa beside her. Syl's nerves are a samba of hesitation and anticipation. She waits to see Robin's lights come on and she swings her Jeep out, ready to follow. Shifting into drive, she catches sight of the two hats lying on the passenger seat, enfolded, her own black one on the outside and, peeking out, the dance of yellow snowflakes around the blue band of Lolly's. Holding her foot on the brake, Syl fishes in her purse for her phone, pecks out a text: Sorry. Would love to come to your place tonight. You have no idea, dear Robin. But Lolly left her hat behind. I fear she'll need it.

ACKNOWLEDGMENTS

I'm deeply grateful to many people and organizations for their support.

Thanks to the following, all of whom read early versions of one or more chapters, in some cases several years ago: Kim Aubrey, Brenda Baker, Bev Brenna, David Carpenter, Terry Jordan, and Alice Kuipers. Special thanks to Brenda Baker, a generous soul whose work inspired a key moment in "The Last Days of Disco." One scene in her story "Puerto Escondido" so intrigued me that ultimately I had to explore it from Sylvie's point of view. Thanks also to Gordon Vaxvick for helping me sort out background and details in several areas where I had questions.

Special thanks to John Pomeroy, Canada Research Chair in Water Resources and Climate Change, University of Saskatchewan, and Director, Global Water Futures Programme, for reviewing short excerpts and answering questions to do with research at hydrometeorological stations in the Rocky Mountains. His work, and that of his colleagues, inspired the setting and the context for some of the questions raised in "Blueberry Hill." The Petrina Ridge station is fictional, and any inaccuracies to do with research and practices at such sites are my own. Other vital members of the inspiration crew for "Blueberry Hill" were intrepid Nordic ski buddies Miranda Jones, Maya Moore, Aldona and Brian Torgunrud, and Judy Winchester.

Under the guidance of Nino Ricci, the Sage Hill Fiction Colloquium 2016 was a valuable—and fun—ten days in the valley. It came at just the right time for *Sylvie*. Deep gratitude to Mr. Ricci and to Patti Flather, Lisa Guenther, Maria Meindl, and Catriona Wright. The singing and dancing were important, too!

Heartfelt thanks to freelance editor Lara Hinchberger for her care, insight, encouragement, and faith in the book. Truly one of the best manuscript development experiences I could ever hope to have.

Thanks to the Saskatchewan Arts Board and the Canada Council for the Arts for grants that helped me along the ten-year road.

Thanks to the Saskatchewan Writers' Guild for the John V. Hicks Long Manuscript Award, and to Marina Endicott and Ibi Kaslik, 2016 award judges.

Chapter 1, "High Beams," under an earlier title, was short-listed for the CBC Literary Award. It appeared in *Grain Magazine* and in *The Journey Prize Stories 26*.

Chapter 2, "How Sylvie Failed to Become a Better Person through Yoga," won the American Short Fiction Contest and appeared in *American Short Fiction*, Summer 2016. I'm grateful to the magazine and to Elizabeth McCracken, judge for the award. My thanks also to Exile Editions, where the same chapter was longlisted for the Carter V. Cooper award.

Two important venues where I drafted and redrafted portions of this book were Studio 330G in Saskatoon (thank you, Marie Lanoo) and the retreats organized by the Saskatchewan Writers' Guild at St. Peter's Abbey in Meunster, SK.

Heartfelt thanks to everyone at Freehand Books, including managing editors Anna Boyar and Kelsey Attard, and designer Natalie Olsen. What a pleasure you've made this experience. Deep gratitude to editor Deborah Willis for her insight, skill, and dedication. She was a joy to work with.

Thanks also to my sisters Beth, Margaret, and Nancy for their support and encouragement. I do hope Sylvie will strike a chord with you.

Thanks to Michael Fulton for love, encouragement, and, of course, valuable technical support.

Finally, to Murray Fulton, it's hard to find words for the depth of my gratitude. For your insights as we talked through ideas and writing challenges, thank you. More importantly, for the decades of love and support in ways too numerous to list, and too big to name, thank you.

AUTHOR'S NOTES

For the purpose of storytelling, I played a little with the time of day for portions of the OJ chase referred to in "Honestly,".

In "What Erik Saw" I refer to a certain commercial and song associated with Coca-Cola as being important to Sylvie during an "everything-sixties" phase. In fact, the commercial is from 1971, which is close enough for Sylvie and her paisley mini dress.

LEONA THEIS's first book, *Sightlines*, linked stories that form a portrait of a town, won two Saskatchewan Book Awards. Excerpts from her novel *The Art of Salvage* were shortlisted for novella awards on both the east and west coasts of Canada. Her personal essays have been published in literary magazines in Canada and the United States, won creative nonfiction awards from the CBC and *Prairie Fire Magazine*, and been nominated for a Pushcart Prize. Her stories have appeared in numerous magazines and anthologies, including *The Journey Prize Stories*, and *American Short Fiction*, where her work won the story prize. She lives in Saskatoon.